TWISTED VINE

PARADISE CRIME MYSTERIES BOOK 5

TOBY NEAL

He reveals deep and hidden things; he knows what lies in darkness, and light dwells with him.

Daniel 2:22

CHAPTER ONE

Corpses shouldn't look like angels.

Special Agent Lei Texeira couldn't get that thought out of her mind as she shot the body with the Canon. A mane of sun-streaked curls haloed the nineteen-year-old's colorless face. His mouth was turned up in a bit of a smile, long-lashed eyes almost closed. Muscular, tanned arms, losing their definition in death, contrasted with the crisp white bed linens. His hands were crossed on his chest.

Her partner, Ken Yamada, usually did the photography work, but he was busy doing that other thing he did so well—calming hysteria. This time, Corby Alexander Hale III's high-powered parents, Senator and Mrs. Hale.

Detective Marcus Kamuela, relegated to the sidelines, leaned his big frame against the wall of a huge bedroom cluttered with surfboards, skateboards, and a mountain bike. He finally spoke, and his voice was tight with irritation. "Don't know why you guys got called in on this one."

"We're investigating a series of suspicious deaths, and with this boy's parents…It's political. You know the drill." Lei spoke apologetically.

1

Taking over the case had been recommended by Sophie Ang, their information-technology specialist. The tech agent had spotted a trend of inconsistencies in a series of suicides and accidental deaths, and she'd flagged the boy's death to FBI Special Agent in Charge Waxman when it came out on the scanner. Given the senator's position, everything to do with his son's death was going to be under scrutiny.

On the bedside table, near the boy's right hand, was an empty syringe, a strip of rubber tubing, and a "cooking kit" with a smudge of black residue left in the bowl of the spoon. Lei frowned as she assessed the scene—it looked too neat, the body artificially laid out.

"What do you think? This looks staged to me." Lei shook curly hair out of her eyes.

"Agree," Kamuela said. His voice was brusque.

"So, who found the body?"

"The maid. Well, whatevahs." The Hawaiian detective pushed off the wall. He left, giving her one last "stink eye," which she pretended not to see, lifting her hand in a goodbye wave. Lei remembered the days of catching a case only to have it snaked by the Feds. Now she was one of them and was relieved to see Kamuela go. She was never entirely relaxed in his company—he was the investigator on a cold case that still had the power to derail her life.

Ken came to the door. "Detective Kamuela's not happy to be bumped off the case. I put him in with the senator, who's had a bit too much to drink. The boy's mother locked herself in the restroom."

"Poor thing. This kid was so young." Lei lifted the boy's right hand off his chest, turned it over, photographed the inside of the arm. No needle marks on the smooth skin, though the mottling of lividity had begun. "Turn his other arm, will you?"

Ken did so. Rigor had begun to set in, so the arm moved stiffly. No marks on the left arm, either, but a tiny blood dot on the recent injection site. They both straightened up, and Lei lowered the camera. "Where's the medical examiner?"

"Fukushima's a few minutes away. The parents swear he wasn't a drug user. According to Senator Hale, he was what this room shows —a top-notch surfer and athlete."

"He was also left-handed, which isn't well known." Kamuela had given Lei the basic profile he'd procured from the first interviews. They both looked at the empty plastic packet, spoon, tubing, lighter, and the needle set on the right side table. There was a second, empty table on the left side of the bed. An injection site into the left arm meant he'd have had to inject himself with his nondominant hand, an awkward position at best.

"Wonder if we'll find prints on the cooking kit," Ken said, his sternly handsome Japanese face set in what Lei liked to call "samurai mode"—straight brows drawn together, jaw tight, mouth a line. "Kamuela might be pissed now, but with the high profile this case is going to generate, he'll be thanking us later."

Dr. Fukushima knocked on the door and entered. Her assistant, pushing the gurney, closed it behind her. A petite woman with a graceful, upright bearing, she padded across the room in proper crime-scene wear—blue paper booties, a coverall, gloves, a hairnet, carrying her black old-fashioned doctor's bag.

"What have we here?" she asked. "Are you ready for me?"

"Looks like a suspicious overdose. Corby Alexander Hale the third, senator's son, aged nineteen. And yes, we're ready to start searching the room," Ken said.

"I'm done shooting." Lei put the camera in its case. Ken slid the items beside the boy's still form into evidence bags as Lei recapped what they knew.

Fukushima gazed at the body. "Looks posed."

"We thought so too."

"Hmm. I'm going to want to rule out homicide," Fukushima said.

Lei didn't have time to reply before the door flew open with a bang. Corby Hale's mother hurtled across the room, throwing herself onto their crime scene. "Corby! Corby!" she wailed.

Ken and Lei pried her off her son's body. Alexis Hale, whom Lei had only ever seen perfectly coiffed beside her husband in media releases, appeared unhinged with grief. Ruined makeup smeared her face, and one ear bled onto the collar of her white blouse where it looked as if she'd ripped an earring out.

She cried the boy's name again and again, "Corby! Corby!" as if she could haul his spirit back from wherever it had gone. The sound brought the hairs up all over Lei's body. She wrestled Mrs. Hale into a nearby chair, keeping her there by crossing the woman's arms and holding them from behind while Ken ran to find Senator Hale. Fukushima fussed around the disturbed body, hastily bagging the boy's hands lest any trace be lost and then pulling the sheet up to hide him.

Lei was able to release Mrs. Hale's arms when she took hold of herself, hands still crossed over her body, and began rocking. She was crying hard now, and Lei patted the woman's back, making inarticulate soothing noises. Every phrase she thought of speaking sounded ridiculous.

Nothing. Nothing could comfort in a moment of loss like this, and Lei had finally learned it was better to say nothing than something insensitive. It had also taken her some years to be able to tolerate the rawness of others' grief without it activating her own— even now, she slowed her own breathing consciously as Mrs. Hale's harsh weeping abraded her emotions.

Senator Hale, pasty under his golfer's tan and reeking of alcohol, wobbled into the doorway with Kamuela holding him up. Mrs. Hale launched herself from the chair, beating at him with her fists. "This is all your fault! All your fault!"

Lei and Ken pushed all three into the hall and managed to get the door shut so Dr. Fukushima could get to work in peace, and the next several moments were a blur of managing the fighting, screaming couple, getting them down the hall and into the huge living room, sitting them on separate leather couches like boxers between rounds.

Lei parked herself beside Mrs. Hale, who had subsided into

hiccupping silence, her red-rimmed eyes fixed on her husband. Senator Hale reached for his highball glass from the coffee table, but Kamuela plucked it away first. "I think you've had enough, sir."

"So, tell us more about yesterday and this morning," Ken said.

Mrs. Hale didn't speak, just kept her venomous gaze on her husband. Senator Hale finally answered, rubbing his eyes with a thumb and forefinger.

"It's like I told you. Corby is a student at University of Hawaii at Manoa. He had classes yesterday; he went surfing in the evening. We don't monitor everything he does anymore, but I knew that because his car was gone." Lei glanced out the window at the black Xterra parked in the turnaround, stacked high with surfboards. Lucky nineteen-year-old. The waste of his death made her heart squeeze.

"Anyway, we didn't know anything was wrong until Jessie went upstairs to wake him for class. She screamed." Hale got up and went to the sideboard, a handsome koa-wood unit, and splashed more Maker's Mark into a fresh glass. The agents looked at each other and at Kamuela. Lei knew none of them wanted to incur the senator's wrath by taking the drink away again.

"I went up and saw him there. I tried to wake him." The senator's hand trembled so violently he couldn't get the glass to his lips. The liquid splashed over his hand and he set it down. "I called nine-one-one on my cell and went out of the room. I wouldn't let Alexis see him. I didn't want her to see him. Dead."

Suddenly the senator clapped his hand to his mouth and ran out of the room. Ken followed him, and Lei heard the man retching in the nearby guest bathroom. Kamuela got up. "I'll go check the perimeter, make sure it's secure."

Lei looked over at Mrs. Hale, pulled a handful of tissues from the mother-of-pearl box on the coffee table, handed them to her. "Your ear is bleeding. I'm so sorry for your loss."

Mrs. Hale put the tissues against her ear without responding, still staring at the spot where her husband had been.

"I wonder, was Corby acting any differently lately? Did you have any indications that he was using drugs?"

"Why is the FBI here?" Alexis Hale suddenly asked.

Lei took a careful moment to answer—she couldn't give anything away right now. "Your husband's high profile immediately bumps the case to a higher level."

"Well." Mrs. Hale seemed to be pulling herself together, having reached some inner conclusion. She smoothed her blond hair, woven with shades from buttercream to platinum, patting it back into some semblance of order, though there was no fix for the spatter of blood on the white blouse from her torn earlobe. She reached over to the expanse of coffee table and tugged another tissue out of the mother-of-pearl dispenser, dabbing mascara out from under her eyes. "He'd been acting different. Quieter. Withdrawn. I thought he was having a tough semester at school, maybe girl trouble. I didn't pry."

Lei had taken her little spiral notebook out of her pocket and she jotted this down. "How long had this been going on?"

"I noticed a change in him around the beginning of the semester. He started locking his door, didn't want to join us for dinner. He was listening to all this angry music. Alternative, you know. I thought it was just a phase." She suddenly hunched forward, as if from a body blow, and covered her face with her hands. "Oh God."

"Please. Mrs. Hale." Lei laid a hand on her trembling shoulder. "Please help me with this. Maybe we can find some answers." Even as she said the words, she knew answers were not always comforting—sometimes they just led to more questions, or more heartbreak.

"It doesn't matter. He's gone." Alexis Hale pulled another handful of tissues out of the dispenser, dabbed her whole face. "Okay. I'll keep it together for a little longer, just to get you people out of my house."

Lei felt the sting of the words but kept her voice soft. "Thank you. I can't imagine how difficult this is. What kind of girl trouble did you think he was having?"

She didn't have time to answer as Ken came back in. "Senator Hale became ill. I helped him to bed. We'll talk another time."

Lei stood up to block Mrs. Hale's view out the window, where Dr. Fukushima and her assistant were pushing the gurney down the walkway, loaded with the strapped-down black body bag. The wheels of the gurney clattered and Alexis Hale looked up, then shot to her feet and ran to the door.

Lei followed her, but Mrs. Hale just stood in the doorway and watched them load the body into the ME's van. The estate was fenced with a monstera-covered coral-stone wall, the giant tropical ivy curling up the ten-foot expanse, and guarded by an electric gate. Kamuela provided some cover from the jostling reporters beyond the gate trying to get the "money shot" with his bulk and intimidating stare. Mrs. Hale turned away as Fukushima slammed the back door of the van and the assistant got behind the wheel.

"Okay. I'll see him later," she muttered to herself, rubbing her arms briskly as she walked back to the living room. Lei trailed her and was grateful when Ken sat beside the grieving woman and picked up the line of questioning.

"So you said 'this is all your fault' to your husband. What did you mean by that?"

Alexis Hale straightened her linen slacks, picking at the creases in the fabric. "This. This life in the fishbowl, where everything we do has to be a certain way and everything we say has to be scripted. This life. It was hard for Corby, and it got harder for him the older he got, but neither of us had a choice. We had an image to maintain. My husband's vision is set high, and we both always knew it."

"You mean the White House?" Lei asked. She'd heard rumors to that effect. Senator Hale was even rumored to have a chance at the presidential nomination in a mere four years.

"Yes. So we lived under a magnifying glass. I had the feeling Corby was getting restless."

"He might have turned to drugs to escape, you mean."

"Maybe. I wouldn't have believed it, but . . ." She seemed unable to go on.

"Why don't we call someone for you? We still have to search his room," Ken said.

They called Alexis Hale's sister, and it wasn't long before they left Mrs. Hale tearfully explaining on the phone and were able to exit. Lei put on a hairnet to restrain her springing curls, unruly in the Kailua humidity.

"That was fun." She grimaced as they put on fresh gloves outside the boy's room.

"You did well with her." Ken rarely praised her, so Lei felt the words' value even more keenly.

"I'm getting better. I don't say what I'm thinking the moment it occurs to me anymore."

"Hopefully we'll find something that tells us more about what went on here." Ken opened the boy's bedroom door and they stepped inside. He locked the door behind them. "No more interruptions."

"Right." Lei had brought a crime kit, and she opened her well-stocked case and clicked on her light. "I'll take the bed."

"I'll start at the desk." Ken headed toward the handsome antique, hidden by a bike propped on its corner.

Fukushima had bagged the sheets and pillowcase, so Lei scanned the mattress, got down on her knees and looked beneath the bed while Ken rooted through the desk. Two minutes later, as she was fishing a magazine out from under the bed, he said, "Here it is." He held up a sheet of paper.

"Yes, here it is," Lei echoed thoughtfully, her brows pulling together in a frown as she looked at the homosexual erotica magazine in her hands. "Don't think Mama knows Corby's taste runs in another direction. This isn't girl problems I'm looking at."

"Interesting. Well, there might be some answers here." Ken cleared his throat as he read from the sheet he pinched by one corner, printed in a bold script Lei guessed was the boy's handwriting.

"Dear Mom and Dad. I'm so sorry for doing this to you, but the pain I'd cause you if you knew the truth, if the world knew the truth about me, is so much worse. This was the best I could do. I love you, and I'm sorry. Love, Corby."

"So this is a suicide?"

"Looks like it could be." Ken slid the paper into an evidence bag.

"Because he was gay?" Lei held the magazine up so her partner could see it. "I don't get it. In this day and age, it's not a big deal for a politician to have a gay son."

Ken's jaw tightened—Lei knew her partner was gay and still in the closet. "No one knows what a struggle it is. Maybe there was more to it. He doesn't say exactly what the 'truth' is."

"Maybe his body will tell us more. Fukushima will find anything worth finding. I'm especially interested in the tox panel and blood work."

They continued on, moving through a room that documented the life of a golden young man who'd had hidden depths, and other than a further collection of homoerotica stashed in a box in the closet, there was little to show what those had been.

"Mrs. Hale will need to identify his handwriting," Lei said, waving the bagged suicide note as they were packing up the evidence that they'd collected—the pile of porn, the note, the drug paraphernalia. "Seems like this is one of those suspicious suicides Ang's worried about."

"More will be revealed."

"Well, I might have done okay talking to Mrs. Hale, but I dread telling her it looks like it could be suicide."

"I'll talk to Mrs. Hale." Ken shouldered the upcoming encounter with his low-key heroism. Lei had come to love that about him—no fanfare or whining; he just did what needed doing whether it was facing down a Mob boss or a grieving mother. In their year and a half of working together, she still learned from him every day.

Lei moved through the living room, carrying the items they were taking back to the Bureau. Alexis Hale spotted her and hung up on her sister, dropping the phone with a clatter into the cradle.

"What did you find?" she cried, eyes wide and fastened on the paper evidence bags Lei carried. Ken intercepted her. "We do have something to discuss with you, but please let my partner put away our equipment first."

He sat beside her on the acre or so of creamy leather couch, and Lei walked out to the black Bureau Acura nicknamed the "bu-car," securing the evidence in a small, locked box in the back. She stowed the crime kits and beeped the vehicle locked, aware of the long lenses of the photographers trained on her through the bars of the gate, the voice of a reporter on camera behind her. They were probably Googling her, and she was relieved that even though Kamuela had left in his beige department-issued SUV, he'd left a black-and-white HPD cruiser parked at the gate, barring illegal intrusions.

Lei hurried back into the house, carrying the small video camera they used for interviews. Mrs. Hale was sipping a glass of water, Ken's hand on her shoulder, when she returned.

"Is it okay if we tape this? We need to get a little more information from you, and if we tape we won't have to reinterview you at headquarters." This usually worked to allow the taping, and today was no exception.

"All right."

Lei turned on the video, and Ken said to Alexis, "Do you have any samples of Corby's handwriting we can see?"

"Why?" Her eyes widened and filled with tears as her hand covered her mouth. "Is there—is there a suicide note?"

"There appears to be."

"No. No." She shook her head. "No."

"It appears to be a suicide note, but there are some inconsistencies at the scene, and we aren't drawing any immediate conclusions at this time," Lei said. Ken narrowed his eyes at her, but Lei's comment worked to distract Alexis.

"What do you mean? Like, someone else killed my son?"

Ken pulled her gaze back in his direction. "This is an investigation, Mrs. Hale. We are trying to figure out what happened to Corby, whether accident, suicide, or something else. Please tell us again what you told Agent Texeira before about his behavior and how it had changed."

"Yes. Okay." Mrs. Hale took another sip of water, smoothing her hair with a gesture that also wiped the pain from her face. Lei was again impressed with the woman's ability to master her emotions. "He'd been withdrawn. Quiet. Pulled away from us. Didn't want to come to dinner, didn't want to tell us where he was or who he was with. Like I said before, I thought it was a phase. He was growing up." She covered her mouth with her hand, closed her eyes. Went on. "I didn't like all his friends. I didn't like the online thing."

"Online thing?" Lei had cursorily looked around the computer in his room, but they hadn't taken it since it hadn't seemed a large part of this outdoorsy young man's life.

"Yes. He had some sort of game or something. When he was home, he was always on there, with that awful hard metal music playing. I complained about it, said it was bad for his social life, and he said he was making friends online. People who understood him."

Lei barely restrained herself from jumping up to go grab the computer. Instead she stood, out of view of the video recorder, and paced a bit. This was what she and Ken had worked out—she had to move when she was agitated, but he didn't want her running off in the middle of an interview. They'd also discovered that Lei's background restlessness seemed to motivate interviewees to talk faster, infusing them with urgency to unburden themselves. Mrs. Hale was no exception.

"I think maybe this is connected with that online thing. I don't know, but he was so secretive about it."

Lei could well imagine that if it was some kind of gay chat room or porn-sharing site, Corby certainly wouldn't have wanted his mother to know about it. "We'll need to take his computer."

"Of course. Just find out what happened. And I'd like a copy of that note, if you can get us one as soon as possible. I want my husband to see what his work did to us."

"Yes. I'll fax a copy to you as soon as we are done processing the paper," Ken said. "But what do you mean about your husband's work?"

"It took over our lives. I think we made too many sacrifices for my husband's ambition. I, for one, am done."

Lei felt conflicted hearing this, hoping Mrs. Hale was just venting her grief in anger. The senator was a popular lawmaker, known for his environmental policies and trying to bring Hawaii into the forefront of ecotourism, even make the little island state a power player in national policy. This loss could derail his bright career and have repercussions on a national scale.

"I hope you will just take some time to grieve," Lei said. "I hope you will turn to each other and not against each other. You've *both* lost your son."

Alexis Hale looked at Lei a long moment, blue eyes narrowed. "You have no idea what I've lost. I'll go get you those handwriting samples." She got up and walked out.

Just then Jessie the maid, a pretty Filipina girl in a bright fitted muumuu, opened the living room door, admitting a weeping blond woman. "Mrs. Hale's sister," she said.

Lei pointed down the hall. "She went to the bedroom."

It hadn't escaped Lei or Ken that the Hales had separate bedrooms. The woman ran down the hall, and they heard the noisy greeting of the sisters. Ken stood, pressed Off on the video camera.

"Let's get back to the office, brief SAC Waxman. I'll get the handwriting samples from Mrs. Hale."

"I'll get the computer."

Back in the boy's room, Lei unplugged his laptop, detaching it from a monitor, printer and Internet ports. Taped to the side of the printer was a Post-it with a series of passwords.

"How handy," she whispered. "Thanks, Corby."

Lei took a last look around the room, the life already gone from it, the stripped bed a stark reminder. She felt her chest go tight with sorrow, and she walked out with the computer in her arms. The only thing she could do for the young man was investigate—but she had a feeling Corby's parents weren't going to like the answers they found.

CHAPTER TWO

KEN CARRIED the computer and Lei, the rest of the packaged evidence, as they rose in the elevator of the Prince Kuhio Federal Building to the tenth-floor FBI offices. The door opened on the gracious lobby with its marble floors, leather couch, and fan of *Guns & Ammo* magazines on the coffee table, a fresh-faced New Agent Trainee behind the bulletproof glass booth. The NAT, Amit Gupta, a clean-cut young Indian man, gave a big grin at the sight of them. "Let me help!" he exclaimed, coming out of the cubicle.

"We got it," Lei said, smiling back. It wasn't that long since she'd been sitting where Amit was, and she still remembered the boredom of answering phones and running background checks, which went with the training period—a period that had been extended especially for her due to some procedural mishaps on a case.

Ken waited, his arms full as she juggled her armload of packages, fumbling for her ID badge. Amit took it from her, swiping it through the lock that opened the steel-cored automatic door leading to Bureau headquarters.

Lei took back her badge. "Thanks, Amit." The NAT nodded and

went back into the booth as Ken and Lei's black athletic shoes squeaked down the hall.

Marcella poked her elegant head out of her office. "Lei, stop a minute. I want you to meet someone."

"Let me drop these off first."

"Sure." Marcella pulled back into her office. Lei noticed the blind was down over the door as she passed, and she frowned. Who could be in there? Marcella sometimes liked to "surprise" her, like the time she'd tried to set Lei up again with Alika Wolcott, whom she'd disastrously dated, at the gym. Lei was still in limbo relationship-wise.

Lei had chosen her career in the FBI and left her boyfriend Michael Stevens behind on Maui. Ever the gentleman rescuer, heartbroken and rebuffed, Stevens had married Anchara Mookjai to help the Thai woman get citizenship. While Stevens and Anchara had tried to make their marriage work, Lei's career choice of the FBI had been rocky.

After they'd worked through the drama of his doomed marriage last year, Stevens had gone back to Maui and she'd buckled down and focused on regaining her credibility at the Bureau while they waited for his wife Anchara's citizenship to come through. They were in touch, but only minimally, as phone calls and Skyping just reminded them both how hard it was to wait to be together. Both of them had plenty to do at work without stirring up emotions.

"Let's use Workroom One," Ken said. "I want to get the case file going, and we can inventory these items before we brief Waxman."

"Okay." They turned into the workroom, a functional space with a locked temporary evidence locker, worktables with bright halogen lights over them, computer stations, and various analysis equipment. Lei was eager to fingerprint the heroin kit and the suicide note, but she'd told Marcella she'd be back. "I'll just be a minute," she said, stowing her armload of evidence in the locker.

"You can leave it unlocked. I still have to inventory it," Ken said, setting down the computer on a table. "I'll take this down to Information Technology in a minute, see how soon Sophie can take a look at it."

"Sounds like a plan. I'll be right back," Lei said. She grabbed a water bottle out of the little fridge and hurried back to Marcella's office. She knocked on the door and gave it a push. It swung inward and bumped into Marcus Kamuela. Wrapped in his arms, looking disheveled and thoroughly kissed, was Marcella.

They sprang apart. "Uh—this is Marcus Kamuela, Lei. My boyfriend."

Lei felt a hollowing under her sternum. "The night marchers walking over her tummy" as her aunty Rosario used to say. Of all the people in the world to be dating her best friend, why did it have to be the detective investigating that nemesis from her past, the Kwon murder? "We've met. Saw each other this morning, in fact. Hi again."

"I didn't realize you were the friend Marcella's always talking about," Kamuela said, looking a little sheepish as he straightened his shirt. "Sorry I was irritated this morning. I hate to miss a case."

"I know how you feel about your cases," Lei said, remembering Kamuela's hard cop face in front of the television cameras on the day Charlie Kwon was murdered. She and Kamuela had had a conversation outside Kwon's apartment a year later about the unsolved case. The murder of her childhood molester still held the potential to ruin her life. Lei pasted a smile on her face. "So this is the mystery detective you've been dating, Marcella. Turns out Marcus and I met when I first got to the Bureau."

"Well." Marcella smoothed escaped bits of hair from what she called the "FBI Twist" back into their pins. "I wanted to be sure Marcus and I were going to . . . you know. Be a thing. Before I introduced you."

"She's commitment phobic," Kamuela said, with that crooked, attractive white grin Lei had noticed more than once.

"Well, happy for you guys," Lei said. "Listen, I'd better get back..."

"So when is Stevens coming over? We need to do something together, a double date or something," Marcella said.

"I'm not sure." Lei lifted the water bottle in a little toasting gesture. "I'll let you know. Well, gotta run. Carry on." She pulled the door shut on Marcella's laugh, imagining Kamuela sweeping her friend back into his arms and continuing to mess up her hair with kisses.

It made Lei feel a little sick with loneliness and worry. What if Kamuela ever connected her with the Kwon murder? It would devastate Marcella and drive a wedge between all of them. Lei had confronted the pedophile in his apartment on the day he was shot, dressed in a disguise Marcella had unwittingly given her.

Lei ducked into the unisex bathroom and flipped the lock on the door. She did a nervous pee, washed her hands. Her oval face with its sprinkle of cinnamon freckles reflected pale in the silver metal of the paper towel dispenser as she yanked out a handful of towels, running a little water on them and patting her face.

Lei's full mouth tightened as she remembered Charlie Kwon: her mother's boyfriend, drug pusher, and pedophile. Just when she started to forget about it, his unsolved murder would bubble up with its taint of the past. Charlie Kwon, on his knees in front of her with his eyes shut, saying, "Do what you came to do!"

The Glock had wobbled wildly as she absorbed the blow that he didn't even remember who she was, and she was frightened that she might actually shoot him by accident. She'd hit him with the weapon and he'd folded up like a beach chair, unconscious but alive.

Someone had come in after her and shot him point-blank. If she was ever identified as the woman seen leaving Kwon's building, all she had was her disguise and a gunshot-residue-free pair of yellow rubber gloves to say she hadn't killed him.

Her curly hair was a disaster after being held captive in a hairnet for an hour or so. She took a couple of handfuls of water and splashed it on, scrunching the frizz back into ringlets. This took some effort, and she couldn't help remembering Stevens's voice, full of affection as he pulled on a curl, watching it stretch and spring back as he said, "Your hair. It's like a pet or something."

Oh, to be in Stevens's arms, stealing a kiss behind a closed door like Kamuela and Marcella. It would be heaven. They'd decided not to sleep together while he was married, but there'd been many times Lei had wished she could just hop on a plane and go over to Maui and spend a weekend with him.

She'd earned this purgatory. Seeing Marcella's happiness just reminded her of all she was missing.

It was just better not to think about it.

CHAPTER THREE

SOPHIE ANG SAT in her computer bay with three large screens ranged around what she called "the cockpit." The low lighting of the FBI's information-technology floor, the sound-deadening walls and carpet, gave the space a womblike feel—but the cool temperature kept the computers humming and agents alert.

And right now, Sophie was feeling more than alert—she was what she'd heard called "wired in." Time seemed to stop, and she entered a state of total synchronicity between the computers, her brain, and her body. Sophie called it "the zone." If she could have, she'd be plugged directly into the mainframe, but such technology didn't yet exist. She knew it was only a matter of time, and she'd be one of the first to sign up.

Sophie had a mug of strong Thai tea at her elbow, and her long golden-brown fingers flew over the keys as she typed in the latest information on Corby Alexander Hale III direct from the scene, piped to her from Lei and Ken through their secure laptop. The photos Lei had taken, their notes, pictures of the suicide note, porn, and heroin kit all flowed through her fingers into the program she'd built.

She'd named it DAVID. The Data Analysis Victim Information

Database was designed to analyze crimes into trend-driven subgroups. Unbound by geography or human bias, DAVID was able to mine law-enforcement databases and use statistical probability to hunt down trends that would be missed any other way—and this time, she was finding a trend with an 80-percent confidence ratio. She could add and take away variables that reconfigured the data based on information as it came in. Nationwide, there was an uptick in suicides. Suicides with inconsistencies. Suicides that weren't really suicides.

Sophie still vividly remembered watching the news report a few weeks ago that had caught her interest—a series of odd suicides in Portland. One of the victims, a woman with chronic depression who'd overdosed on sleeping pills, looked uncannily like Sophie's mother.

When she'd entered all the data and hit Submit, DAVID hummed a long moment, the screen blank.

DAVID didn't produce conclusions. It used a probability algorithm that had taken her almost a year to write to provide a percentage of confidence that a given hypothesis was true or false. She had typed in the code for "suicide," having ruled out accidental death herself because of the note and posed quality of the body.

A window popped open: "30-percent chance suicide."

That made it 70-percent probable that Corby Alexander Hale III had been murdered, or assisted in his suicide by someone else—still technically murder.

Sophie pushed back from her bay and stood up, stretching her arms high above her head, arching her back. She bent back down to lay her palms flat on the plastic chair guard on the floor. Other agents dotted around the room didn't look up; they were used to Sophie's frequent workout breaks.

At five foot nine and a hundred and fifty pounds, Sophie Ang was a tall woman with a rangy build and the long muscles of an athlete. She wore loose black rayon pants and a stretchy white blouse with black rubber-soled athletic shoes, well within Bureau guidelines but an outfit that was all about comfort.

Sophie rolled an exercise ball out from under her desk and lay backward, arching all the way over it to stretch. She picked up and crossed two dumbbells on her chest and began a series of sit-ups. When she'd done a hundred, she put down the weights, turned over on her stomach, rolled the ball down to her feet, and did a hundred push-ups.

It was hard to keep fit at a desk job, but Sophie loved mixed martial arts too much to let sitting all day make her soft. After she joined the FBI and learned combat skills, she discovered the Women's Fight Club at her local gym, and she'd been hooked on the intense sport that was a combination of boxing, wrestling, and martial arts.

As Sophie did the push-ups, her busy brain ticked over this new information on the Hale case—information she knew Special Agent in Charge Waxman wouldn't like. In fact, she still had the DAVID program under wraps. She dreaded the moment she had to tell the SAC she was running her own software on the Bureau servers. Truth was, she'd hoped to get some results before she disclosed how she'd come to them.

Any defense attorney would have a field day with the fact that an untested, unsanctioned computer program had generated results pointing to their client. Which was, in fact, a good reason to keep the program secret for the moment—there wasn't a suspect yet to point to, just a confidence ratio that said the boy's death wasn't suicide.

The suicide note appeared to be in his handwriting, though frustratingly general. The fact that there was a note claiming suicide was consistent with those other odd deaths—she'd started a subfile on them, and so far there were forty-eight. Forty-eight suicides across five states with oddities, inconsistencies, evidence others had been involved—but they all had solid, uncoerced-looking suicide notes.

DAVID thought that constellation of factors was statistically improbable with an 80-percent certainty.

Sophie pushed herself up off the ball and did a brief sun salutation, stretching out her arms, shoulders, neck, and hands, ending with her palms flat on the padded carpet again. She straightened and strode across the "lab," as they called it, to the water dispenser with its handy cabinet of glasses. She downed a healthy eight ounces, thinking about the environment of wealth and privilege that young Corby Hale occupied.

Sophie was familiar with that fishbowl life. Her father, an American diplomat posted to Thailand, had met and married her mother there, and Sophie had grown up in a palatial home surrounded by servants. She'd been cared for by a nanny, her every movement supervised and magnified in terms of how it reflected on the family. Not only was she the daughter of a diplomat, but her mother was a cousin to the king. She was related to royalty.

Educated at boarding school in Switzerland, Sophie discovered a knack for three things: languages, athletics, and computers. None of these was particularly encouraged by her family, and she'd graduated with little recognition of her talents and a lot of value placed on her beauty.

She knew she was what the Americans called a "knockout"— even tall enough to do modeling. With her triangular face, tilted eyes, curly black hair, and golden-brown skin, she was the essence of exotic. Her mother had arranged a marriage for her upon graduation, and by then her parents were separated.

"Come back to the States with me," her father said. "You don't have to do this."

But Sophie thought she did. She'd wanted to please her mother, an elfin beauty afflicted with chronic depression. She'd hoped that by doing what Pim Wat Smithson wanted, she would gain some closeness to a woman who'd always been unreachable.

It hadn't worked, and the marriage had been a disaster she'd barely escaped from.

Sophie was at home here in this cool cave. Her mind and her skills made her fortune, not looks or bloodline. She'd discovered hand-to-hand combat and was now an expert with weapons, from the standard-issue Glock to throwing knives.

Assan Ang would never beat her again.

She leaned her forehead on the cool plastic of the water dispenser. Assan hadn't even looked for her. Instead, she'd received a packet of divorce papers in the mail. He'd kept the settlement her parents had given them upon their marriage, and Sophie considered it a bargain to never have to see him again. She refilled her carafe and drank another eight ounces of water with her usual focus.

She had Womens Fight Club tonight. It wouldn't do to be dehydrated.

CHAPTER FOUR

LEI UNLOCKED the gate of her little cottage on the outskirts of Honolulu. Keiki, her Rottweiler, and Angel, the teacup Chihuahua she was dog sitting, joined forces in a rhapsody of welcome as she pushed the gate open, stepped in, and relocked it.

The yard was enclosed in a six-foot chain-link fence draped in orange trumpet vine that did a great job of bestowing beauty as well as ensuring privacy and security. She always gave a deep sigh of relief to be home, and today was no exception.

Lei squatted down and rubbed the dogs' bellies, scratched under their chins. If she didn't do exactly the same thing with each of them, they found a way to wriggle under her hands and compete. She scooped tiny Angel up and patted Keiki's big broad head, rubbing behind the silky triangle ears as they walked to her little porch. More unlocking here and a quick deactivation of the alarm, and she was really home.

Lei walked into the bright yellow kitchen with its little table and orchid plant. She fed the dogs and left them happily munching, a comical echo of each other with their matching black-and-tan points.

In her room, she stripped out of her black slacks and unbuckled her weapon harness, hanging it off the iron bedstead of the king-sized bed she'd finally replaced after the fire on Maui. She'd rented the little house furnished but for the bed, and it was big enough for her and the dogs to sleep in without bumping into each other.

Looking at the pristine bed linens reminded her of the sad crime scene this morning; she unbuttoned her white button-down blouse, standard FBI "uniform" wear, as she thought about her conversation with Sophie Ang just before the workday ended.

"I don't think the Hale boy is a suicide." The tech agent had come into Workroom One, where Lei was using her fuming chamber, a glass aquarium-like cube, to raise fingerprints on the heroin "cooking kit" found beside the boy's bed.

"We don't think so either," Lei said. "Come see." They both squinted into the fuming chamber. "See anything?" The spoon, lighter, plastic packet, and hypodermic were all in the chamber.

"No." Sophie Ang wore a short-sleeved shirt, and Lei noticed again the curlicued foreign-writing tattoos that traced down the inside of the agent's toned arms. She'd always wondered about them.

"That's the point. Looks like the kit was wiped. Why would Corby Hale wipe his prints off the drug apparatus?" Ken, crisp in his gray suit, leaned down beside them. "So why don't *you* think this is a suicide?"

"Computer analysis of the scene information," Ang said.

Lei was still looking at the tattoos. "What are those kanjis on your arms?"

"They aren't kanjis—they're Thai writing." Ang stood, and Lei was struck again by her height, the leashed power of her movements. Marcella and Sophie seemed to be addicted to the Women's Fight Club they went to together. "I'm half Thai, half American."

"Oh." Lei wanted to ask what the tattoos said but already felt like she'd overstepped herself with the very private tech agent. "What's the computer saying about the case?"

"Seventy-percent confidence ratio that the boy's death is murder. This additional information will likely bring it up into ninety."

"What kind of program are you running?" Ken switched off the power to the hood and the lit interior flicked off. "I asked you that earlier during the team briefing on looking at these suicide cases, but I don't think I got a straight answer."

Lei heard a defensive note in Sophie's voice. "Classified."

Ken gave a bark of laughter, putting his hands on his hips. "Got clearance just as high as you, Ang. You running something off the books?"

"I plead the Fifth Amendment." Ang's foreign birth sometimes showed up in how she used colloquialisms. "Something I'm working on. I'll tell Waxman at the right time."

"Well, so far we're all on the same page. There's something *kapakai* with this one. It's weird." Lei told Ang about the boy's left-handedness and imitated the tricky position needed to inject oneself in a major vein with the nondominant hand.

"What about the suicide note?" Ang frowned.

"That's what we're all wondering," Lei'd said.

Lei pulled her eyes away from the bed and her obsessive thoughts and tossed her blouse and bra into the laundry hamper. She rolled an athletic bra down over small round breasts and pulled on a pair of nylon running shorts and a mesh top, bundling her curling hair into a ponytail.

The suicide note. In a scene that looked staged, it was clearly in Corby's writing and yet it didn't reveal any of his real motivation. The note had a stilted, form-letter feel to it that concealed as much as it revealed—like someone had given the boy the words.

Keiki, done eating, saw these signs of imminent departure and began a low rumbling whine of eagerness, intelligent brown eyes tracking her mistress as Lei slid her feet into short athletic socks and laced up Nike Air running shoes. Angel, not so restrained, lapped circles around Lei, yapping with excitement.

The little dog was too small to keep up with Lei and Keiki on their runs but was devastated to be left behind, so Lei had rigged up a secondhand baby carrier that she wore on her chest. She'd been caring for the little dog for more than a year while her owner, a teenager Lei had forged a bond with, served a sentence in Hawaii Youth Correctional Facility in Ko`olau. She scooped up the dog and tucked her in, leaving the little domed head and large pointed ears protruding. She slid a heavy chain collar over Keiki's head, patted her pockets for her house keys, phone, and pepper spray, and took the dogs outside for their evening run.

The cottage was about a mile from the west end of Ala Moana Beach Park, and Lei and Keiki made good time jogging along the urban sidewalk to the long stretch of lawn at the beginning of the park. They ran past picnic structures, spreading banyan trees, a long yellow-sand beach, and several homeless tents.

Lei took the dogs to the fenced dog park area. The big Rottweiler lay down panting when they arrived, while Angel made darting runs at the other dogs, barking when she had a mind to. Lei did some stretches off the park bench, watching the families and other dog owners.

A couple sat on the bench near her, their arms twined around each other, sneaking kisses as their dogs, a Shih Tzu and a pit bull, wandered and sniffed the fenced area. The sight of the couple brought Lei's loneliness back in a rush as she remembered Marcella's flushed face and sparkling eyes, Kamuela's dimpled grin.

Love was in the air, and Lei wasn't getting any.

It was too much. Lei took out her phone and held down the number seven, Stevens's speed dial. The phone rang and rang. She listened to his voice tell her to leave a message. Just to hear his voice brought tears prickling up, a dreaded weakness. She hung up, sliding the phone back into her pocket without leaving a message.

She wasn't tired enough; that was it. Maybe she should give the Womens Fight Club another try, but she didn't like the idea of seeing Alika Wolcott, who coached there. They'd dated back on Kaua`i, and she was still uncomfortable with him.

Some more running would help. She went to the nearby water fountain, splashed water over her face and hands, sucked down all the liquid she could hold. Made sure the dogs each got a good drink in the little basin designed for them, clicked the leash back on Keiki, and loaded Angel into the front carrier.

This time she went down to the beach and jogged laps back and forth. Tiny, clear turquoise waves lapped at the sand. The sunset blazed orange against the depthless blue sky, gilding clouds mounded near the horizon. Palm trees lining the beach clattered their fronds in the light breeze, and mynahs squabbled in a towering plumeria tree.

Lei jogged until the restless darkness of her mood was drowned by the thunder of her heart. Finally Keiki began hanging back, tongue lolling, and Lei took the dogs back uptown at a brisk walk.

The phone rang in her pocket, a buzzing vibration. She took it out, checked it before she answered.

"Hi, Michael."

"Lei." Just the sound of Stevens's voice as he said her name made her throat tighten. "You called."

"I did. I had to tell you—Marcella's dating someone. It made me miss you."

"Glad to hear your voice, whatever the reason. Who's the lucky bastard?"

"Marcus Kamuela. The detective working Charlie Kwon's case."

A long pause. "That's awkward."

"You think?" She made herself give a little laugh, like it didn't terrify her. "Anyway, seeing them together—they're really happy. It made this even harder."

This. Waiting. Their long separation. She heard the sigh of his exhale.

"God. I miss you too." She could tell he was running a hand through his dark curling hair. She could picture the shadow of his lashes falling over those blue, blue eyes, his long fingers rubbing them. "Things are moving along."

"Really?"

"Yeah. Really. Anchara told me her citizenship application was approved. I met with a divorce lawyer today."

"Oh." Lei stopped, leaning against a building, the sharp shadows of evening falling on the windows of the city all around her, Keiki tight up against her side as she bent her head, closing out everything in the world but his voice and the phone. Angel tilted her pointed nose up in the baby carrier and licked Lei's chin. "So...how long?"

"Couple weeks. Could be sooner."

"Oh my God." After waiting so long to be together, the imminent end of their separation seemed like a mirage.

"I know. It doesn't seem real."

"I can't believe it either."

"So what are we going to do? Are you coming here?" Stevens was embedded in his job on Maui, promoted to lieutenant of the Haiku Station where Lei had once worked under Captain C. J. Omura.

"I don't know." Lei stroked a finger over Angel's head, and the tiny dog closed her eyes in bliss. "I was really hating the Bureau for a while, but things are better. Waxman's lightened up on me, and we've always got interesting cases. Let me tell you about this latest one." She described the contradictory evidence in Corby Hale III's death.

"We've got interesting cases here too."

"I don't know what to do. I just know we need to be together. Don't you think it would be easier for you to come to Oahu? More opportunity here for you too."

"I'm just getting settled in as commanding officer. I'd have to see what was available for transfer. You can be sure I wouldn't have my own station."

Another long pause. A horn blared nearby, startling Lei. She straightened up from the wall, continued up the cement sidewalk with Keiki at her side. The lush green mountains behind Honolulu seemed to glow in the setting sun as her eyes wandered over them, unseeing.

"We don't have to have all the answers now. Just...we have to be together. When you're free." Lei felt her throat closing on longing, a physical sensation like a fist squeezing her chest. It was beyond lust. It was a parched dryness. Only being tucked under his collarbone in her special space against his side could restore her.

"I love you." His voice was ragged.

Her eyes closed for a second, and it was in that second that she walked into another pedestrian.

"Watch where you going!" Angry words put her back into her body and in this moment on the busy street. She waved apologetically at an older woman pushing a cart.

"I have to go. Call me when you know anything."

"I will. The minute I know."

They hung up at the same time. Lei wanted to cry at the severing. Instead she broke into a jog, Angel bouncing in the carrier against her chest. There was respite in the movement and in caring for her dogs, and that night, in getting online to find out everything she could about Corby Alexander Hale III.

CHAPTER FIVE

SOPHIE UNLOCKED the red lacquered door of her apartment, carrying her gym bag. In the posh Nuuanu area of Honolulu, her place was the penthouse suite atop a high-rise building. It was her father's, one of his many real estate investments, and he'd insisted she be his "caretaker" now that Honolulu was her home, a situation she was grateful for. Her FBI pay wasn't bad, but she could never have afforded the wide-open expanse of gleaming teak floor and the view, glass unbroken by anything but an occasional steel strut all the way across the wall facing the ocean.

At thirty stories up, the city was spread below in an entrancing tapestry of movement and glittering lights, trimmed in beach and ocean. Diamond Head was an iconic silhouette in the indigo distance with the moon a glowing coin behind it.

Sophie toed out of her athletic shoes and carried the gym bag into the laundry room just off the sleek modern kitchen. Standing in front of the washer, she tugged off sweaty Lycra workout gear. Naked, she unzipped the gym bag and pulled out her FBI clothes from the day, loading everything into the washer and turning it on. She clipped her gloves and padded helmet to a hanging drying rack and walked across the apartment to the bathroom.

Sophie loved the feeling of being nude—cool air wafting across her flushed skin and tired muscles. She wasn't worried about anyone seeing her; besides being thirty stories up, the expanse of glass was both tinted and foiled so that it lightened and darkened with the sun.

The bathroom was all marble and gold-plated fixtures. No one could accuse her father of restraint in the area of luxury. She stepped into the glassed-in chamber of the shower and turned it on. A large showerhead set to "rain" poured a gush of warm water over her, and under that flow she soaped herself, tracing the curliqued letters of the tattoos running down the insides of her arms and outsides of her thighs, places where they could be easily concealed.

One arm said *hope* and *respect*. The other read *power* and *truth*. On one thigh was *freedom* and the other, *courage*. Circling her narrow waist, where no one saw them, were *love, joy*, and *bliss*. She had no trouble reciting the words she'd had inked on her skin after her divorce was final. They were words she tried to live every day.

She microwaved a dinner of brown rice and stir-fry the house-keeper her father employed had prepared and left frozen in individual ceramic containers and carried it to her bedroom. She'd rigged one side of the room to duplicate her office, and she fired up her workstation with the touch of a button.

DAVID was archived and networked to the Bureau computers so that anything she did here was automatically replicated there. For a woman who lived her work, it was a seamless transition.

She'd just settled into eating and putting DAVID to work on comparisons of the many suicide notes, looking for commonalities, when her FBI-issued smartphone rang—it was Lei.

"Hey, Texeira." She was surprised to hear from the other agent.

"Hey, Ang. Sorry to bug you at home, but I brought home my laptop, and I've been researching Corby Hale, just searching him by his name. He's popping up on Reddit, advocating for right to death in several chats. He went by the name of SurfHawaii, so you can run him under that, see what you find. Did you get started on his computer yet?"

"Not yet. I saw you left it at my station. I had to get through some stuff on my other cases before I could start on it, and I just ran out of time."

"Yeah, I know you and Marcella had Fight Club tonight." There was an odd note in Lei's voice that Sophie, with her sensitivity to nuances and language, picked up.

"Marcella canceled, so I went alone. You never came back to Fight Club after that first time. Why?"

"Alika. You must have heard we used to go out, when I was stationed on Kaua`i." Lei blew out a breath, a noisy gust. "It didn't end well."

"I think he might still be interested in you." Sophie had heard about Lei's dating fiasco with her coach from Marcella. She liked Lei, and it didn't surprise her that Alika might still be in love with Lei's unforgettable face and physical bravery.

"God, I hope not. Stevens and I are getting back to together the minute his divorce is final. Alika's a great guy, though—you guys should go out."

"Ha," Sophie said, her fingers flying as she opened a window and ran background on Alika Wolcott, something she usually did with anyone she spent time with. She'd cloned all her FBI programs on this workstation, so it was easy to do exactly what she did at work. "He's my coach. It's not like that."

"Marcella said you wouldn't mind it being like that."

Sophie frowned. "I'll give her an extra beat-down for that. I've got a little crush, that's all. He's not interested in me except as a fighter."

"Well. No let me stand in the way. All I stay sayin'." Lei's playful pidgin made Sophie smile. "Back to the case. Corby's mom said he was really into some online activity that kept him busy when he was at home; he said he had people who 'understood him' online. So that points to gay friends, maybe, or maybe something to do with drugs."

"Or maybe just Reddit. That site is one big time sink," Sophie said, shrinking the window with the search on Alika and opening a new one in Reddit, the massive real-time chat and news site. "I'll see what I can dig up. Thanks for the heads-up."

"Welcome. Sooner we can get to Corby's computer, the better."

"I'll try to get to it tomorrow. Marcella's still bugging me to do hers too, though. The embezzlement case."

"You know, the cases we get at the Bureau—so much less dangerous than regular cop work. It's not something you read in the brochure."

"Not necessarily. Marcella's been shot, assaulted, and strangled. I heard you've been through a lot as a police officer; maybe you're ready for things to be calmer. Our criminals are more sophisticated, that's all. I'll let you know as soon as I find anything in Corby's computer."

"Okay. Later then." Lei clicked off.

Sophie set her phone down. She leaned forward, eyes intent and fingers flying, the stir-fry forgotten. Corby Hale and *the zone* sucked her back in.

CHAPTER SIX

Lᴇɪ's ᴘʜᴏɴᴇ woke her at six a.m., never a good sign. It bounced around on the side table on ring and vibrate, anchored by the charge cord. The noise brought Keiki and Angel's heads and ears up from sleeping on their ratty old blanket at the foot of the bed.

Lei grabbed it. "Special Agent Texeira."

"Caught a new case, Lei." Ken's voice was crisp. "Suspicious death. We're called in because Corby Hale's prints were found at the scene."

"What the hell?" Lei tossed the blanket aside. She walked in her thin tank top and boxers to the preloaded coffeemaker in the kitchen, punched it on. She'd learned it was best to make the coffee the night before or she was liable to have to do without—and the blast of caffeine was really necessary this morning after her heavy exercise and late night.

"I know. It's weird." He rattled off the address. "Meet me there."

Lei hopped under the brisk flow of the shower, reordering her wayward curls with a few handfuls of water. She dried off and dressed in her version of the FBI uniform in less than five minutes— white short-sleeved shirt, black chinos, black athletic shoes. Her badge clipped to her belt, shoulder holster strapped on, Glock loaded up. In the kitchen she made sure the dogs' water bowl was full, threw a couple of handfuls of food in their bowls to tide them over, and unlocked the dog door.

Keiki looked at Lei plaintively as she filled a lidded travel mug with coffee, and Angel did a few experimental whines to see if Lei would pick her up. Lei succumbed, picking the tiny dog up and stroking her head.

"Be good. Keep an eye out for bad guys." She put Angel down and gave Keiki an ear rub. "See you girls later."

They followed her out into the dewy yard, a few stars fading from the sky with the morning blooming in the east—another gorgeous Honolulu day. Lei took in the sounds of morning as she unlocked her truck: a few cars, a rooster crowing, the chatter of mynahs and the rustle of a tiny wind in the nearby palm tree.

Lei drove her truck through streets too early to be choked with the commuter traffic that would come later. She'd plugged the address into the on-board GPS, and her navigator guided her across town to an older neighborhood near Punchbowl. She pulled the silver Tacoma up behind a couple of HPD cruisers parked in front of a ranch-style home with an orchid-bordered walkway.

Lei slipped a pair of latex gloves on from a box under her seat and picked up her crime kit. She made sure her badge was clearly visible and identified herself to the uniformed officer guarding the yellow tape across the garage, signing the log and entering the time: 6:27 a.m.

The retractable garage door was still down, but the side door was ajar, and she pushed it open with a finger, poking her head in to see what she was getting into. She'd walked too fast into a few crime scenes in her time and had learned to go slow and let herself take in all the details before she zeroed in on the body—and Ken's message had been devoid of detail.

Her partner had his back to her, looking into a parked beige Toyota Highlander. The garage and interior lights were on, and he was looking around the motionless driver with a penlight. Detective

Ching, Marcus Kamuela's partner, gave her a little salute from the wall. "You're getting another of our cases," he said. "Alfred Shimaoka, aged fifty-nine."

Ken had the door ajar, and he pushed it all the way open and moved back so Lei could see into the vehicle. "Looks like a suicide."

Lei could smell auto exhaust and a whiff of decomposition. "Asphyxiation, then?"

Ken nodded. Ching was still looking surly, doing something on his phone.

Lei approached, her eyes scanning across the tidy cement floor in "see mode." The walls of the garage were lined with some sort of craft supplies: bundles of bamboo, clippers, cutters, saws, and bottles of glue, stacks of what looked like paper. Against the wall that faced the house was a washer, dryer, sink, and workbench. She spotted what Shimaoka did in his spare time: a tidy row of small square paper lanterns stood in a row.

She walked around the SUV, past Ching, to look into the driver's side, but without opening the door all she could see was a man's profile, his head tilted back, and the yellow interior lights of the vehicle gleaming on salt-and-pepper hair.

Ching pointed. "Your boy's prints were on the tape connecting the hose to the exhaust pipe."

Lei saw that the tape had been removed. The hose was detached and lay on the floor beside the SUV. "I'll bag that." She took a large paper evidence bag out of her kit, snapped it open, then coiled the hose carefully and inserted it into the bag, sealing it with paper tape and initialing it with the date and time. "Where's the tape with the prints on it?"

Ching pointed. The evidence bag was already sealed, so Lei set hers next to it and rejoined Ken at the door of the car. Her partner was scanning the interior of the SUV with a forensic light. "Can I open the door on the other side?" Lei asked.

"Long as he doesn't fall out," Ken said.

Lei walked back around. The window was up almost all the way, and traces of duct tape still clung to the edge of the window and the doorframe.

"Thanks for securing the scene." Lei addressed Ching. "I think we've got it covered."

Ken spoke up from the other side of the vehicle. "Your commanding officer called us himself when you identified Corby Hale's print. Quick work on that, by the way."

"I scanned it in and it came right up—not much to it. We're not in the Dark Ages, you know."

"Well, do you think you could get started gathering some statements from the neighbors? We'd really appreciate it." Lei tried a smile, wishing her dimple worked as well as Marcella's.

Ching pushed off the wall abruptly. "Might as well air this place out."

He punched the button on the wall and the garage door rumbled up. Lei opened her mouth to protest but spotted Fukushima's van pulling up at the end of the driveway, breaking up the cluster of lookie-loos craning their necks at the end of the driveway.

She turned away. The air did feel a lot fresher with the door open, and what did she care if there were a few gawking neighbors?

Ching stomped off.

Lei looked at the driver's side door. An ashy-looking drift of fingerprint dust decorated the ground beneath the door, but there was nothing on the handle. Odd. The dead person should have left a lot of prints. "Ken, do you know anything about the victim?"

"Alfred Shimaoka. Aged fifty-nine, an architect. This is his house. He's Japanese and single."

"Who found the body?"

"Neighbor. Heard Shimaoka's dog barking inside, and he's religious about walking it, according to what the neighbor told Ching. She peeked through the glass in the garage door and saw him. The SUV had run out of gas and turned off, so she thought he'd passed out or something until she approached the car."

"That must have been a shock." Lei heard a far-off yapping. "Did anyone deal with the dog?"

"Couldn't. House is locked."

Lei sighed. That would be next, as soon as they were able to leave the body to the medical examiner. She finally really looked at what was left of Alfred Shimaoka.

Shimaoka's skin was pale but patched with red in the lips and extremities, an effect of the carbon-monoxide poisoning. His head was tilted back, mouth ajar, and most interesting, his hands were resting upright on his thighs, the thumb and forefinger close to touching, in a Buddhist meditation pose. The slender Japanese man, beginning to swell as decomposition began, was dressed neatly in a muted aloha shirt and chinos. Other than the strange coloration of his skin, he looked peaceful.

Ken pointed his penlight at a square of white paper propped up against the gearshift. "Can you bag that?"

"Sure." Lei took out another evidence bag and picked up the paper carefully, leaning past the dead man to retrieve it. The fruity smell of decomp, faint but powerful, rose from the corpse. "If Corby's prints are on that tape, he's got to be dead at least two days."

Ken had his camera out and shot the scene. "Just what I was thinking."

Fukushima appeared, the gurney's clattering wheels, pushed by her assistant, announcing their arrival. "What have we got?"

Ken told her, while Lei read the suicide note. It was written in beautiful calligraphic script on a translucent square of the paper used to make lanterns.

Dear friends. I have no family to shame with this choice to avoid my last months of suffering. I have pancreatic cancer, as many of you know, and I'm ready to go now—not in another three months when the doctors say I will. Please accept that I chose not to burden anyone with my end-of-life care and recognize my right to choose how to die.

And to my friend Soga, I finished my lanterns. Please light one for me at the Floating Lantern Ceremony.

Alfred Shimaoka

Lei felt her heart do a little flip as she looked back at the row of lanterns. Chances were very good the Soga he referred to was her grandfather Soga Matsumoto, whose home was mere blocks away. Her grandfather also volunteered at the Shinnyo temple, helping to build and repair the beautiful lanterns lit annually and floated out to sea in Waikiki on Memorial Day.

She slid the paper into the evidence bag without comment, sealing and marking it, as Ken and Fukushima continued their conferring and Ken took more pictures, circling around to her side and shooting the body from every possible angle.

"We're going to want to go over this vehicle inch by inch," Ken said. "If there's anything else Corby left, we need to find it."

Lei nodded, setting the bag with the others next to her kit. "I want to deal with that dog."

"Poor dog," Fukushima said. As usual, the fastidious ME was swathed in sterile wear and even wore a particle mask. Ken gestured to the keys, still in the ignition. "Chances are the door key is there."

Lei lifted them out carefully, holding the side of the main key. She'd fingerprint that later—but for now, she walked across the garage to the back door and inserted a silver Schlage into the lock.

The dog that charged the door, yapping fiercely, was a wire-haired Jack Russell terrier, white with brown spots and a good deal of attitude.

Lei squatted down, lowering her voice and extending her closed fist for him to sniff. "Hey, boy. You hungry?"

The dog tentatively sniffed at her hand, and his tail wagged. She slowly stood up and advanced into the kitchen, spotting his bowls (both empty) against the wall. She picked up the water bowl first, turning on the sink and letting her eyes roam around the room, looking for anything out of place.

It was spotless and pristine except for a corner near the trash bin where the dog had succumbed to biology and defecated. She refilled the bowl and located a lidded trash bin filled with dry food. She refilled that too as the dog frantically lapped water.

Ken came up into the doorway. "We should search the house."

"I know. Got a lot of detail work ahead, but I want to figure out something for this little guy."

"Strange that Shimaoka didn't give him away before he died. People planning their suicide usually do that. Another oddity."

"Maybe he didn't have time. Maybe it came up suddenly," Lei said, frowning thoughtfully as she set the dog's bowl down. The little terrier chomped down the food as fast as he could. "Did Ching find out the dog's name from the neighbor?"

"Ask me yourself." Ching approached across the garage with his clipboard.

"Hey, Detective. Did the lady who found the body say what the dog was called?" Lei ignored his attitude.

"His name's Sam." They all looked at the little dog with his nose in the bowl. "She said Shimaoka usually took good care of the dog."

"I wonder if she'd be willing to take care of him until a relative or something can be located."

Ching leafed through the papers on his clipboard, removed one and handed it to her. "Here's her contact information." He was clearly not volunteering for dog care duty. "She seemed attached to Shimaoka. Cried a lot over the discovery. Said she knew about the cancer."

Sam finished eating and darted out the open doorway and through the garage, past the open door of the SUV, where his master's body was being awkwardly wrestled into a body bag by Dr. Fukushima and her assistant. Ching and Ken hurried to help while Lei ran after the dog. Sam trotted into the immaculate little front yard and did his business. Lei scanned the neighbors still clustered on the other side of the tape Ching had put up at the end of the driveway.

One woman, dressed in purple sweats and a T-shirt with a lei hand painted across the front, was crying into a dish towel. Lei approached her, glancing at the paper Ching had handed her. "Hi there. You wouldn't be Sherry Thompson, would you?"

"Yes." The woman looked up, brown eyes streaming. She had the kind of complexion that didn't age well in Hawaii, tissue-like freckled skin patched with red. "I was a good friend of Alfred. I can't believe he did this to himself."

"Tell me what happened, please."

She listened to a recap of what Ching had already told them, with embellishments of shock and grief. Finally, when Sherry was winding down, Lei gestured to the little dog doing a patrol lap of the front yard. "Any chance you could take care of Sam? I'd hate to see Animal Control have to come take him to the Humane Society."

Sherry squatted and opened her arms in reply. "Sam! Come here, boy! I'm happy to take him and at least try to find a home for him." The terrier ran to her, and she scooped him up. "Can I get his leash and food?"

"Just a moment," Lei said, trying to physically turn the woman away from the sight of Fukushima and her assistant loading the black body bag and gurney into the ME van, but she was unsuccessful. Sherry watched with her mouth ajar, color draining from her highly colored face. As if sensing her distress, Sam licked her chin until she looked back down at him.

"I can't believe he didn't do something for Sam," Sherry said. "He loved this dog. Took such good care of him."

"You seem like you're surprised Mr. Shimaoka took his own life, but Detective Ching said you knew he had cancer."

"I knew he had cancer, but not what kind. He was in pain, and he didn't like to take medication. We'd talked about that several times. I guess if I'd known it was pancreatic cancer—which is painful and terminal—I wouldn't have been so shocked." She stroked the little dog's fur. "I better get his things."

Lei led Sherry and another helpful neighbor into the kitchen to pick up the dog's food, leash, bed, and toys. "Thank you, Agent Texeira. You're very kind," Sherry Thompson said.

"Just want to find him a good home." Lei couldn't remember anyone calling her kind before—she must be mellowing with age. She kept the women from going any farther into the house and rejoined Ken at the SUV as the ladies walked off with the dog and his accoutrements.

"Whew. Got that taken care of. Got a little more information on our victim too."

"Good." Ken handed her the handheld vacuum with its special trap for fibers. "Back to work. Let's get this car done."

Evening bloomed a salmon glow over clouds above Punchbowl when Lei was finally able to drive out from the Bureau headquarters into her grandfather's neighborhood near where Alfred Shimaoka had lived. She'd told Ken about the likely connection to the name in the note, but it had taken hours to go over Shimaoka's car inch by inch and then to search his house. They'd then taken samples, fibers, prints, and photos back to headquarters and spent more hours processing the evidence in Workroom One. Finally Ken had dismissed her, saying, "I want you to interview your grandfather. He's the only person mentioned by name in the note."

Lei drove through the quiet neighborhood with its neat lawns and monkeypod shade trees, passing Shimaoka's house and going on to Soga Matsumoto's. She'd made a photocopy of the suicide note after they'd analyzed it—no prints but Shimaoka's were on it.

Lei continued to wonder how Corby's prints could be on the duct tape off the tailpipe, indicating an assist with the suicide apparatus. Yet important areas where other fingerprints would have been, like the suicide note and the keys, were marked by none but Shimaoka, indicating the death was by his own hand.

How could two such different people ever even meet, let alone join in executing Shimaoka's death? And then someone had assisted in Corby's too.

There were still too many missing pieces in both cases.

Lei pulled her silver Tacoma up to the curb in front of her grandfather's low, modest ranch home. The grass of the front yard was a beautiful, putting-green quality Bermuda, decorated with a small cement temple and a single, clipped bonsai juniper.

Lei usually met her grandfather for lunch at his favorite noodle house. She'd been over to his home only one other time, at the holidays, when her grandfather had invited her and her visiting aunt and father over for tea. It had been a tense hour for Lei, full of awkward pauses, but an important gesture on Soga's part as her parents' marriage hadn't been supported by the Matsumotos. They'd never tried to find or contact Lei after their daughter Maylene died, and without her aunty Rosario's intervention, Lei would have ended up in foster care.

Aunty Rosario had brought her famous poi rolls, a Tupperware of the Portuguese bean soup her restaurant was known for, and a mouth tight with disapproval—until she'd had several cups of warm sake and Soga had patted Lei's hand. "Having Lei in my life has made me so happy. I wasn't able to see her before my wife died."

The delicate inflection confirmed what Wayne Texeira had told Lei and Rosario—Yumi Matsumoto, Lei's grandmother, was the author of the separation between the Matsumotos and the Texeiras. Now she was gone, dead of a heart attack more than a year ago.

Lei had witnessed the visible relaxation of adults affected by a powerful presence she had never been able to know. The tension was also eased for Lei. The remaining members of her family were willing to find common ground with one another for her sake.

Lei walked up the cement path to the shiny black-lacquered front door with its geometric knocker. She had to knock hard, several times, before she heard her grandfather's footsteps—deliberate but not shuffling. He opened the door and smiled at the sight of her, his stern face lighting up. "Lei!"

"Hi, Grandfather." She'd decided on that slightly formal appellation a while ago—it suited him best. "Can I come in? I have to talk with you about something."

"Of course. Let me put on some tea." The door opened into a dining area, with a sunken table flush with the floor, preserving the Japanese seating tradition. The colors of the room were quiet grays, muted in dim lighting. A black leather couch against the far wall set off a framed watercolor of Mount Fuji.

Lei followed him through the room into the kitchen, an immaculate space filled with golden evening and shiny surfaces. She seated herself at the round table for two beneath the window while he filled an electric kettle with water. She took a moment to look into the backyard with its tiered rows of orchid shelves and open workshop, a dangling bulb lighting a workbench covered with materials for making lanterns.

The Floating Lantern Ceremony was a huge event organized annually by the Shinnyo Buddhist Temple to honor the fallen and lost on Memorial Day. Her grandfather had invited her to participate last year, and they'd lit three lanterns at the ceremony: one for her mother, one for her grandmother Yumi, and one for her friend from the Big Island, Mary Gomes. Lei would never forget the sight of the lanterns in the Canal in Waikiki, the magical way the yellow candles had glowed by the thousands reflected in the water.

Her grandfather and Alfred Shimaoka were among the many volunteers who retrieved, repaired, and built new lanterns each year for the event. She reached into the backpack that doubled as her purse and took out the photocopied suicide note, placing it facedown on the table as her grandfather returned with a bamboo tray set with small ceramic cups and a teapot.

"It is good to see you." The evening light shone on his silver hair as he set the tea tray on the table. "The water will be a few more minutes."

"Okay. I see you've got a lot going in the workshop." Lei pointed out the window to his lit workbench.

"I have many lanterns to get ready by the end of May." It was mid-March. He opened a canister of loose tea leaves and scooped some into an empty hand-thrown ceramic pot.

"Well, that's in part what I'm here about. Did you know Alfred Shimaoka?"

"I know him, yes." Soga looked at her. Dark eyes, shadowed by the fold of his eyelids, revealed worry in the creases. "He is my friend."

"I'm very sorry to tell you—but he's died."

The teakettle began a high-pitched squall, and Soga got up. She saw his shoulders draw up tightly and then drop, a deliberate loosening. As he returned to the table, his face had smoothed into neutral. He poured the boiling water into the teapot.

"I knew he was sick."

"Yes, he was. But he didn't die of cancer. He committed suicide." She slid the letter in its plastic sleeve over to him. "He mentioned you."

Soga ignored the note lying in front of them like an accusation. He stirred the tea with a bamboo whisk, placed the lid on. "It must sit for a few minutes."

Her grandfather was deliberate in everything he did, especially tea. She wasn't surprised at his lack of reaction to Shimaoka's note— he always took time to adjust to things. He'd read it when he was ready.

Soga got up. "I have something for you too. I was waiting for the right time to give it to you." He walked out.

Lei took the simple handleless cups, with their translucent green glaze, off the tray and placed one in front of each of their places. She'd heard of the Japanese tea ceremony but didn't know anything about it, assumed her grandfather did.

He returned, carrying a large wooden box with a slanted top and handed it to her. "This was your grandmother's writing desk. She kept some keepsakes of your mother's and photos in here. I thought you should have it."

Lei felt her stomach clench. She might as well be holding Pandora's box. Her voice was pitched high as she replied. "Wow. This is special. Thank you, Grandfather."

"You're welcome."

Soga set a strainer over Lei's small cup and, using both hands, carefully poured the tea into the cup. "I would like to take you to Japan sometime. Show you a real tea ceremony."

"That would be wonderful." Lei inhaled the delicate fragrance of the tea, scented with jasmine, and watched as he transferred the strainer to his own cup, poured, then set the teapot down on its trivet. Each movement was precise and economical.

She set the box of memories down by her feet and turned to face her grandfather, copying his movements as he folded his hands and made a slight bow to her; then they both picked up the cups and sipped.

The tea was hot and tasted like toasted flowers. "Delicious."

Her grandfather got up and fetched a small box of rice crackers. "A little taste of something. We always try to balance the taste of the tea."

"Thank you." Lei took a cracker. It burst with the salty flavor of nori seaweed on her tongue. "These sort of melt in your mouth."

"Yes." They ate and drank for a moment as Lei felt the stress of the day drain away in this peaceful setting. What did it matter whether the meeting took five or thirty minutes? She was with her grandfather in his world. Finally, when his tea was gone, Soga reached over and drew the note to him, turned it over. His face was stoic as he read.

"What can you tell me about Alfred Shimaoka?" Lei asked at last. "Why do you think he mentions you in the note?"

"I knew Alfred for many years." Soga poured himself another cup of tea, refreshed Lei's. "He was a good man. A man of his word. He had an obligation to fix the lanterns, and he fulfilled it. He mentions me only because he wanted to be remembered that way, and it doesn't surprise me. He has no family, no children."

"I know he was an architect. Tell me about his work."

"He was a good architect. He worked for a big firm, Matsei and Company, for many years. He was very good at his designs. He retired when he got sick." Soga ate a cracker. "I will go to his house and bring the lanterns back here."

"Not yet, Grandfather. It's still a crime scene for a little longer."

"What do you mean? He died by his own hand."

"Anytime there's a strange death, we investigate it. And there are oddities about his death."

Soga looked up at her with eyes so dark they were almost black. "Oddities?"

"I can't say more than that, and really there's nothing more to add. But did you know of anything in Alfred's life that . . . didn't fit? That would lead him to suicide?"

"No, other than he was sick with cancer and became withdrawn. He was in pain, but he disliked medicines. This does not surprise me, his choice." Soga looked down at the note, but his hands remained in his lap. "He would not talk about it. But he did not like medication."

"Did you know his little dog, Sam?"

Soga smiled, a fan of creases folding from the corners of his eyes. "Yes. So energetic, his dog."

"Well, one of the oddities is that he just left the dog in the house. Did not give him away or have anyone care for it. It seems inconsistent."

"Yes." Soga picked up his cup with two hands, his gnarled fingers delicate on the rim. "I think that's strange too. He loved that dog."

"A neighbor is taking care of Sam right now, but she already has a dog. What do you think of adopting him?" Lei asked impulsively.

Her grandfather set down the cup. "I have a quiet house. I don't have time."

Lei looked around the spotless kitchen. "He seems like a good, sweet dog. He'd shake things up around here a little, that's for sure. But I love my dogs. They keep me company, and I never feel alone with them around. Speaking of, I have to get home to them before they chew the house down. Is there anything else you can tell me about Alfred?"

"He had a computer. He spent a lot of time on that when he was home."

Lei thought of the sleek black Mac they'd carried into IT and left in the lineup for Ang to look at. "That's good to know. Did you know what he was doing on there? Did he ever say?"

"No. Only that he knew people through the computer. That he wasn't as alone as he seemed. Sometimes I would tell him he should find a wife; he was still young enough. That was before the cancer."

Lei blinked, surprised at the sight of a tear making its way down Soga's impassive face. She fussed with her tea things to give him time to compose himself, and when she looked up the tear was gone. "Well, thank you. For the tea, for grandmother's lap desk." She picked up the wooden box. "I'm a little afraid to look inside."

"I hope it brings some happy memories and thoughts," Soga said, rising to follow her as she walked to the front door. "And that it helps you know your mother a little more."

"I hope so too." She leaned over and impulsively kissed his leathery cheek at the front door. "I'll call you when Alfred's house is okay to enter. Do you know who his next of kin was, by the way?"

"A nephew. Saiki Shimaoka. He lives in Honolulu."

"Thank you." She carried the box out to the truck and set it as gently as a bomb on the passenger seat. In a way, that's just what it was. She turned the key, waved goodbye to her grandfather still standing in the doorway, and pulled away for home.

With herself and the dogs exercised, fed, and showered, Lei was finally ready to have a look at the contents of her grandmother's lap desk. Sitting at her little round Formica table with the orchid plant on it and a fortifying local-brewed Longboard Ale at her elbow, Lei lifted the glossy lid.

The smell of sandalwood wafted up from a pile of photos and letters lying in wait for her. The contents of the desk had probably been neatly stacked at one point, but they had become jumbled in transport. Lei took out some Japanese writing implements: a set of sumi paintbrushes with bamboo handles, bound with a fraying rubber band; a green jade stone with a well in it for mixing the ink stick she found in a little plastic bag.

A stack of thick, deckle-edged writing paper filled with Japanese characters and tied with string was next. Lei couldn't read Japanese. She felt cheated as she lifted her grandmother's correspondence and set it aside.

A pile of photographs greeted her next, and in them she recognized her mother's pale lily of a face, black hair long and straight, her clothing simple and immaculate. In the series of photos of Maylene that progressed from babyhood into high school, her mother's face was always serious, her posture demure.

A good little Japanese girl until she met Wayne Texeira, the wild *paniolo* cowboy, at that fateful long-ago rodeo.

Lei found a picture of Maylene wearing what Wayne had described meeting her in—a white eyelet sundress, flounced to the knee, her slender torso and legs set off by the full skirt and red cowboy boots she wore with a cautious smile. She'd been married in that dress, at age eighteen, holding an armful of wild orchids. Lei still remembered the rain-swept night on Kaua`i when her father had told her the story of her parents' whirlwind romance.

The next picture was of a baby. A baby with big tilted brown eyes, a full rosebud mouth, and a tuft of curling brown hair.

Lei turned the photo over. Written on the back, in her mother's round precise writing, was *Leilani Rosario Matsumoto Texeira, b. Nov. 27, 1985*.

Was this really the only photo her grandparents had ever had of her? The photo was yellowing, its edges curled as if it had been handled a lot.

At the very bottom of the box was a letter. Lei opened it, and a slip of paper from a fortune cookie fell out. *Shape your destiny*, the fortune said. On the back was written a phone number in her grandmother's calligraphic handwriting. She picked the letter up and read it.

Dear mother and father,

I wanted you to have this picture of our beautiful daughter, Lei. She is healthy and happy, and I am too. I know you said I was not in the family since I married Wayne, but I wanted you to know that the family will go on anyway. Our name is a part of my daughter's name and heritage. I hope you will consider being in her life. She is a gift to us and will be to you too.

Sincerely,

Maylene

Lei folded the paper, feeling bittersweet emotion tighten her chest. Her mom had tried to connect her with her grandparents, but they had chosen to keep them cut off, and in the end, Wayne had been a bad influence on Maylene. He'd been dealing, and she'd become addicted.

Thank God for Aunty Rosario. Being adopted by her at age nine, after Maylene's death, had been best thing that could have happened, given the situation. Still, Lei wished that she'd at least met her grandmother, wished she'd had her grandfather in her life even longer. She picked up the slip of fortune thoughtfully and slipped it into her wallet, a reminder.

"Shape your destiny," Lei said aloud. Keiki and Angel, snuggled on the rag rug at the back door, both lifted their heads to look at Lei. "We're doing that. Aren't we, girls?"

She folded the letter, stacked the photos, repacked the writing items. At the bottom of the box, she spotted a slender silvery chain decorated with a tiny child-sized cross. She'd bet it had been her mother's, and it was just right for that other important pendant she'd been needing a chain for.

Lei walked to her room and picked up the little black jewelry box from her bedside table. Inside, nested on the white cotton, was a disc about the size of a nickel. A hole with a loop had been drilled through it. Polishing had removed the last traces of black and char on white gold embedded with a roughness of diamonds.

Melted in the fire they'd been through, Stevens's grandmother's wedding ring had been pounded down and given to Lei by Stevens when she left for the FBI—a talisman for rubbing when she was anxious.

Lei no longer needed that comforting habit and had cleaned the piece up to wear as a pendant. She slid the disc onto the chain and fastened it around her neck. It felt satisfyingly solid resting there, the tiny silver cross dangling over the white-gold circle. She'd wear it always, she decided. Against her throat, resting on her pulse, reminding her of what really mattered.

CHAPTER SEVEN

SOPHIE ARRIVED at her workstation dressed in her usual easy-movement clothes and carrying a thermos cup of strong tea. She glanced over at the row of computers beside her computer bay: A sleek black Mac had been added to the lineup, with an evidence tag attached identifying it as coming from the recent suicide site of Alfred Shimaoka.

The suicides needed to slow down. She barely had time to keep up with all the tech stuff as it was.

She took a sip of tea and opened a window in the DAVID database. Her fingers flying, she inputted all the new information on the most recent case, including the fingerprint from Corby Alexander Hale III, mysteriously captured on duct tape from the tailpipe of Alfred Shimaoka's SUV.

DAVID agreed this was an anomaly, along with the fingerprint-free door handle and the existence of a small beloved dog left to starve in the house. Confidence interval of 78 percent that Shimaoka's death was an assisted suicide, or murder.

The answer to how these two disparate victims were connected lay in the computers stacked up on her desk. She was sure of it.

Sophie saved and closed DAVID. She hooked up two small,

square black write-blocking units to Corby's and Shimaoka's computers. The devices cloned and saved a complete record of the computers' hard drives, and even Internet use patterns, allowing her to virtually access the computers without disturbing the data and time stamps. Defense attorneys had successfully argued that computers were tampered with by forensic technicians, but with the data imaging systems they currently used, nothing on the original computer was marred by a single keystroke.

The write blockers needed several hours to copy everything, so she turned her focus to finishing the work for Marcella's embezzlement case.

Some hours later, that work done, Sophie rose and went through her stretching routine. She did some push-ups and sit-ups, finished her tea, and unplugged the completed write blocker copy of Corby's computer. She had three computers she'd nicknamed Amara, Janjai, and Ying, and Ying had the most powerful processor. She plugged the write blocker into Ying's back port and dove into the virtual clone of Corby Alexander Hale III's computer.

A lot of what Sophie was looking for would be found in his online searches, and sure enough, the boy hadn't deleted his cookies. She was able to trace his online activity, and using the handy set of passwords on the Post-it, access his most-frequented websites. The kid had been active on several gay sites, done some dabbling in World of Warcraft, been a regular on Reddit. He'd had a fair amount of gay porn highlighted. She wondered if the Hales had had any idea about their son's sexual orientation. She'd heard Senator Hale was targeting the White House, and this would have been an interesting but not insurmountable situation to winning the election.

A pie chart generated by her FBI-issued software analyzed online site visitation time. It showed that the majority of time he spent logged in was on a site called DyingFriends. Sophie had developed a template to categorize users' online usage, and she developed his profile as she went, including links to his most-visited sites, his profiles and access codes. His main email was cluttered with spam, indicating he didn't use it much.

She began backtracking through his online activity and logged into DyingFriends.

A portal screen opened. "About Us: We are a community of people who are wrestling with the knowledge that our lives are ending. We offer an agenda-free supportive atmosphere to explore issues we are facing." A series of exterior links on the front page led to various resource websites. Accessing the actual site with its inter-active forums required a password.

Sophie tried various username variations on Corby's name to no avail. Finally, she hit "Lost Username" and asked for a new one to be sent to email. "Username sent to email" appeared, but when she went back to his email, nothing had arrived.

Little bastard had a secret email. She hated when that happened, but fortunately she had another program for that. Sophie dragged and dropped that program from another monitor, and it began tracing companies with storage containing Corby Hale's IP address. After some minutes, it dredged up Yahoo, Bing, and Gmail.

"You sneaky boy," she muttered, entertained by this mild challenge.

On the three major search engines, she was able to identify and hack into Corby's various identities and retrieve the username for DyingFriends on his Gmail account, surferboyOahu@gmail.com.

Once she had that, it was easy to reset the password and log back into his account on DyingFriends—only to find herself at a dead end: "Account deleted by admin" flashed at her from a blank screen.

Sophie sat back from the desk, automatically beginning to exercise as she regrouped. She lifted her knees to touch her chest for forty core-strengthening exercises, stretched backward and cracked her long golden-brown fingers. Realized she was hungry and it was almost ten a.m. She stood, did a sun salutation, and ended folded over with her forehead against her knees, thinking.

"Deleted by admin" implied that the site administrator had

removed the account, something that hadn't happened with any of Corby's other accounts. All of them were still active, and the boy's body was barely cold.

So it was quite possible the admin of DyingFriends had known he was dead.

She stayed jackknifed over and unzipped her backpack on the floor, removing a fortified protein drink and a hard-boiled egg. She walked across the felted carpet to stand in front of the floor-to-ceiling tinted windows.

Something wasn't right about the DyingFriends site—why would his account, which had been used the day Corby died, be deleted already? She didn't need DAVID to tell her that was unlikely. She hoped the write blocker on Alfred Shimaoka's computer would be done soon; DyingFriends could be the link between the two men. In any case, it was time to bring Waxman up to speed.

She drank the protein drink, ate the egg mechanically, refilled her plastic cup at the water dispenser, and tapped the Bluetooth headset at her ear. "Chief? Can we hold a team meeting on the suicide cases? I have some information and ideas I need to discuss."

CHAPTER EIGHT

L<small>EI</small> <small>BROUGHT</small> her coffee into the spare conference room, with its window overlooking the ocean, wraparound white boards, and large FBI plaque over the head of the table. Special Agent in Charge Waxman was already seated. He had a way of always being there first; Marcella said it was so he could assert dominance over the pack.

Marcella had a theory that his leadership style was to "copy the wolves" and had told her he'd let it slip that he was a sociology major in his undergrad program. Lei sat one seat down on the left from the SAC. In the eighteen months she'd been with the Bureau. Waxman seemed to have turned his critical attention to working over the NAT, Gupta, instead of her and Marcella.

"Good morning, Chief." He was even letting them get away with such loosening of protocol as a nickname title.

"Good morning, Agent Texeira." Waxman, immaculate in a light gray gabardine suit, adjusted his laptop microscopically to the right and pushed a button. A screen trundled down over the FBI plaque against the wall behind his head. "Where's the rest of the team?"

Ken slid into the seat beside Lei, a faint scent of lemony after-shave in his wake. "Good morning."

Sophie Ang, moving with the grace that had always reminded Lei of a cat, sat down with her laptop at his right side. "Can I start, sir?"

"You may. You asked for this meeting. But first I want to tell you that we need to give our full attention and effort to solving what happened to Corby Hale. The senator and Mrs. Hale have powerful friends, and either they or their connections been calling the office daily and demanding updates. I just got off the phone with the mayor, and that's no way to start the day."

Lei was glad, in that moment, that she hadn't had to see the Hales again—she didn't think she'd ever forget Mrs. Hale's white face contrasting with the blood on her collar from the torn earlobe.

Ang punched some buttons on her computer, and a website, DyingFriends, popped up, appearing on the screen. "I know there's a lot of pressure, sir, and I asked for this meeting because I thought it was time that discussed what's happening with these 'odd' suicide cases." She made air quotes. "I was the one to ask that we take the Hale boy's case. There's a reason for that, and I'll get into that in a minute—but for now, I wanted to tell you that in addition to the anomalies at the sites of the two suicides, both Shimaoka and Hale belonged to a website called DyingFriend.com."

A pause as the team digested this. "DyingFriends? Why would a healthy young guy like Corby Hale belong to something like that?" Lei asked. "I didn't find his name or that site when I was just searching his name in general."

"I don't know why. Don't you have a meeting with Fukushima about his autopsy later? Maybe there will be some answers there," Ang said.

"So this is the commonality between them? Did you find anything else connecting the two?" Waxman asked. "I haven't had time to read all your case files so far."

Ken spoke up at that. "We got the call for the Shimaoka site when one of the HPD detectives lifted a print of Corby Hale's off duct tape on Shimaoka's tailpipe. We did a full search of the house and car yesterday, but so far, no other trace of Corby Hale."

"My guess is that they'll be connected somehow on this website. The problem is, Corby's and Shimaoka's identities have already been deleted by the system admin of DyingFriends. Which implies knowledge of their deaths, something none of their other online accounts seem to have." Ang typed rapidly, and they were able to view the error message 404 pages. "There's something about this site that's fishy. I'd like permission, sir, to develop a profile and impersonate a DyingFriends member. I will see if I can figure out what really is happening on this site behind the fire wall and track the system admin."

"Permission granted. Please submit all particulars on this to me —identity, details, et cetera—before you initiate the impersonation. Yamada and Texeira, where are you with your part of the investigation?"

Ken cleared his throat. "We're still sifting through the trace and evidence collected at both the crime scenes. Now that we're aware there was some sort of crossover between Hale and Shimaoka, we're planning to go back through everything we found at Corby Hale's. We also have some follow-up interviews to do, including one with Senator Hale. We didn't find any foreign trace at Corby's scene— what's notable was that there were no prints at all on his heroin kit. The syringe had his prints on it, but awkwardly placed. The setup was for a right-hander when Corby was left-handed, a difficult maneuver to pull off."

"So these are the anomalies." Waxman switched to photos of the scene on his computer, and they flashed on the screen overhead. Lei was struck again by Corby's beauty, the posed quality of his body like an angel on a tomb.

"We're also still waiting for toxicology reports from Dr. Fukushima's office," Lei said. "She can give us preliminary findings on the autopsies as early as today."

"What about the suicide notes?" Waxman pulled images of those up—the enigmatic handwriting of Corby's beside the elegant finality of Alfred Shimaoka's. "They look genuine—what did handwriting analysis reveal? Any trace on the paper?"

"No trace but the vic's prints," Lei said. "Handwriting analysis came back as consistent. These notes are real, and they were handled only by Corby and Shimaoka."

"So what's going on here, exactly?" Waxman looked up at them over the narrow steel rims of his reading glasses. His icy eyes tracked their faces and made Lei's bladder cramp, reminding her of her old boss, Captain Omura on Maui. Omura's exacting standards had both challenged and improved Lei's work—and Waxman's had too. "I'm still not getting a clear enough picture of what happened to these two victims and why. Let's have these dots connected by the next briefing. And how did you come up with this trend in suicides, anyway?" That sharp, pale gaze had come to rest on Sophie Ang.

For the first time Lei could remember, the tech agent shifted in her seat and looked uncertain—though with her exotic features set in an immobile mask, it was hard to tell. Ang kept her gaze on her laptop screen while her fingers worked their magic, and the overhead filled with a log-in portal over a plain white screen labeled "Data Analysis Victim Information Database."

"This is how I detected a trend nationwide in suicides with oddities. I decided to narrow my search to local suicides, and DAVID twigged the Hale case."

"DAVID." Waxman had become very still. "I am not aware of that software. And I'm aware of all of our Bureau software."

A flush stained Sophie Ang's high cheekbones. "DAVID is my program. I have been building it on my own time for the last two years." Lei knew Ang had been at the Bureau in Honolulu for three years, and until this moment, she was the only agent Lei had never seen come under Waxman's hammer.

"So this is an unsanctioned, untested program."

"Yes, sir." Ang's eyes stayed down.

"Are you running our confidential data on it? Are you using

Bureau computers to run it? Have you taken any of our information off-site to work on at home?"

The flush deepened. Lei could see stress in Ang's wide brown eyes as she looked up at their boss at last, and Lei felt the tech agent's anxiety as Ang answered. "Sir, I'm aware this is a breach in protocol, and I'm willing to submit the program to the most stringent of reviews with the national tech department. I didn't want to do that until I was confident of the value DAVID could offer the Bureau and had worked out the bugs in the program. I was waiting for the right time to talk with you about it."

Waxman let a long beat go by as he stared at Ang. Then he turned to Lei and Ken. "Go see the medical examiner. Get a rush on those tox results. Agent Ang, you stay here while we discuss the repercussions of this."

Lei wished she could find a way to show the Sophie Ang some support or sympathy— Ang was brilliant, and she had no doubt that the DAVID program was going to be a huge asset, no matter how it worked. Lei looked over at Ang, but the other agent had folded her hands in her lap and looked down. There was nothing Lei could do but say, "Yes, sir," and follow Ken out.

The click of the conference room door shutting behind them had never sounded so final. How well Lei knew the feeling of being under a superior's scrutiny. She said a little prayer for Ang as she walked down the hall.

CHAPTER NINE

Sᴏᴘʜɪᴇ ᴋᴇᴘᴛ her hands folded in her lap and her eyes down as the conference room door closed behind the other agents. Her back was to the gorgeous view of a sunlit ocean dimmed by shaded glass. She wished she hadn't sat with her back to the window. It might have calmed her racing heart to sneak a look at it now and then.

"Agent Ang." Waxman waited a long beat until she looked up. "I'm disappointed in you."

Hurt showed in the tightness at the corners of Waxman's light blue eyes, the line of his mouth, the way he removed his glasses, tossing them down.

"I'm sorry, sir. I only ever have wanted to help the Bureau and our cases."

He cut her off with a hand gesture. "I'm not disappointed that you used your considerable gifts to try to build something new to help the Bureau. That doesn't surprise me at all. It surprises me that you didn't tell me about it early on. It would have made this stage, when we tried it out on a case, so much easier."

"I'm..." Sophie opened and closed her mouth a couple of times, her fingers twisting in her lap. "I didn't think you'd approve. I wanted to show you it could work." She looked back down at her log-in screen. "I thought you'd shut me down if I didn't prove DAVID's worth first."

Waxman shut his eyes, rubbed them with his forefinger and thumb. "I'm doing something wrong as special agent in charge that you don't know how much I value you. How much confidence I've come to have in your skills and your integrity."

"I'm sorry, sir," Sophie said again, feeling her face heat up. She didn't know how to respond to Waxman's praise, his personal disappointment. She'd misread him, and it wasn't the first time she'd done that. Once again she wished she understood people half as well as computers.

The SAC sighed, replaced his glasses, sat forward. "From here on out, you get an idea, come to me. Right away. I promise I'll hear you out and try my best to facilitate your project, whatever it is. The Bureau is getting hammered these days because we've created a bureaucratic culture where individual incentive isn't rewarded. Our best people are leaving for other agencies or the private sector. I've tried hard not to be that kind of director, but I see I've failed, and that's for me to correct." He tapped his laptop. "Now, damage control. This program has to be submitted through the proper channels or defense attorneys will have a field day—we always have to keep the end in mind as we pursue a case, right?"

"Right," Sophie agreed.

"So, if DAVID generated the original lead, what we need to do is come up with another reason we were 'twigged' to the Hale case, which is pretty easy—the senator's high profile. And we need to submit DAVID to the review process. As to you working with confidential data off-site, that has to stop immediately."

"But, sir. I often work at home late at night..."

"I can't allow that. The premises of your building may not be secure, and if our data were stolen somehow, it's an unconscionable security breach."

Sophie couldn't tell him she'd replicated her entire lab at home and that everything was networked together. She'd known it was against regulations, but to her mind the efficiency justified the risk, and she had a good alarm system in a high-security building. Sophie had long ago moved to a cloud computing mentality: Individual computers were merely outlets plugging in and out of a seamless information flow rather than individual repositories, which was how the Bureau still operated in many areas.

"Yes, sir."

"So tell me how this program works. Walk me through what you did to come up with the Hale case."

Sophie felt herself regaining confidence as she entered her password and broke open DAVID to her boss, explaining how it mined the other criminal databases, including local and state police. She demonstrated how DAVID searched out commonalities depending on variables entered in search parameters and how the confidence ratios worked. She walked Waxman through her process with the suicides, which she'd begun running in DAVID after a news report on an upswing in suicides caught her attention.

"So this program can basically go hunting for types of crimes nationwide, looking for common MOs and other variables such as weapons, et cetera?" Waxman clarified at last.

"Yes. But it can work only with what's been inputted, so the more we digitize criminal records, the more effective DAVID is going to be."

"What about DAVID's unauthorized access to local and state police department records?"

"I'm sure that's going to be something to be worked out, sir, but don't you think the greater good justifies it?"

"Of course it does. That doesn't mean we'll all be able to sit down and play nice in the sandbox." Waxman sighed, rubbed his eyes again. "Save a copy of the software and deliver it to my office by the end of the day. I've got to make some calls."

"I'm sorry, sir," she said again.

This time the look he shot her was hard. "One apology is enough. Never apologize more than once."

"Yes, sir." Sophie unplugged her laptop and fled as he reached for the triangular conference phone in the center of the table.

CHAPTER TEN

KEN PUSHED the door handle bar to open the hermetically sealed door of the morgue. Ever since Lei's friend had died on the Big Island, Lei had trouble with morgues. She'd begun her relaxation breathing in the hallway—in through the nose, out through the mouth, counting to three—but even with that and with a dab of Vicks under her nose, every muscle in her body tightened at the chemical-over-biology smell.

Several draped bodies decorated wheeled tables in the big, chilly room with its range of sinks and steel wall of closed box doors. Dr. Fukushima and her assistant were bent over the brightly lit chest cavity of some unfortunate as they entered. The medical examiner looked up, her gloved hands covered with gore. "I'll be right with you."

"We'll be over here," Ken said. They pulled back against her desk, an island of normality behind a transparent shoji. They sat on a couple of folding chairs until Fukushima arrived, her mask lifted onto the top of her head, snapping off the gloves and tossing them into a biohazard bin.

"We were able to get the posts done on your two suicides— luckily things haven't been busy lately, though there was a big pileup on the H-3 and I'm backed up now. I sent your blood and tox results off; we should have them by tomorrow since you told me to put a rush on it."

"Thanks, Dr. Fukushima," Lei said as the doctor sat down in her wheeled chair.

"Well. I'm curious too. Suicides that look like suicides but just aren't right." The doctor picked up a file. "I'll email these to you, but so far it's looking much as we suspected. Alfred Shimaoka died of carbon-monoxide poisoning. All the physical signs are there for that. And Corby Hale died of heart failure, no doubt due to a heroin injection. But what was interesting— and will be confirmed in his blood work—is this." She passed Ken the file on the young man and opened it to a picture Lei wished she hadn't had to see. "Lesions inside his mouth. The boy likely had AIDS. Signs just weren't generally visible yet."

"Ah," Ken said. Lei noticed a slight tremble in his hands as they held the folder.

"Maybe that's why he took his life. Didn't want to go through that. Though people can live a normal life span now. It's not the death sentence it once was," Lei said.

"The point I'm making is that both of these men, while they might have been ill, died well before they would have naturally. Alfred had pancreatic cancer, and according to his records kept here at the hospital, he refused treatment. Wouldn't do anything—chemo, radiation, nothing. By the state of his pancreas and the cancer I found elsewhere, I'd have said he had six months. Most people want every day they can get." Dr. Fukushima set the folder down. "I'm ruling these deaths as assisted suicides."

"That gives our case some momentum," Lei said. "We think there's some sort of online connection that they made. Our tech department's looking into it."

"Well, I'm glad you agree. I was really in two minds about this, but the amount of time both of them would have had left makes this a crime worth pursuing."

Lei noticed Ken was still gazing down at the images of Corby Hale. His face was pale and rigid. She took the folder out of his hands and set it back on the desk. "Thanks, Doctor. We'll look forward to the tox results."

Ken followed her out into the shiny, fluorescent-lit linoleum hallway. The whoosh and click of the morgue door behind them felt like liberty to Lei. She turned to Ken and put a hand on his arm as they walked down the hall.

"Want to get some coffee?"

"Okay." They turned in to the cafeteria, one floor up. Lei got a tray and loaded it with coffee as well as some Portuguese sausage, a scoop of rice, and scrambled eggs from behind the cafeteria counter. It was almost midday, but she hadn't eaten yet today. She joined Ken with his lone Styrofoam cup of coffee in one of the vinyl booths.

She tore open packets of salt and pepper, sprinkled them over her breakfast.

"Something's up. What's going on with you?"

"Bugs me. That kid." Ken stirred creamer into his coffee with a red-and-white-striped stir stick. He tapped the stick, lay it down, took a sip of the coffee, grimaced. He set the cup down. "So young. Shouldn't be dead that way."

"Or sick that way."

"Or sick that way," Ken agreed. "He should have known better."

"He was so young." Between them lay the awkward topic of Ken's sexual orientation, the fact that he was in the closet about it. "Kids always think they're going to be the exception."

"Someone might have infected him on purpose. I've heard rumors of someone doing that. Here in Honolulu."

"That should be a crime we could investigate."

"It should, but it's not." Ken took another sip of the coffee, winced. "Man. This stuff is really bad."

Lei had made short work of her breakfast and now she sipped the coffee. It really was bad. "Lot of us with our own side projects going on." She'd never told Ken about her connection to the Kwon murder. "What do you think of Sophie's DAVID program?"

"It's going to be amazing when it gets okayed. Though I'm trying to imagine a world where DAVID gets to freely roam through all the criminal databases of all the states—I can't see that getting approved. Everyone wants to guard their cases and data."

"We should keep the bigger picture in mind, though. I think of one of my cases early on, before I was a detective. Serial rape case. The perp had been preying on girls on different islands. If we'd had that communication easily available, we could have seen it was all connected sooner." Lei took a sip of the coffee for something to do, and regretted it.

"Well, it will be interesting to see how Waxman handles the DAVID thing."

"I felt sorry for Sophie. Maybe I should call her, see how it went."

Ken looked up. His face had lightened a bit. "She'd be shocked. You aren't exactly the BFF type."

"Hey." Lei stood, picked up her empty tray. "Marcella's teaching me some manners. I'm getting better."

"Speaking of Marcella. Did you see who she's dating?"

"I did. They seem pretty into each other."

"Yeah. So when's your boyfriend coming over from Maui?"

Lei tossed her trash, stowed the tray, pushed the glass door open with her shoulder, Ken right behind her. "Don't know. But I'm hoping soon. How about your boyfriend?"

Ken raised a brow at her, and she laughed. "Fine then. Back to work."

Sophie arrived at her workstation and felt the dim coolness of the IT lab, her comfort zone, bring her heart rate down after the stress of the meeting with Waxman. She stowed the laptop in the slotted shelf she'd set aside for it. She liked to have her work area clear. She fired up her computers, and while they booted, she got out the big ball, lay facedown on it, rolled it down under her feet, and began doing push-ups.

"Everything okay?"

Sophie continued her push-ups without looking up. "Sure. Why wouldn't it be?" Sophie sped up, feeling the exertion discharge stress from the meeting. "Pull out another ball and join me."

Bateman, a pudgy geek fresh out of Quantico, seemed to have developed a crush on her. He swung by her station way more often than she'd like, on one pretext or another.

"No, thanks." Bateman watched her as she flipped back over and began her sit-up routine. "I don't know how you make yourself do those all day."

"Keeps me in shape for the gym."

"What gym is this?"

"Fight Club down on Kalakaua."

Bateman was silent. He had to have enough physicality to have made it through the Academy's rigorous tests. She took pity on him. "You can come down sometime. It's good for our tech skills for us to stay in shape, keep a balance."

"I'd like that."

Sophie resumed her sit-ups, and he drifted away to his station.

IT was like that. Everyone had their quirks—and now she'd challenged Bateman to something that he might even consider a date, which would be awful. Sophie felt a stab of loneliness. She'd definitely felt a tingle the other day as Alika demonstrated a hold, his steely arm around her waist…She suppressed the feeling by sitting on the ball in a V shape, carefully balancing, holding her legs straight out for a count of a hundred and fifty. Finally, trembling, she did some stretches, refilled her big water cup, and settled into her cockpit, all her screens humming.

She cracked her supple fingers and opened up the entry screen of DyingFriends.

Copying each piece of information as she developed it, she planted a dummy IP address in case the system admin was watching for law enforcement and began a profile: Shasta McGill, aged forty-three, sick with leukemia and not expected to live. Two children, divorced. Username ShastaM, password a transparent combination of numbers that were a fictional birth date. She imported a photo from the FBI stock photo archives of a wan-looking pretty blond woman.

All these details she saved into a text box and sent to Waxman per his request.

When her profile was complete, she hit Enter and was admitted to DyingFriends. Within the home screen were various topic areas, chat threads, and pages with links and resources. So far, nothing more than morbid, she thought, surfing a catalog of burial choices, featuring everything from caskets to crematoriums.

She supposed, for the dying, it must be comforting to be able to freely talk with other dying people. She cruised through the thread discussions: "When do I tell the kids I'm dying" to "I want out early."

She zeroed in on that one. After all, their cases had involved suicide, and their two victims had met each other here.

The chat conversation started off lively, with a debate about the worth of such a choice and petered out with one respondent, Cancer-Curmudgeon, saying, "You have to live out the number of days God gives you."

She typed in a response: "Hi, I'm Shasta, and I've got terminal leukemia. I'm sick and miserable and, frankly, I don't see the point of many more days."

She felt a twinge, the phantom pain of her own losses and the depression she battled with exercise. This wasn't easy, imagining herself in this woman's shoes.

CancerCurmudgeon responded. "Make your peace with God and accept his will. You'll have more peace."

"God has nothing to do with cancer, and if he does, I have a few words to say to him," ShastaM typed back.

"God is sovereign, and we are eternal beings. It's this life and cancer that are illusions."

"I don't buy that. I believe in reincarnation. This life is a revolving door, and I want out." Sophie had to pause to consider what Shasta's position was—and she realized she didn't really know her own. It brought a hollowness to the pit of her stomach. She'd been so busy trying to live, she'd never really considered death.

"You'll die, and it will be too late. You'll burn in hell, and I'll be laughing from heaven."

"I get to believe what I believe," ShastaM said, even as Sophie wondered how she'd so quickly locked horns with a "troll" on a forum. They were everywhere on the Internet, and dying or not, they were opinionated, rude, and hiding behind anonymity. Just as she was, she reminded herself.

Sophie abandoned that thread, hoping she'd planted some bread crumbs that would lure the system admin. She dropped other suicidal hints on a few more threads, then posted her email in yet another chat room, asking for "emotional support."

That done, she navigated around the site until she spotted "DyingFriends in Your Area." She plugged in her zip code, and a list of identities popped up, along with how recently they had been active and their zip codes. She copied the zip codes and names into another window to track down. DyingFriends had at least twenty Hawaii members.

Armed with that information, she logged back out of the site and then set to work tracking down the identities of the Hawaii members. Their zip codes and fake names weren't much to go on. She'd have to lure them into revealing more.

Sophie tracked the names to the emails listed and sent each of them a sweet introductory email with a picture of the pale, smiling, pretty face of dying Shasta McGill, appealing for friendship outside the site in the big lonely town of Honolulu, where she'd moved to live her last days in paradise.

Sophie wondered how often that really happened. She felt her worldview shift just a tiny bit—lonely people, waiting to die, were all around and invisible. It made her wonder if she was just a few cancer cells away from being one of them.

The depression and loneliness Sophie had battled on and off fluttered black wings at her from the edges of her mind, and she had to look down at the tattoos on her arms to remind herself she was living life on her own terms. In *freedom*, with *courage*.

Setting up an online sting was like an elaborate form of cooking to Sophie, ending in a meal that brought her targets to the table. Cooking in Thailand was a lengthy production she'd watched their servants perform: first, harvesting the food. From the garden, farm, or sea came the raw ingredients. Then washing, hulling, seasoning, marinating, and prepping. After that, individual mini cooking of elements of the dish, and then the collection of all the ingredients into a cohesive whole, and finally, the presentation.

Right now, her "meal" was at the hunting, gathering, and prep stage. She'd left all those lures out there. Hopefully, a few would respond to the dummy email address she'd set up. Then she could track their computers, find their addresses, and send Ken and Lei to check them out.

She switched back to digging into the innards of the black Mac that had belonged to Alfred Shimaoka. She tried not to think of his sad end in the SUV with his beloved dog barking a few feet away.

CHAPTER ELEVEN

LEI PULLED into the Youth Correctional Facility. She held up her ID badge at the gate, and Vinnie, the guard, gave her shaka and waved her through. She was a weekly visitor here, a fact unknown to anyone but Marcella, who'd declined to come as she was having dinner with Marcus Kamuela at her parents' restaurant in Waikiki.

Keiki and Angel sat on the passenger seat of the truck. They loved the drive over the Pali to Kailua, where the youth jail was snugged up against the wall of a green mountain. A slight breeze came down the valley, and Lei cracked the windows and left Keiki in the truck in the cool blue of evening.

Carrying Angel, who wore her therapy dog vest, Lei went through the security admission steps and finally arrived in the group rec room, where she visited the girl she'd captured last year during a burglary spree. She'd forged a permanent bond with the orphaned Consuelo Aguilar.

The pretty Filipina girl bounded up off the battered couch where she'd been lounging with some other adolescents. Lei set the wriggling, ecstatic little Chihuahua down, and Angel ran to Consuelo. Several girls waved to Lei from the couch. "Titas" all, the tattooed tough girls clustered around Consuelo, exclaiming and petting

Angel's little domed head as the seventeen-year-old clasped the dog close.

Lei sat on one of the molded metal stools bolted to the floor. The corrections officer, a sturdy woman they called Aunty Marcie, came up and greeted her. Her graying hair brushed her waist in a braid as thick as Lei's wrist. "So good you come fo' see her," Aunty Marcie said. "Consuelo, she look forward to you all week."

"She jus' like see her dog." Lei had impulsively agreed to care for Angel last year when Consuelo was taken into custody, and so far she hadn't regretted that decision for a minute.

"No, she talk about you all the time. She always in one better mood after you come."

"That's good. Me too."

"You make all the girls feel good, like they can be somebody because you come," Aunty Marcie said, her brown eyes warm. "These kids, they need role models."

"Thanks, eh." Lei looked up at the woman. "I'm sure you help all you can."

"I do, but I only one CO, and sometimes I gotta bust them for something. You young, you one big-shot FBI agent, and still you come every week and bring the dog. It means more than you think."

"Okay." Lei was embarrassed, and Aunty Marcie walked off to break up an argument brewing in a far corner.

She sat quietly waiting at the round Formica table, and as she always eventually did, Consuelo came and sat across from her. The girl had left Angel with the other teenagers on the couch. She tucked glossy hair behind a small ear and smiled. "Hi."

"Hi. How are things this week?"

"Pretty good. Almost done with my English class. When I finish, I'll be ready to get my diploma." Consuelo wore the bright orange overalls with a natural elegance that belied their coarse message. Her big dark eyes flashed something like defiance as she looked at Lei. "I'm going to college."

"'Course you are. I never had a doubt."

"Hey. I could just be a deadbeat, go back to a life of crime." Consuelo pushed her bottom lip out in a mock pout.

"Ha. You know you never were a normal criminal."

"Well, did you know my English project is my memoir?"

"I knew your lawyer was negotiating with all those Hollywood people interested in it."

"I know I can't profit from it, which is fine…But I like the challenge of writing." She produced the introductory pages and handed them to Lei. Lei had noticed the stark beauty of the girl's writing when she read her journal last year, and now the opening pages of the memoir brought a lump to her throat.

"Wow, Consuelo. You really have a way with words."

"So that's what I'm going to major in. Journalism."

"That will make Wendy Watanabe happy." They grinned at each other. Watanabe was a ruthless but passionate TV reporter, and she too visited Consuelo regularly. Her fundraising efforts had procured Consuelo the best defense lawyer in the state.

"Yeah, and now I've got Wendy doing writing workshops with the girls here. She's organized editorial help for us. We're all writing our memoirs, not just me."

Lei glanced up and looked around the room at girls of every size, shape, and shade—all troubled teens who'd hit the wall of the law. "I bet there are some good stories here." She felt her own chest tighten with a moment of memory—if her aunty Rosario hadn't taken her in, she might well have ended up here herself.

There but for the grace of God go I, she thought. It was something her father, converted to Christianity in prison, often said.

She set the pages back down on the table. "These are very good. But then, you knew that."

"Thanks. It's my chance to explain everything, and I don't want to miss it. Mr. Fernandez is sort of acting as my agent; he said I can choose any charity to give the proceeds to. That's perfect. I can always write something else and make money on it."

"That's the spirit. So do you hear from Tyler?" Tyler, Consuelo's boyfriend, had been subject to some tougher sentencing and was incarcerated in California.

"We write. But he's kind of depressed. We're just friends now."

Angel had fought her way free of the clutches of the other girls, and she trotted back to Consuelo. Lei watched their affectionate reunion.

"Do you still ever think of suicide?" she asked suddenly. Her mind had wandered back to the case.

Consuelo looked up, her dark eyes hard. "What do you think? I'm in prison, and I've got a record that will follow me when I get out. I'm broke and my parents are dead."

"I'm sorry. I didn't mean to be so abrupt. I have a case that involves suicide, and I'm trying to understand it better." Lei had had her own brushes with those dark thoughts, but they'd led in other directions—to self-injury. She looked down at the faint white lines of scarring on the insides of her arms.

Consuelo stroked the little dog, who'd flopped on her back in the girl's lap. "I wanted to die when I was first captured. I thought my life was over."

"I remember."

"I actually thought I could will myself to die. But that's not how it works, is it? Every day I kept waking up. Now I just let the thoughts pass by. I observe them. Dr. Wilson taught me how. Thoughts are not reality. They're just thoughts. It's helped me to realize they aren't the truth."

"Told you she's a good therapist." Dr. Wilson, Lei's former therapist, had worked with Consuelo on and off since her capture. Lei thought about the Hale case. "If you'd been feeling that way, and you'd had someone agree to help you commit suicide when you couldn't do it yourself for some reason, would you have taken advantage of that?"

A long beat passed while Consuelo stroked Angel's belly, scratched under her tiny pointed chin. Finally she looked up at Lei. "I wouldn't be here today."

"Thanks," Lei said. "This actually helps me with a case."

"Weird convo, but glad I could help."

"Back to your rooms; it's the boys' time!" Auntie Marcie called, and with good-natured grumbling, the girls got up from the couches. Consuelo stood, handed Angel to Lei.

"Thanks for coming."

"You're welcome. Thanks for loaning me Angel." They smiled at each other, and Consuelo straightened her uniform and walked back to her friends, hips swinging, shiny black hair bouncing.

The girl had style, there was no doubt.

Lei waved goodbye to Aunty Marcie and left, a little surprised at the glow of happiness she felt to be in Consuelo's life, to be making even a little difference with these tough teen girls through her limited contact.

On the way back over the steep and winding ribbon of the Pali, Lei put her Bluetooth in her ear and speed-dialed Stevens.

"Twice in one week," he said. "I'm going to get spoiled."

"I know. I missed you. Just got done visiting Consuelo. She's working on her memoir."

"That's going to be worth reading."

"I think so too. Wouldn't be surprised if someone wants to make a movie out of it. Anyway, she's doing well."

"Was there a doubt? The girl's tough."

"Not really. You know, she kind of gave me food for thought on my case." Lei told him about the situation with the suicides. "She confirmed that if she'd had someone to help her die, she would have. And just think of these suicides. If there's some sort of assistance going on—many of them will be dying too soon. Or when there might have been a solution of some kind."

"Are you sure there isn't just one 'angel of death' offing people who say they want to commit suicide?"

Lei considered this new idea, tapping her fingers on the top of the steering wheel as she navigated a steep curve. Far away below, the ocean gleamed under a silvering of moonlight, Honolulu spread out before it in a net of lights. "I don't think we considered that scenario because of the print of one victim appearing in the scene of the other one."

"Well, maybe the doer knows there are enough inconsistencies to draw some attention. The print could be some sort of misdirection."

"I don't know. Really, all we have are two dead bodies with anomalies—nothing conclusive—suicide notes that are genuine, and both victims having memberships on this fishy website. I'm not even sure the case is hanging together at this point. Ang seems convinced, though. What would you think of a program that could mine all the different law enforcement databases for commonalities in a case? Nationwide?"

"Impossible," Stevens said. "Too much security, too many different and incompatible databases. But if it could be done, and the interagency problems resolved, incredible."

"That's what Ang's working on. Girl's some sort of genius with computers."

"Awesome potential. You fixing to have another friend?"

"Don't know. I like her, but she keeps to herself."

"Speaking of keeping to yourself, and being sick of it, have you given any more thought to what we're going to do when I'm free?"

"I don't know. It's so hard. One of us has to give something up with work."

"I know. But I've been thinking about you. Remembering." The deep note in his voice activated longing, a throb that spread outward and beat in her veins. The feeling, instant as fire blazing through a dry field, rippled down the insides of her arms, and she squeezed the steering wheel, hard.

"I've been trying not to think of you. That way. Any way."

"It's not working. What are you wearing?"

Lei laughed. "I'm driving. I have two dogs as chaperones. And I'm wearing the usual Bureau pants and shirt."

"I meant—under that." His voice dropped lower.

Lei gulped, speechless. "You first." She couldn't believe they were having this conversation. Phone flirting had never been their thing—but desperation led to invention.

"Well, I got off work and went surfing. I just got back, took a shower. Got a towel on."

Lei's nipples tightened with a tingle akin to pain as she pictured his long corded arms, the light sprinkle of chest hair over his wide chest, the ripple of his abs ending at the towel.

"This is torture. I hate you," she said.

"Yeah. I wish you were here. If you were, I'd put you in front of me and unbutton that white blouse. Slowly. One button at a time."

"No," she breathed, turning off the freeway onto the side street that would eventually lead to her house. "I'm driving. Stop."

"You have to call me back. Later."

"Okay. I will. And keep the towel on until then. I've always liked you wearing less."

This time he was the one to hiss though his teeth. "Don't know if I can wait for you."

"You better." She put her foot down and sped home.

Sophie circled her mixed martial arts coach, Alika Wolcott. Marcella had canceled again, some excuse that meant she was seeing her new boyfriend. Sophie kept her stance low, and when Alika finally made a move, throwing a roundhouse kick, she caught his leg and tripped him to the ground.

She wore a boxer's padded helmet, split-fingered, open-palmed gloves, and tight Lycra athletic wear—not out of any vanity but to keep the clothing from getting caught and used against her.

Alika was large, at least six foot two and a hundred and ninety pounds, all muscle, from what she could tell, and considerably stronger than her pound for pound. That's why she had to be more tenacious and agile—and she felt a frisson of triumph as she succeeded in wrapping herself around his back in a hold called the spiral ride.

Alika's thick muscles bunched beneath her, and he flexed, breaking her grip. He held up a hand, indicating a stop to the action, and she moved away, sitting up on the mat and circling her arms around her knees.

He unclipped his headgear and took it off, kneeling on the mat. Black hair rippled back from his forehead; he was a light brown color too, but more golden than she. His heritage was Hawaiian and Caucasian, what they called *hapa* in Hawaii.

"When you do that hold, grasp your arm above the elbow." Alika shook his head briskly and combed his hair out of his eyes. Sophie wished she didn't keep noticing how handsome he was.

"Right," she said.

"Let's walk through the move. Grab me from behind, like you did." They both got up. She moved in on him, feeling tentative as she noticed the ridges of muscle in his back. She reached across his shoulder—and the breath flew out of her lungs as he flipped her, to land hard on her back on the mats.

"Again!" he exclaimed.

Sophie sucked air back in, feeling a burst of anger, and bounded back up. This time she threw her weight and strength into grasping him. They grappled intensely for several moments, but Sophie ended up having to concede.

She rolled away from Alika and stood up. "I think I've got it."

"We'll try it again sometime. When you work out with Marcella, I want you to try that hold on her. It should work with someone closer to your size."

Sophie narrowed her eyes at him. "You saying I can't take you?"

"Not yet. And the day you can, I won't have anything to teach you anymore, and that will be a sad day for me." He grinned, and she smiled back, taking off the headgear. Her hair was cropped short, so there was no rearranging to be done. He was looking at the tattoos on the insides of her arms.

"What's that writing? What do they say?"

"It's Thai. I did it so I wouldn't forget some things I've been through. They are just words." She mopped her face with one of the thin gym towels, turned away toward the showers, but he followed her.

"What do they say?" he asked again.

"Hope. Freedom. Power. Respect. Courage." She had no trouble reciting the words she'd had inked after her divorce was final.

"I like it." He gave her shoulder a brotherly pat. "Thanks for telling me. I've been wondering about them for a while."

That made her look down at her gym bag. The tattoos ran down the outsides of her thighs and insides of her arms—not the most suggestive of places; she'd done that so they could be easily concealed in a professional setting. But that meant he'd looked at her body.

He'd thought about it.

Sophie, don't be ridiculous. The voice in her head sounded like her mother. He'd never be interested in someone so unladylike, a brawler like you.

"I was wondering about something. Are you going out with anybody?" His voice sounded a little uncertain. "You must be."

She stilled, her hands in her gym bag as she stowed her gloves. She turned to look at him. "No."

"I can't believe it," he said. "Greg was right. Are you gay, then?"

Greg was the gym manager. Sophie felt a wave of heat roar up her chest, and her rigid fingertips shot out to stop less than an inch from his throat, a gesture capable of crushing his larynx with a blow.

"You think because I'm single and a fighter, I must be gay? Take a look at your biases." She spun to grab her gym bag, striding across the large warehouse space. Her ears felt hot.

They'd been talking and speculating about her. She could imagine the crude joking. She wished she could have a relationship, but the truth was she hadn't been interested in anyone since her divorce—until this silly crush on Alika.

And now all she felt was angry and embarrassed. Better to go back to her computers, where she was never misunderstood or misjudged.

She was unlocking her car, a white Lexus SUV her father had given her for graduation from the FBI Academy, when she felt a hand on her shoulder. She didn't think, she reacted—shot her elbow back into her attacker's solar plexus, spun to swing the gym bag.

Alika had doubled up from the blow, and the gym bag caught him on the side of the head.

"Oh no!"

Alika tried to smile as he rubbed his head. "Should have called your name. My bad, sneaking up on you."

"Sorry, Coach." Sophie picked up her bag. "I just reacted."

"Call me Alika. Well, I'm not going to worry about your defense skills, that's for sure. I wanted to apologize. I shouldn't have just—asked you like that. You're so private."

"I'm in the FBI. We don't go around discussing our lives." She stowed the gym bag in the SUV's backseat. "I'm sorry too. I overreacted. I don't like people talking about me behind my back."

"It wasn't like that." Alika leaned on the car next to her. "You're a great fighter, really talented. I was going to suggest we put you up in some matches. I wanted to see…what might be factors to deal with before I asked you."

"There are no 'factors' but my job. And I'm pretty sure going into matches would just draw attention to myself, which isn't good for an agent. So regretfully, I have to decline."

Sophie found she really did regret it. She would have liked to see how she could do in the Women's MMA fight circuit, but she was sure Waxman would consider it inappropriate. In her head, her mother agreed wholeheartedly.

"Too bad." Alika pushed away from the side of the car. "You've got talent."

"So I've been told." But not with men. Not with relationships, and especially not in bed, where Assan had said, "Fucking you is like banging a mannequin."

The words still hurt, though she knew, as a professional adult, that it was no reflection on her that she couldn't get turned on by a man who beat her. Still, it had stolen her confidence at a time when she was too young to know better. Having Assan as her first and only relationship was no good measure of anything but heartache.

"See you next week." He raised a hand as he walked away. "I'm off to ice my injuries."

She smiled, but it didn't make it all the way to her eyes.

Fresh from a shower and clad in a towel, Sophie microwaved a glass casserole dish of pad thai noodles prepared by the housekeeper. She took off the towel and tossed it in the washer with the rest of her workout gear. The conversation with Alika, on top of the setback about using DAVID and her home computer setup, had left her with a dark feeling, a flatness. Tonight, and the days ahead, seemed without interest.

She padded naked across the living room, noticing the stellar sky, the twinkling lights, the ocean a black smudge in the distance. None of it did a thing for her. In her bedroom she pulled on a silky sleep tee and underwear and sat down in front of her home computer rig and fired it up, but the frisson of anticipation she usually felt getting "wired in" was gone. Tonight she was disabling the network.

It felt like facing an amputation.

"This is ridiculous," she told herself aloud. "I have plenty I can do. I have a life." The way the words sounded—like empty bravado —didn't help.

DAVID beckoned, but instead of playing with the program, she saved it to an external drive as Waxman had asked. She logged into her departmental email—and saw several emails from the Dying-Friends site.

Targets had responded to her lure.

It wouldn't hurt, just tonight, to respond to them from home. She could disable the network afterward.

She responded in ShastaM's identity to three emails that Dying-Friends members in Hawaii had sent. A few clicks of the mouse and inputting the email addresses into her search program later, and she'd traced their computers and had three names and addresses for Lei and Ken to follow up on tomorrow.

Sophie felt energy come back at this bit of progress, and that gave her the strength to log into her network and disconnect her home computers from the FBI ones. DAVID was now neutralized and "on ice" for the review process, and she also no longer had access to her FBI workstation data—but there was no reason she couldn't spend some time on DyingFriends, strengthening her identity there.

She left her angst behind as she disappeared onto the Internet, where she roamed free, powerful and bodiless. The world of her computers often felt more real, and certainly more comfortable, than any human company.

CHAPTER TWELVE

Lᴇɪ ᴡᴀʟᴋᴇᴅ into the Starbucks near Ala Moana Shopping Center the next morning. Her curls were still damp from the shower, but she'd managed to get to the meet with Ken and Ang within fifteen minutes of the phone ringing and waking her up from the best sleep she'd had in days.

"Hey, you looking sassy," Ken said as she joined the agents at a table off in the corner, away from other customers.

Lei knew her grin was huge. Exploring the new world of phone sex had done wonders for her mood. "Life is good, that's all. What's up, Sophie? You wanted to meet us here?"

"Yeah." In contrast, Sophie Ang didn't look like she'd slept well, her dark eyes circled by shadows. "I got some names and addresses of Honolulu members of DyingFriends, and I thought we could save some time by meeting here. I was hoping you could go out right away and interview these people."

"Definitely," Ken said. "How did you get that so fast?"

Ang explained her process of phishing on the site. "My identity is getting a lot of sympathy and attention. I keep saying I want to 'get out early,' and so far, no bites from the system admin or any organized effort to encourage suicide. But there are more people right here on Oahu in this group than you would believe."

"Is that bothering you?" Lei asked, concerned by Ang's demeanor.

"It's depressing, that's for sure. But no. I'm having to disconnect my home network and not bring work home anymore, and DAVID is offline for the review process, so I'm kind of at a loose end."

"I wondered what Waxman was going to do to you."

"It actually wasn't that bad." Sophie sighed, took a sip of her tea. "It's just a buildup of things. Alika asked to put me up in some bouts in the MMA women's fight circuit; I had to say no. I'm sure it's not something I should do as an agent."

Ken's straight brows drew together. "You're probably right. It could make you a target, and you know the Bureau policy of keeping a low public profile."

"I think it sucks," Lei said. "You should be able to do what you want." Sympathy for the tech agent, stymied on several levels, rose up. Sophie had so many talents, and it bothered Lei to see so few of them expressed.

"Life is never that simple," Sophie said, with a grateful glance at Lei. She slid a paper over to them. "Here are the names and addresses."

"Thanks." They watched her go, her tall, lithe figure weaving through the coffee shop.

"If I weren't gay, I'd have a crush on her," Ken said.

Lei smiled. "If I were, I would too. Okay, what's the plan?"

Ken looked at the list, pulled up his navigator app on his phone. "Let's figure out where they are, plot a route."

The first address was in the ritzy suburb of Kahala. Lei enjoyed warm morning air blowing by her through the open window and the sun on the ocean as they rounded Diamond Head and wound into a neighborhood of gracious estates. She let her mind wander back to Stevens and her building need to see him, as they drove up to an Asian-styled mansion with a cobalt-blue tiled roof.

They parked the Acura in a pea-gravel turnaround and walked over a tiny arched bridge spanning a koi pond. Fat fish in oranges and yellows swam lazily in the water below.

Ken rang the bell. A sound of celestial chimes rang somewhere deep in the house. He rang the bell again and finally a third time—and when the lacquered door finally opened, they understood why. A tiny man stood there, shrunken and frail as a Chinese Yoda, swathed in a lustrous brocade smoking jacket that brushed the floor. "Yes?"

"Good morning. My name is Special Agent Ken Yamada, and this is Special Agent Lei Texeira. We have a few questions for you regarding an investigation." They both held open their cred wallets.

"What is this about?" Yoda peered at the wallets. He appeared to be clinging to the door for support. Lei glanced at the note in her hand. "Clyde Woo" was written in Sophie's distinctive hand.

"Perhaps we could sit down? And you'd be more comfortable, Mr. Woo?" Lei asked. Without a word, the gnome let go of the door and shuffled off, leaving them to follow him into the dim recesses of the house. A vast living room opened up before them, with a bank of sliders framing the view of a sculptured garden. Mr. Woo made a short gesture to a low red couch and settled himself into a motorized wheelchair.

Lei looked around at the collection of exquisite sculpture against one wall and the shrine to Buddha on the other.

"What is this regarding?" Mr. Woo asked again. He had a wet rattle in his voice.

They'd decided on what to say back at the coffee shop. "We are investigating a website—DyingFriends. We understand you are a member on it," Ken said.

"Yes." Mr. Woo dug in the pocket of his robe, pulled out a pair of startlingly thick plastic-framed glasses, and put them on. "What are you investigating?"

"Well, that's confidential. All we can say is that DyingFriends may be involved in some unethical practices. Can you tell us what the site has been like for you?" Ken asked.

Mr. Woo took a while to think this over, and Lei found herself squirming a bit under his magnified gaze as it switched between herself and her partner.

"Well, as you may have guessed, I'm dying," he said. "I have a caregiver, but she's out. I have no family that I am speaking to, and DyingFriends is a place where I can be dying and not be shame." He gave a phlegmy cough. "I don't get out much anymore."

"We understand," Lei said. "It seems like it's a place where people who are in the same situation can get support. Has anyone ever talked with you about suicide on the site?"

"There are always people talking about it. We're dying. Suicide is a way to take control of that."

Lei was struck by the power of that simple sentence. She'd thought she was definitely against suicide, but she was finding the issue much more complex and heartrending than she'd ever known.

"Do you feel like suicide is being promoted at all on the site?" Ken asked.

"It's a chat site. There are all kinds of people there—and lots of religious people who think suicide is a sin. So no."

"Have you ever been approached by an administrator of Dying-Friends?"

"No." Even the small effort of talking seemed to be wiping Mr. Woo out, and he hunched in a storm of coughing. Lei stood up. "Can I get you a glass of water?"

He nodded, still coughing, and she went into the vast kitchen and filled a glass, brought it back. His liver-spotted hand trembled as he drank, but he calmed his breathing.

"Thanks so much for helping us," Ken said. "And sorry to disturb you."

"High point of my day, having FBI agents come to my house," Mr. Woo said. "I'm sure I won't see you again, but good luck with what you're looking for."

They let themselves out, and Lei took a deep breath of fresh, sunshiny air. "God. What a way to end. You can tell by all this he was a successful man at one time." She gestured toward the house as they crossed the bridge.

"I know. Depressing." Ken unlocked the SUV and they got in. "This is brutal. I think I understand why some people want to 'get out early,' though he didn't seem to be one of them."

"That's a kind of courage. To live to the end, looking death in the eye." Lei sighed. "But I'm beginning to understand the reasons better, and why people might even want help ending their own life."

"It's a slippery slope," Ken said. Silence fell as they got on the road, each occupied with their thoughts. Lei spent the drive researching Clyde Woo. A businessman worth millions, he owned a chain of convenience stores. According to the most recent news article she could find, he was "graciously retired and enjoying his days golfing."

It looked like it had been a long time since Clyde Woo had golfed, but the article was dated only a year ago.

She looked up their next listing, a woman named Betsy Brown. There was no information in the system but the driver's license basics and nothing on her personally. She was a thirty-two-year-old Caucasian female who shared a residence with her mother.

The house they pulled up to was modest, and Betsy Brown was in bed with a laptop on her lap when the caregiver let them in. She was puffy, with the indoor look of someone who hadn't seen the sun in months. The smile she gave them was strictly for form's sake.

After they'd stated their purpose, she made a little gesture to the keyboard. "I can still type, and I can still eat and breathe on my own —but I don't know how long that will last. I have ALS. Lou Gehrig's disease."

Lei must have looked blank because Betsy continued. "It's a neurological disease that causes progressive paralysis until finally all the body's systems shut down. However, I'll have all my marbles up until the very end."

"We're very sorry to hear that," Ken said. Lei felt any words she could think of clogging her throat, "oh shit" being the first thing that had come to mind.

"So yeah, DyingFriends is a place I can rant and rave; I can network with other people in my situation. I've found a whole ALS subgroup, since ALS is its own special hell and is virtually always fatal within five years. So frankly, if I decide to get a little help getting out early, I figure I'm doing myself and the world a service."

Lei and Ken left without anything specific, but Lei knew she'd never forget the woman's hopeless but defiant eyes. She was only a few years older than Lei and had been living an athletic life up until she began stumbling and falling on her daily runs.

Back in the Acura, Lei did some relaxation breathing and restrained herself from rubbing the pendant around her neck. "Didn't think it could get worse than the old guy, but that was worse."

"I know. I think we need a break." Ken drove them to a nearby Zippy's. Lei ordered a bowl of chili and a salad and made herself eat. Being sad for these people and their horrible situations wasn't going to solve the case—though she'd begun to wonder if there was going to be any real criminal that could be brought to justice.

Ken held a mug of coffee and looked at her over the rim. "Awfully quiet, Texeira."

"I know. I'm really...I don't know. Betsy Brown. She was a runner before the ALS."

"I know a little about it. It actually occurs a little more frequently in athletes. Terrible disease." He set the mug down.

"So do you think it's criminal for her to have someone kill her before she eventually smothers to death, trapped in her own body?"

"Not for us to judge." Ken shook his head. "Just for us to figure out who's setting this up and catch them."

"That's true, and I get that. Thank God our position is clear. But shouldn't people have some choice, some control, as Mr. Woo said, in how and when they go when they know they're going?"

"I guess. And probably, functionally, there is a degree of that through families receiving end-of-life care." Ken blew on his coffee.

"I'm sure there's a bigger dose of morphine than normal here and there that no one's looking into. But legislating that? It just opens a door with potential for too much abuse."

"I'm just sick, thinking about Betsy." Lei stirred the remains of her chili. "Corby too. Why did he want to die? It's so weird."

"That's what we're here to find out. Glad we got involved with these cases—I think they're going to get way too complicated for HPD to track."

Lei was still thinking about a young athletic runner struck down with progressive paralysis. "I wish I'd never heard of ALS. I was better off not knowing about it." Her hand trembled, and she reached up and held the pendant at her neck, rubbing it. "Think I need a cup of coffee too."

"I'll go call Waxman and check in." Ken set a couple of bills on the table and stepped outside.

Lei waved the waitress over and ordered a coffee to go. She opened her wallet and spotted the fortune from her grandmother's lap desk. *Shape your destiny.*

She turned it over, looked at the phone number written on the back in her grandmother's precise handwriting.

Life was short. Maybe this was someone who had known her grandmother, someone special who could help Lei know Yumi a little more. On impulse, she took her phone out and punched the number in.

It rang. And rang. And rang. No voice mail came on the line, and she punched off, feeling deflated.

She took her coffee in the to-go cup and left cash on the table, pushing out through the glass doors to get on the road to the next DyingFriends member's house.

Robert Castellejos had once been a tall man, but age and pain had bent him over. He was bowed with a tension that was evident in deep grooves beside his mouth and tightness around lashless, browless eyes. He served them tea, hot and sweet with honey from his own hives in the avocado orchard out back.

"Lost all my hair a month ago. Chemo." He rubbed his shiny pate. There was a tremor in his hands that never quite went away. "DyingFriends is a godsend. I can just be real on there. No one knows how to talk to a dead man walking." He gave a little bark of a laugh.

Ken began his spiel on what they were looking for when Lei's phone toned. She looked down and saw it was the mysterious number from the back of the fortune. She held up a finger.

"Gotta take this." She strode rapidly through the modest house and out onto the front porch. "Hello?"

"Hello." A deep voice with a little bite to it. "Who is this?"

"You first. Who is this?"

"You called me. So you first."

Lei frowned. He didn't sound very friendly. "Okay. My name is Lei. I found this number in my grandmother's things. I was calling to see if you knew her. Yumi Matsumoto."

"Lei? Lei Texeira?"

A frisson of alarm shot through her at being recognized. "Yes," she said cautiously.

"This is Marcus Kamuela. Why are you calling this number again?"

"Marcus! Is this your phone?"

"No. Please answer the question." His voice was all cop.

Her brain raced. The phone must have been picked up somewhere in the course of a crime if Marcella's boyfriend the detective had it. The less she said, the better. She decided to go on the offensive.

"Why do you have the phone if it's not yours?"

"Police business. Answer the question, please."

"I already did."

A long pause. He must have decided to back off, because when he next spoke, his voice was conciliatory. "Lei. Listen, I was just surprised to have this phone ring and have it be someone I knew. So, you said something about the number and your grandmother?"

"You still haven't told me why you have the phone."

"Well, it's a burner. And it was in the possession of a man who's been murdered. So you can see why I need to find out why you were calling."

Lei's throat closed. She couldn't think. A long moment went by, hissing in space, and she saw the ghost of Kwon laughing at her. Anything she said could make things worse.

She hung up on Marcus Kamuela with an abrupt punch of the button.

Somehow she got through the rest of the interview with Robert Castellejos, which was mostly over by the time she went back in. She accepted the jar of honey he insisted each of them take. "I've got a month or two to live, and it makes me happy to give this to you. Would you deprive a dying man of feeling happy?"

Throughout, she felt numb and terrified. Her muted phone vibrated repeatedly and angrily in her pocket.

CHAPTER THIRTEEN

KEN DROVE as they headed back toward Honolulu. Their last interview had ended them up near Sunset Beach on the North Shore, so they'd done a complete circle around the island. The wide-open fields between Haleiwa and the downtown Prince Kuhio Federal Building where their offices were located gave Lei's dry, gritty eyes somewhere to rest. She leaned her head against the doorframe and watched the bowl of sky and sea of green flow by.

"What's going on with you?" Ken asked, darting a glance over at her. "Something's wrong."

She'd never told her partner about the debacle with Kwon. "Nothing. It's just these dying people. So depressing."

"You got that right. Rich or poor, doesn't seem to matter. Everyone is alone in the end."

Lei looked over at him, concerned by an odd note in his voice. "You won't be alone. I would never let that happen."

"You'll be off with Stevens. Probably raising a family. I'll still be working. Hopefully I'll go down on the job." His jaw was bunched as his hands squeezed and released the wheel.

"You're thinking you're never going to find someone to love.

You will." Lei didn't know how she knew, but she did. "You might have to come out of the closet, though."

"You don't know what's at stake. It would kill my parents."

"I'm sure that's what Corby thought too, but I think his mother, at least, would have wanted the truth." She looked over at her partner. Maybe unburdening herself to him, sharing her fears, would lighten his. She was tired of keeping secrets from someone so close. Ken, in spite of his sometimes-rigid adherence to protocol, was someone she knew she could trust. "Okay. I'm going to tell you with something big, and you're going to have to believe me."

"Lei, you're not a good liar." His grin was a flash that made his face startlingly handsome. "I'll be able to tell."

"Well, this situation began a long time ago. Remember I told you I was abused as a kid? It was sexual abuse. The doer was my mom's boyfriend, a guy named Kwon. She was an addict, and he moved in on us after my father was popped for dealing."

Ken frowned. "Wow. I knew you had it rough, but that's quite a story."

"Yeah. Prepped me for a job in law enforcement. Anyway, Kwon raped and abused me over a period of six months when I was nine. After he left, my mom died of an overdose. I still don't know if she meant to or not." Old pain made Lei's hand steal up to rub the white-gold pendant hanging around her neck. "After I became a cop, I found Kwon. He was in prison for pedophilia."

"At least they got him. So often, they don't." Ken glanced at her, frowning.

She filled him in on her confrontation with Kwon, his murder. "It's Kamuela's case. He's getting nowhere with it, but the guy's like a dog with a bone. I'm afraid something will connect me to Kwon and that day."

"Jesus. And I mean it as a prayer."

"Yeah. So then I decide I need to find out who murdered him so I can stay ahead of it. Kwon had a lot of people with motive after him. My dad thought maybe my grandfather Soga Matsumoto had something to do with it, so I got over myself and reconnected with him. Which has been good, until he gave me this box of my grandmother's things. And today I called a number I found in the box."

"Yeah?" he prompted when she wound down into a long silence.

"Today I called the number. No answer. Then my phone rings and it's Kamuela. Says my number came up on a murder victim's phone."

"Shit," Ken said. They'd entered the maze of freeways that marked the edge of the city. "You don't know whose phone it was, then."

"No."

"So you don't know if there's any connection to Kwon. All you know is you found a number in your grandmother's things, you called it, and it's the phone of a murder vic."

"Right."

"Not good," Ken said. "But not necessarily anything to do with Kwon."

"I know. Kamuela's not going to believe I didn't know anything about it. Especially with the source of the number. It's on a fortune that says 'shape your destiny.'" She fumbled it out of her wallet, held it up. "I hung up on him, but I know I have to talk to him, explain." Lei's stomach knotted. "I can't be telling Waxman all this. Another skeleton in my closet, like the Changs."

"What do you mean? The Chang crime family?"

"Yeah. We have history—my dad killed the Chang family head in prison. Self-defense, but that didn't stop them from trying to take him out over the years—and one of their sons came after me too."

"Your life is kind of a crime soap opera, you know."

"I know, right?" She smiled at Ken. "Even though we scooped up a lot of organized crime connections in that big case on Maui, the Changs managed to wiggle out of any prosecution. I've been dreading a case that brings that old history out to bite my ass, like this Kwon thing is threatening to."

"Nothing could be further from organized crime thugs specializing in gambling and drugs than an online suicide club. This case is a lot of things, but it's not dangerous to anyone but the already dying."

"I know. I'm just so freaked out about it all, with Kamuela breathing down my neck. Feels like those skeletons want to come out of the closet and dance. Wreck my career, wreck my life." Lei pinched her leg through her pants.

"I'll help you. We'll keep it on the down low. For all you know, it's a coincidence that your grandmother had the number in her belongings. That's all you know right now."

"You're right." Lei sighed. "I'm paranoid. I'm getting ahead of myself."

"I'm glad you told me. Imagine how much worse it would be if you had to keep sneaking around, lying to me while you tried to deal with it yourself."

"Stevens knows, but he can't help me over here." She reached over, touched his arm. "I'm sorry I didn't tell you sooner."

"I'm just glad you did. Big thing to carry and get through alone."

Lei felt affection suffuse her, an unfamiliar feeling that made her eyes prickle with tears. She had people who loved her—and better yet, people she'd let herself love back. Ken had just joined that select group.

Back at the Bureau, Lei contacted Ang and the three of them converged on Waxman's office to brief him on the activities of the day. Lei looked out the window, where late-afternoon sun sparkled on the ocean and poufs of cumulous cloud scudded across the bowl of sky. All of it was tinted gray by bulletproof glass. She couldn't stop her mind from wandering to the call she needed to make to Kamuela, how it could make her a suspect and stress her friendship with Marcella.

What a mess.

"Agent Texeira!" Waxman's voice snapped her head around. She'd tuned out Ang and Ken's summary of their findings so far. "What are your thoughts here?"

"The situations of the DyingFriends members we visited are terrible," Lei said, thinking fast. "The site seems to be providing some much-needed support and interaction for them. So far, no hint of any wrongdoing."

Ang cleared her throat. "Actually, while you guys were canvassing, I was burrowing around in the site and planting suicidal threads under my identity. I got a ping on it just before I came here. An email from a masked location." She'd printed the email and looked down to read it.

"'Dear ShastaM, you have been invited to a deeper level of commitment and sharing on DyingFriends. If you accept this invitation, you commit to keep all interactions and communications confidential.'"

Ang looked up. "I accepted. I'm waiting for a confirmation link that will take me into this deeper level. This could be the door we're looking for."

Lei didn't envy Ang her role impersonating a dying person, making virtual conversation and trying to lure the administrator out of the shadows—doing techie things on a computer all day. Once again she was glad of the diversity of roles within the FBI.

"Good." Waxman steepled his fingers, pale blue eyes tracking them. "So to summarize: We are looking for a group or individual practicing assisted suicide. The people who are participating are so far already dying. Have you come across any garden-variety depressed people so far? Not dying?"

"No, sir. The ones we've visited so far were definitely dying," Lei said, remembering each face with a tiny internal shudder.

"I have come across people in the chat rooms who call themselves 'existentially dying,'" Ang said. "The parameters of the site are such that actually having a life-endangering disease or condition is part of joining. But these people found a way around that. They have their own subgroups."

"Okay. So when I account to my district director, I know what he's going to ask me. Is this case the best use of the FBI's time and resources? Is there a crime worth pursuing, that we can prosecute, being committed by an individual or individuals we can bring to trial?" Waxman narrowed his eyes.

The three of them looked at one another. Ken finally answered. "This is going to be one of those shades-of-gray cases, sir. It's criminal to assist in another person's suicide as the law stands. In the case of Corby Hale, his death was at worst a murder and at least an unnecessary suicide. The boy had AIDS but could have lived a normal life span with proper care and medication, which his family would have provided. Alfred Shimaoka still had up to six months to live—granted, painful and unpleasant, but still life he was entitled to." Ken steepled his fingers, unconsciously imitating Waxman. "I don't think we have enough information yet to say if it's a good use of the FBI's time and resources. I do know that this is a case that crosses state lines, may have a ripple effect and cause other sites to spring up, and at least once has resulted in a premature or unnecessary death: Corby Alexander Hale the third, a senator's son."

Waxman smiled, sat back. "Good. I wanted to hear our rationale articulated. I think we need to get to the heart of this site, who's behind it—and that person or persons are whom we will bring to trial. Dismissed."

Out in the hall, Lei glanced at Ken, relieved the meeting was over but apprehensive about where she was going next—to meet Marcus Kamuela. "I'm going to take off a little early. Got some personal business."

"It's Friday, so I won't see you until Monday. Want me to come with you?" His eyes told her he knew what that business was.

"No, but thanks for asking. I'll call you."

Lei walked away and heard Ang. "What was that about?"

She didn't hear Ken answer, but she knew he'd keep her secret. That's what friends and partners did—and maybe someday she could add Sophie Ang to that handful of friends.

CHAPTER FOURTEEN

Lᴇɪ ʜᴀᴅ ᴀʀʀᴀɴɢᴇᴅ to meet Kamuela at the dog park. Keiki was feeling frisky, at least as frisky as a middle-aged Rottweiler ever got. The sight of the big black dog lumbering and snorting with the tiny matching Chihuahua bouncing beside her as they played gave Lei a much-needed lift—that and looking out across the yellow arc of beach at the radiant sunset beginning, piercing the clouds over the ocean with golden arrow rays.

She closed her eyes, tipped her head back, did a couple of relaxation breaths, letting the freshness of a tiny breeze off the water ruffle the curls on her forehead, wicking the sweat from the run down off the mesh athletic shirt she wore. She longed for Stevens with a sudden hungry fierceness, wishing for his solid, calm strength beside her, his arms around her.

"Hey, Lei." Marcus Kamuela's deep voice. Her eyes snapped open. She sat upright as Marcella's boyfriend, with his intimidating physical presence, sat beside her on the bench. "You were a million miles away."

"Yeah, just thinking about our latest case," she lied, feeling her cheeks heat up with that awful blush she'd struggled with all her life. "Long day."

"Yeah, well, imagine being me at the scene of a homicide, picking up the vic's phone, calling the last number, and having it be you."

"Freaky it was a homicide." Lei's heart had jumped to trip-hammer speed. *Stay calm*, she reminded herself. *You don't know anything yet.* "I kind of freaked out talking to you today. I was in the middle of a witness interview when I took your call, and the personal business was throwing me off. I apologize for hanging up on you. I knew I needed to talk in person to explain."

Kamuela had a handsome Hawaiian face with classic features: broad brow, wide nose, full chiseled lips. Those lips were set in a line, and there was another one between his angled black brows. He hunched big shoulders. "I'm meeting you here and not at the station because you're an FBI agent and a former cop and my girlfriend's best friend. I really don't want this to be something I have to bring you in for, but you hanging up on me didn't help."

"I know. So here's the deal." She sat forward, leaning her elbows on her knees, giving him a lot of eye contact. "My grandfather gave me a box of my grandmother's things last night. That number was written on the back of a fortune cookie slip. On impulse, I called it. I've been trying to find out more about her because she's dead and I never got to meet her."

"Fortune cookie," Marcus repeated, incredulity in his tone.

"Yeah." She'd brought the slip of paper, already in a small paper evidence bag. She handed it to him. "The number's in her handwriting. I included samples for analysis if you want that. Didn't seal the bag because I knew you'd want to look."

Marcus nodded. His big brown hands were gentle and deft as he slid the slip of paper out without touching it, held it by its sides, and read it. "Shape your destiny."

"I know, right? So it would really help me to know a little more about this strange man whose number my grandmother had."

He ignored this, setting the slip on the bench and easing the letters she'd included in the bag out as well, giving them a quick once-over. Lei had included letters with characters, English phrases, and even some numbers. "Looks the same. She Japanese?"

"Yes. Full blood. She's gone now, like I said."

"How did she die?"

"Heart attack, a year ago."

A long pause as he put the items back into the bag, still not touching them except by the edges, and folded down the top of the bag in a neat, ruler-straight line.

"I'll take these in," he said. They both looked at the sunset that had decided to go glorious, a Technicolor display of light and color against the purpling sky. Keiki and Angel belatedly realized their mistress had been approached by a stranger and bounded back, sniffing Kamuela thoroughly. As usual, Angel was the most suspicious, yapping. She looked like she was considering latching on to his ankle until Lei scooped her up and scolded her.

Finally the dogs took themselves off for more playing, and Kamuela turned to Lei. "So here's the weird thing, other than this bizarre situation. I think I solved my old homicide case. Remember that one a year ago?"

Lei kept her face blank. "We both have a lot of cases."

"Two years ago. Cold case. Charlie Kwon, child molester, shot dead in his apartment with a nine millimeter. This stiff we found today—his gun matches that bullet. Kwon and at least three other unsolved homicides. This guy was a professional, and someone offed him."

Lei had to lean down and tie her shoe because she felt the hot blush prickling her chest at hearing Kwon's name. Thank God she was off the hook for his murder! She had to get better at subterfuge in her line of work. She wasn't that easily rattled anymore, but interviews didn't get more stressful than this one.

"That's a good day for you," she said to her toes, tying her other shoe. "So great when criminals off each other and save us taxpayer dollars."

"Yeah. Of course, I'm trying to solve the dead assassin's case, but even more stoked to cross off four cold ones. My closure rate just bumped big-time."

She glanced at him, smiled. "Congrats."

"So what was your grandmother doing with a pro hitter's number on a fortune cookie slip in her box?"

"No idea," Lei said, and the blush that she'd just fought down surged up her neck. She jumped to her feet, dug a ball out of her pocket, and threw it for the dogs, who took off after it in a rush of excitement.

"You know something." Kamuela had not been distracted by her camouflage.

Lei considered her options. If he dug deeper and found a connection to her some other way, lying to him even by omission at this early stage would look even worse. Her career could be endangered by being formally interviewed in connection with multiple murders even if she was cleared.

"I do know something, but nothing about this guy whose number it was." She sat back down. "I know something about Charlie Kwon. You aren't recording this, are you? Because you better turn it off if you are."

"Holy crap. You think I came to talk to you in a park wearing a wire?" He sounded outraged, his eyes wide and nostrils flared.

Lei squinted at him. "It's possible."

Kamuela ripped the subtly patterned aloha shirt he wore off over his head, holding it bunched in his fist. "No wire. I don't operate like that with my friends." Lei was a little alarmed by the expanse of broad, muscular brown chest. No wonder Marcella was looking so happy and distracted lately.

"I'm glad you called me a friend. And I'm sorry." Lei averted her gaze. She tried not to notice the other park visitors staring. Kamuela unbuttoned the shirt and shrugged back into it. She did some relaxation breathing. "This is really hard for me. Personally and professionally. Marcella might have told you I had a rough childhood."

Kamuela seemed a little mollified as he finished buttoning up the shirt, a relief to her sensibilities. "She did. Said your dad was in the game and you grew up with an auntie because your mom died of an overdose."

"Yeah. So the reason my mom died was Charlie Kwon. He had a score to settle with my dad, targeted us when Dad was in prison. Raped me while he was manipulating my mom and feeding her drugs."

"Damn," Kamuela said. "He really deserved what he ended up getting."

Somehow she was able to glance at him with a bit of humor. "I know, right? I tracked him in prison, and right before I joined the FBI, I paid him a visit. I was in disguise. It didn't go like I'd hoped, with him being sorry for what he did. I clocked him with my weapon and left him alive."

"So that was the goose egg on the body's head."

"Yes. And I hope the ME could tell that happened several hours before he died."

No answer. Kamuela just stared at her, brown eyes inscrutable, the gaze of an investigator in "cop mode." She was very familiar with that look.

Lei hurried on. "So, anyway. I was horrified to see on the news that he'd been shot that night, and I've been trying to figure out who did it ever since. I hid my clothes, gloves, and wig in a safe place, and they will exonerate me—they don't have GSR." She didn't point out the obvious holes in this explanation. He would do that himself if he wanted to. "I want to help solve this, and that's why I'm telling you all I know. Coming clean. I hope we can figure it out, because I'm tired of living with this hanging over my head."

"God. Lei." He leaned back against the bench, rubbed his face. "I want to believe you. Abused by Kwon. Shit." His eyes narrowed. "But just because you didn't kill him yourself doesn't mean you didn't call a professional hitter who did. My dead guy from today. And the hitter's number written in your grandmother's handwriting doesn't mean a thing except that maybe she was the one to give it to you."

Lei felt her throat dry. She'd been so focused on the physical evidence connected to the visit she'd made to Kwon that she'd forgotten how this other connection, her number on the assassin's phone, would look.

"But I didn't," Lei whispered, and felt the blood drain from her head as his face telescoped into the distance, black encroaching from the sides of her vision. She felt despair swamp her. She'd thought these blackouts were over, and to have one in front of Kamuela felt like suicide.

Keiki's bulk leaned against her leg, a heavy, warm weight she could feel, anchoring her back in her body. The rasp of Angel's tiny tongue on her calf made the blackness recede.

"I didn't do it," Lei repeated. "And I didn't hire anyone to do it. I don't have a thing I can say or do to convince you. I know it looks bad."

A long moment. Kamuela was still looking at her as if searching inside her head. She'd just revealed everything to him, and she was vulnerable. The flow of blood under her skin—the flush when she lied, the ebb of it when she almost fainted with terror—were easy to read. Her demeanor could add up to her innocence or solidify her as his prime suspect.

His cell phone rang. "Kamuela here." A pause, and he stood up. "I'll be right there."

Kamuela holstered the phone, turned to her. "Caught a fresh one. I'll be in touch." He turned and loped away.

Relief warred with anxiety as Lei watched him go, the evidence bag in his hand.

CHAPTER FIFTEEN

Sophie had decided to just stay at work until she got tired. Not having her network at home had removed all interest in even going there. She'd gone earlier to the workout room, done an hour running on the treadmill, skipping rope, and doing free weights, then showered and changed into her "home" clothes, a racer-back tank and a pair of yoga pants. She sat upright on the large exercise ball and logged back in to DyingFriends.

The email link to the "deeper level" on DyingFriends had finally arrived in her in-box and she clicked it, a smile of anticipation tugging up one side of her mouth.

The next level opened to a portal where she had to read and agree to a nondisclosure clause and a "leave-no-footprint" policy in which she deleted her cookies nightly off her computer. She hit "agree" even as she kept a tracker program open in a window in the corner of her monitor.

After clicking the box, the next level of the site opened. A blog post greeted her, a treatise on right to death written by someone with the handle "KevorkianFan." It was the first open reference she'd come across to assisted suicide and the famous "Dr. Death" who'd battled hard for rights to death in the 1990s.

Tabbed down the side of the page were different forums, and she popped onto "Suicidal Thoughts." Browsing among the threads, she was glad that she hadn't had to go out with Lei and Ken to the canvassing—it would have been very hard to put a face to the names and stories she was already finding heartrending.

ShastaM contributed some comments here about how bad her pain was and that she wanted to spare her children visits to the hospital as she died. The deeper level seemed to have shucked off trolls like CancerCurmudgeon with their antideath rhetoric. After an hour or two of exploring, she still had no way to track down the site admin.

She started a thread: "Whose brilliant idea is this? My dying wish: to meet the visionary behind the site! email me!" She provided ShastaM's fake email.

Almost immediately she was replied to by someone calling themselves Lightbody: "It's dangerous for him to reveal himself. He doesn't contact you or anybody."

ShastaM: "I just want to thank him personally. What's the danger? I'm a dying single mom all by myself in Honolulu!" Sophie felt a little adrenaline boost at this bite from someone close to the fish she was after.

Lightbody: "There are close-minded people who would love to shut us down, and the greater good is served by having DyingFriends available to all who need its support."

ShastaM: "I don't get it. I just want to thank the site administrator. Surely someone is in charge here."

Lightbody: "Take no for an answer or I'll report you."

Sophie paused, gazing into the bluish glow of the screen as she considered how her "character" would respond and what bait might work.

ShastaM: "Go ahead and report me. I want him (or her!) to know I'm dying, and I just want to thank him."

Sophie waited minutes, her long fingers poised—and nothing happened. Lightbody had disappeared.

Sophie found herself irritated. Impatient. Annoyed. She rolled the ball away from the desk and did her push-ups and sit-ups. Checked the computer again. Still nothing.

She did stretches now: rolled backward off the ball into a bridge. Did hamstrings, splits. She was bent over, her face between her knees, pulling hard behind her calves to get herself completely jack-knifed, when she heard a delicate throat-clearing behind her.

She straightened up immediately. Waxman was standing there, looking uncomfortable. "That is nonregulation attire," he said.

"Sorry, sir. Now that DAVID is disabled, I saw no point in going home. I worked out at the gym downstairs and ended up changing into my after-work clothes. No one's here, so I thought it would be okay. I'm phishing for the site admin of DyingFriends, and he's ignoring me."

"You can't live here, Sophie." There was a chiding note in Waxman's voice. "I came down to give you a sit rep on the DAVID software."

Sophie waited, hands on her hips. She saw her boss's eyes on her well-developed biceps and triceps, and she crossed her arms self-consciously. He made a half turn and addressed a spot over her shoulder.

"The national tech department is very excited about DAVID's potential, but the legal and privacy ramifications are a real tar baby. So while the techies are looking at it, our defense counsel is getting involved. This is going to take a while."

Even after many years in the United States, Sophie still came across phrases she wasn't familiar with. "Tar baby?"

"It's from an old folk tale. Br'er Rabbit. Google it when you get home. It'll give you something to do. Did the site admin respond?"

Sophie leaned in, looked at her in-box. "No, sir."

"Well, go home. It's Friday night. Find another interest besides computers and working out, Agent Ang. Life is short; you're young. Don't let it go by before you know it."

Sophie cocked her head. There was a harsh note in her boss's voice, but he'd spun on his heel and walked away before she could be sure.

"Go home, Sophie. That's an order!" he said over his shoulder.

"Yes, sir."

The pneumatic door of the lab slid shut behind him. She frowned, checked the email in-box again. Still empty. She sighed and shut down her most faithful friends. Amara, Janjai, and Ying whirred into silence, and as Sophie padded across the felted carpet, she wondered what the hell she could do besides work out and her computers.

There was only one other place she wanted to be—Fight Club.

Sophie managed to ignore the flatness that Alika's absence had brought to sparring at Fight Club later that evening. She and Marcella finished their bout, bumping fists in padded gloves. She'd trounced her friend fairly well, as usual. "Want to get something to eat?" she asked.

"Let me check something first," Marcella said, swiping escaped strands of chocolate-brown hair out of her eyes with her forearm. Sophie felt the simmering irritation she'd been battling all afternoon rise to the fore. She poked Marcella's shoulder, not lightly.

"Checking with the boyfriend?"

Marcella looked up, narrowed her eyes. "Hey. We already sort of had plans."

"Whatever." Sophie turned away, ripped her gloves off, and stuffed them in her bag. "Let me know when my friend Marcella gets back."

"Geez," Marcella said. "Touchy, aren't we? Okay, I'll cancel." She worked her phone with her thumbs. "There. You happy?"

Sophie turned back. "I don't need your pity date. Seriously. Go bang your boyfriend already."

Marcella poked Sophie's shoulder back hard. "That was bitchy. What's gotten into you?"

Sophie picked up her bag and walked away. She could hear Marcella following, and she blinked tears out of her eyes. She was jealous, and it hurt to know it. She kept walking across the parking lot, Marcella following. She heard the other woman's phone ring and a one-sided conversation. She was too intent on getting to her car, getting inside, and escaping to listen to it.

Sophie beeped the Lexus open, and Marcella jumped in, throwing her gym bag into the well between their bucket seats. "God, you're so high maintenance."

Sophie set her jaw, turned the key. "You aren't going to get out of my car, are you?"

"No. I know I've been blowing you off since Marcus and I went public, and I feel bad about it. Let's go out and have girl time with pool cues and beer. I'll give Lei a call, see if she can join us."

Sophie glanced over at Marcella's dimpled white grin and felt a tug of gratitude—she'd canceled plans with her man to spend time with a friend.

"Since you insist," Sophie said. She wasn't about to show how much it meant to her.

CHAPTER SIXTEEN

LEI RAN HOME POST-SUNSET—THAT time between day and night, which, in Honolulu, was warm, flower-scented, and filled with tourists on foot in the downtown areas and commuter traffic everywhere else. She had to concentrate on getting herself and the dogs home safely, distracted as she was from the meet with Kamuela. She played an endless feedback loop of the conversation between herself and the detective, wondering if she should have tried to lie, should have asked for legal counsel—anything but what she'd done.

Told all and trusted him.

Turning into her own quiet side street at the edge of town was a relief until she saw the black Ford Explorer parked outside her gate. Her heart lurched—another detective here to interview her? Had Kamuela turned her in already?

She drew abreast of the car and the door opened. "Lei."

A familiar voice. The one voice that could bring joy surging through her body.

Lei threw herself into Stevens's arms as he got out, squashing Angel in the baby carrier between them. Those long arms embraced her, hard and gentle. Her head fit into the space measured for it, just beneath his jawbone. She breathed in the smell and heat of his body, and her world tipped to where it wanted to stay.

Now and forever.

"I can't believe you're here!" She burst into tears, letting go of the stress of the day.

"Wow." He hugged her again, set her away from him so the wriggling Chihuahua could get some air. "I guess you're glad to see me?"

"Yes." Lei sniffled, letting Angel out as Stevens greeted Keiki, giving the big dog ear rubs. Angel, freed from her carrier, bounced around yipping. "Let's get out of the street."

In the yard, the rapturous greetings between Stevens and the dogs continued as Lei took the little dog's carrier off, hung it on a hook, and unlocked the front door. She grinned, watching them, brushing the tears off her cheeks with her hands, combing hair out of her face, self-conscious about her sweaty workout wear.

Finally, he advanced toward her. "A proper greeting," he whispered, looking down into her eyes.

Her lashes fluttered shut as his mouth descended to touch hers, gentle as a night moth. She reached up to encircle his head with her arms, stroking his hair as they deepened the kiss, exchanging all the promises that could be shared between lovers sworn and long-parted.

She remembered their first kiss in that moment. Her fear a cloud around her, so easily triggered by the past. That kiss so tender, so careful—yet full of hope and possibility even then.

The passion she felt now was so full and ripe it seemed her skin would split with the juicy power of it, that he could make her burst with the tip of a finger or the touch of his tongue.

She broke away with a little gasp. "I have to get these clothes off, get in the shower. I'm gross."

"I like you sweaty. This mesh shirt—you were running through Honolulu in this? And no one got in a car accident?" He managed to sound genuinely scandalized, and she laughed.

Lei ran her hands up and down his arms, savoring their dense texture, the light springy hair beneath her fingertips. "You're here. Does that mean what I think it means?"

"Got the papers in my back pocket. I'm free. And so is she."

She. Anchara. Stevens's ex-wife. Lei could never think of the other woman's lovely face without a potent cocktail of regret and jealousy. How Lei wished she'd been able to deal with her shit and make a commitment to Stevens before she left for the Academy two years ago—but she hadn't, and the three of them had suffered for it.

But he was here now. And he was free.

She looked up into Stevens's blue eyes, shadowed under dark brows. "Thank God."

He reached down to hook up the pendant at her throat with a finger, and he brushed the skin of her neck. It ignited at his touch, heat spreading across her chest. Her nipples tightened painfully, and she sucked in a breath.

"You're wearing my ring." His voice was rough as he looked at the humble medallion and cross dangling from his finger, her pulse fluttering beneath it. His grandmother's antique ring, given to her long ago on their first engagement.

Burned. Melted. Beaten. Shaped and polished. Beautiful because of its history.

"Yes."

The kiss then was fierce, and claiming, and it carried them stumbling through the house, shedding clothes and frantic. They ended up in the shower with hot water washing away darkness, tears, loneliness, and deprivation.

Lei sat curled against Stevens on the couch in her yellow terrycloth robe. Slack-key guitar music filled the little cottage along with Keiki's snores. The big Rottweiler was curled on the rag rug at the back door, Angel tucked into her flank while they waited for pizza delivery.

She sipped her Corona. "This reminds me of when we first got together on the Big Island. Pizza and beer, sitting on the couch."

His hand wandered into the neck of her robe, leaving a trail of sensation like phosphorescence on the tide. "Not quite. I remember a lot of awkwardness back then. Not to mention worrying about a stalker."

Lei sighed. "Oh yeah." She put her head back against him. "How long can you stay?"

"Got to go back Sunday. But I had to see you now that . . ." He pulled one of her damp curls out straight, watched it spring back as he let go.

"The divorce is over."

"Right."

"Should we talk about it?"

"I'd rather not."

"Agree."

They each took a sip of beer. The pizza delivery van drove up, and the dogs leapt to their feet, barking. Lei and Stevens untangled from the couch, and Stevens, clad in his jeans, went out onto the porch and across the yard to pay.

Lei savored the sight of him returning, the overhead light of the porch gilding dark hair, his wide shoulders and chest as he carried the box. The jeans rode perilously low on his hips. She enjoyed the shape of him—a graceful build, lean and well developed.

"What?" he asked.

"Just looking at you. I can't stop looking at you."

"Keep that up and I won't be able to eat."

"I'm already not hungry."

He pounced on her with a growl, and this time they ended up in the bedroom.

Morning wasn't kind to her hair, and she looked at the storm of frizz as she entered the bathroom.

She'd been in a storm all night.

A grin pulled up one side of her mouth, and it hurt. She touched lips chapped by kissing, chest pink from razor burn. Aches from various other places reminded her they were happy to have been touched, and she smiled some more. Good problems to have, in the scheme of things. She got into the shower, and the sensual fog lasted until she remembered Kamuela and that he'd said he'd be in touch.

She finished her shower quickly. She had to talk with Stevens about the situation.

Stevens was still sleeping, and wrapped in her towel, she looked at the great sprawl of him filling her bed. White linens contrasted with the tan of his skin. One long foot was exposed, the mountain peak of his shoulder, ruffled brown hair stark on the pillow. Big as a work truck parked in the pristine garden of her bedding, and just as perfect there.

Her chest tightened as she reveled in the sight of him. She hadn't known that love could be so intense, so complicated. Feeling this way about a man was a triumph over everything that had been done to her, and still it was heady and terrifying. Knowing he'd be gone soon distilled each moment, intensifying its sweetness.

They'd have the weekend together at least.

She decided to let him sleep and surprise him by fixing breakfast —but in the kitchen, her refrigerator was empty as usual. She threw on sweats, scrunched some CurlTamer into her hair to prevent last night's unfortunate 'do, and walked to the little grocery store on the corner.

She had eggs and toast going, the dogs a rapt and hopeful audience, when Stevens came out of the bedroom in his jeans. He brushed his teeth and filled a mug with coffee, came to stand behind her. He distracted her, trying to bite her neck as she worked the spatula.

"Now I know you love me," he murmured in her ear. "Texeira going domestic. What is the world coming to?" His breath stirring the hair over her ear sent a shiver down her spine.

"Hey, I can scramble an egg," she said, elbowing him.

He turned, looked back at the bedroom, at the rumpled, pretty white bed. Sipped his coffee. "I never stopped thinking about that bed after I spotted it last year. I like it."

She leaned up to kiss him before she served them. "Let's spend some more time in there, making sure the mattress is up to speed."

Digging into the eggs and taking a bite of toast, Stevens gestured to the pizza box, still on the table unopened. "No wonder I'm hungry."

She refilled her coffee mug, joined him, opened the pizza box, and sniffed. "It's still good. I have an instinct for how long it takes for pizza to go off—we ate a lot of it when I was a kid."

Keiki, looking on, gave a great sigh—nothing had fallen to the ground. The Rottweiler lay down with her big square head on her paws, soulful eyes tracking them. Angel remained upright, ears pricked. "We have an audience. Ignore them."

"I'm the noncustodial parent." He dropped a bit of egg and Angel nabbed it. "Oops."

"Hey." She smacked his shoulder, got distracted by the feel of it, reached over to stroke it, massaging the hard muscle.

"Stop that. I'm an old man, I have to fuel the machine." He picked up his mug of coffee and reached for a slice of the pizza.

Lei sighed, addressed her breakfast. "We have to talk."

"Same as last night. If it's about the divorce, I'd rather not."

"This is something different." Stevens was the only other person who knew about her visit to Kwon. She described the discovery of the number in her grandmother's box, how she'd called it with no answer—and then how Kamuela had called her back from the phone of a homicide victim. Stevens set the slice of cold pizza down, eyes narrowing as he frowned.

"So that was why I cried when I saw you. I'd just met with him, and I told him everything," she finished. Took a bite of her tasteless eggs and made herself chew.

"I knew that Kwon business would bite you on the ass." He stood with that coiled grace and set the dishes in the sink. "God, Lei."

His words were an ironic echo of Kamuela's. Stevens turned

back, ran hands through his hair in that way he did when he was upset. "I'd almost forgotten about that whole thing—I guess I hoped it would just blow over. Kamuela's got to do something about your number on the hitter's phone. It's a strong lead, and if I were him, I'd be all over you. Talk about means, motive, and opportunity!"

"I know. It looks bad." Misery and terror roared back worse than before, and she pushed her plate away, covered her face with her hands. He took her half-eaten breakfast and threw the eggs outside, causing a mad scramble by the dogs. Put the plate in the sink. Returned to sit beside her, drawing her into his arms.

"We'll get through it together."

"How? You're leaving tomorrow."

"We could go talk to Kamuela today."

"That won't do anything, just put pressure on him, remind him what a tough spot he's in." Lei sighed, straightened up out of his arms. "I can't help seeing it from his perspective. Here's this Federal cop, his girlfriend's buddy, and she looks guilty as hell of hiring the hitter. She's called and left evidence on a victim's phone. He has to document and act on it, even if he wants to believe me. I mean, I feel bad for him. Let's not make it worse."

Stevens tipped her chin up. She couldn't look into those sky eyes a minute longer, and her lashes fluttered shut. She could feel him looking at her mouth, then the tender brush of his lips on hers.

"I love you," he said. "You've really grown up."

She smiled, pulled her chin out of his hand. "Lotta good that does me."

"So if we aren't going to go talk to him, we need to get our minds off this."

"I can think of one or two things we can do." It wasn't far from her chair to his lap, her favorite place in the world.

Lei didn't check her phone until much later as they were taking the dogs to the beach with a couple of longboards she'd borrowed from the landlord. Marcella had left a message last night inviting her to come shoot pool with her and Ang.

Her chest tightened with anxiety. Lei knew Kamuela wouldn't say anything to Marcella, but she felt trapped. Telling her friend would deepen the conflict of interest; not telling her was a betrayal by omission. A breach of trust. These sobering thoughts dampened her mood as she navigated the downtown traffic in the truck, Stevens beside her, headed for the beginner waves in Waikiki.

"I'm wondering if I should tell Marcella about what's going on."

Stevens just looked at her, his eyes hidden behind Ray-Ban Aviators. "Shitty situation. Damned if you do, damned if you don't."

Lei squeezed the wheel, turning onto the small side road weaving between skyscrapers that ended at the marina. "That's it exactly."

"Just wait and see what develops."

"She called me to go out last night. Girl time at the pool hall with Ang."

"Woulda been fun. But we were having fun too, weren't we?" He reached out, tugged a curl. It stretched out, sprang back. "I never get tired of this hair."

"I have to call her back."

"You don't have to say anything right now. Let Kamuela do what he does. See where it goes. This could end up taking care of itself."

"I just don't know how it could end any way but badly."

"We were supposed to be getting your mind off it." They'd pulled up at the parking lot by the Waikiki Yacht Harbor. On the left was the towering rainbow-tiled Hilton, further down the serene beach the famous pink Royal Hawaiian Hotel. On the right, sparkling white boats anchored in the harbor. And straight ahead, perfect little waves with only a few people out. "Shake it off, Texeira. Bumbye you come stress out."

Stevens's attempt at pidgin made her smile.

"As how, brah," she said, getting out. She wore a bikini with a Lycra surf shirt over it; Stevens was in board shorts. "I've only been surfing for a little while, so you get to laugh at me."

"I've been surfing only a little while longer. We can be kooks together."

They carried the boards down to the beach.

In the concentration of mastering a difficult skill involving clear water, gorgeous scenery, and more fun than she could remember having learning any sport, Lei was finally able to forget the ghost of Kwon.

CHAPTER SEVENTEEN

SOPHIE WOKE UP LATE, though it was hard to tell with the blackout curtains closed. She'd always had trouble sleeping, and a completely dark room with no sound but the hum of air-conditioning was the only way she could truly rest.

She felt the throb of a hangover in the base of her skull, and the sandpapery dryness of her mouth confirmed it. She cleared her throat, and someone stirred beside her in the bed.

"Is it morning?"

Marcella's voice.

"I don't know." Sophie tried to remember how that had happened —they'd had a lot to drink; that was it. And taken a cab home. And gone to bed together.

She swung her feet out of the bed, padded to the bathroom. She didn't turn the light on; it was too bright. She brushed her teeth in the glow of the night-light, then got in the shower.

She soaped her body, read her tattoos, reminded herself it was just a hangover and she'd feel better eventually. Clad in a silk robe, she walked through the room as Marcella was sitting up in the dim light from the bathroom. Her friend wore last night's shirt and panties, a tumble of long brown hair brushing her waist. "God, what a hangover."

"I know. Shower helps. I'll go fix some coffee."

In the kitchen, Sophie put her teakettle on and dug out the drip filter for guests. She knew Marcella didn't find life worth living until the second cup of coffee.

She had her own tea ready and had drunk two large glasses of water with aspirin by the time Marcella came out, wrapped in a towel with another one wound turban-style around her hair.

Sophie had set a cup of inky, drip-filtered coffee and two aspirin beside a halved papaya with a slice of lime and a silver teaspoon. She'd opened the slider to the little balcony off the kitchen, letting in fresh morning air above a dizzying view. Marcella walked across the expanse of teak flooring to face the bank of windows looking out over the city to the ocean, Diamond Head in the distance.

"What a spread. I couldn't see anything last night between the late hour and drinking too much. I had no idea you had a place like this."

"It's my father's. Just caretaking for him." Sophie busied herself with organic sprouted wheat toast and homemade passion fruit jam from the housekeeper.

"I'd never leave if I had a place like this. It's amazing."

Sophie didn't reply, thinking of the irony. She hated being home now that her network was down. Waxman was right; she needed some other interests.

Marcella returned, sat down at the modern, brushed-steel table. "Oh, thank God for coffee. You're an angel."

Her phone rang and she looked down. Sophie could tell by the color that rose in her cheeks that the caller was Kamuela. "I have to take this." She got up and walked away across the expanse of hard-wood, the phone cupped like a shell against her ear.

Sophie got up, mixed honey in her tea, picked up her toast, and carried it back into the bedroom, turning on Kamala, her home computer, and pulling a cord so the blackout drapes folded open on another glorious Honolulu day.

She sat down and logged in, sipping her tea and munching the toast as Marcella came to the door. "Hey." The other woman carried her coffee in. "Mind if I get dressed? I've got to get on the road."

"No problem," Sophie said.

Marcella dropped her towel, picked up her clothes from the night before. "Ugh, I hate wearing dirty clothes."

"Look through my closet." Sophie kept her eyes on her computer, but a reflection in the corner showed Marcella's lush outline as her friend opened her closet and riffled through.

"Do you mind if I grab some underwear too?"

"You won't fit into my bra."

"No, just bottoms. These yoga pants and shirt are fine."

"Take anything." Sophie watched the reflection as Marcella dressed, feeling guilty and aroused at the same time. She remembered how angry she'd been when Alika suggested she was gay—she didn't think so. She was just lonely and miserable, not getting action of any kind nor likely to at the rate she was going. She logged into her email as Marcella unwound the towel from her long hair, combing it out with her fingers.

"What are you working on?"

"Still hoping to lure out the system admin from the DyingFriends site." Sophie scanned the emails as Marcella sat on the bed behind her, picking up the half of papaya and digging into it.

"Mmm. This is good. The lime makes all the difference. Thanks for letting me crash."

"Anytime. What are you and Marcus up to today?"

"Oh, you guessed that was him. Yeah, he wants to take me to the zoo." Marcella blew a little raspberry. "I've never been. He wants me to see all the major Oahu sights. We made a list and we're checking them off. I didn't realize until we started going out how little I had seen of Oahu."

"That sounds fun." Sophie knew her voice was wooden. She'd

been exactly three places in Honolulu on a regular basis: Fight Club, work, and the apartment.

Marcella finished the papaya, sipped the coffee. "Mind if I take the toast to go?"

"Not at all."

"My hangover's getting better by the minute. There must be something magical in papaya and aspirin. So, I'll see you Monday?" Marcella got up, toast in her hand, plainly eager to leave.

"I'll be there." Sophie got up, walked her friend to the door. "See you Monday."

Sophie shut the door behind Marcella, shot the bolt, and turned back to pick up the small traces of their breakfast. She made the bed, and the usual silence descended over the apartment. She tried to ignore the heaviness that came with it.

She went back into her email, where she'd spotted something from DyingFriends. She opened it. Another invitation, to the "next level of deeper sharing and support." She read the disclosures, hit "agree."

Now what? There was no DAVID to work on, no network to extend her work to, and the system admin had responded to her challenge with one of his own, a sensible precaution on his side. He probably had IP address tracking software too. She wasn't worried—she had a blocker on her computer's location, the most effective one government contract money could buy.

Sophie could disappear, become ShastaM, and see what she would see in the forums. Work on her DAVID software, at least check through it some more. Or she could get outside this apartment and do like her boss had told her: find some other interests. Life *was* short. DyingFriends was a potent reminder of that.

Sophie had never hiked Diamond Head, that famous volcanic landmark visible from her windows. She didn't need a boyfriend to make the plan to do one new thing a week a good idea. She should experience the beautiful place she lived in. She'd heard the hike up the famous crater was fairly rigorous and uphill—she might even get some cardio in.

Feeling the first anticipation she had all day, Sophie put Kamala to sleep and got into running clothes. Maybe she wasn't capable of finding another interest outside of exercising, but at least she'd be doing it outdoors in a new place.

There might even be other people there.

CHAPTER EIGHTEEN

LEI GOT into the office early on Monday morning after dropping Stevens off at the airport for the earliest flight out to Maui. He'd ended up changing his reservation so they could spend one more night together, and not only was her hair disorderly this morning, but her eyes and lips were puffy from tears and kissing.

The loss of goodbye felt like a flu coming on, heaviness in her very bones..

Lei reached into her desk for her emergency Visine, dosed her eyes, and wound her rebellious curls into the FBI Twist, which her hair was finally long enough to do. Smoothing lip gloss on, she booted up her computer just as Ken stuck his head in the door. "Got another suicide. Let's go."

Lei felt the hit of adrenaline that made law enforcement so addicting light up her body. "Who? Anyone we know?"

"Yeah. Betsy Brown."

"Oh no," Lei said as adrenaline turned to the nausea of dread. She reached for her crime kit, freshly restocked after the Shimaoka death. "Dammit."

Betsy's body was dressed in a silky white nightgown, and she was laid out in a pose that was eerily familiar. Head on the pillow, hands crossed on the chest, hair curled and brushed. She even had makeup on. Other than her pallid face, she looked like she'd wake up at any moment, pretty and young.

Lei exchanged a glance with Ken as he got out the Canon and began photographing. "What made you call us?" Lei asked Detective Reyes, a mid-fifties Portuguese man with a weathered face and a basketball midsection. She took out her pencil and spiral notebook.

"We have a general alert on all suicides right now. We're supposed to look for inconsistencies and call you guys in, especially if there is an association with a site called DyingFriends. When Betsy's mother told me she was an active member, I called Dispatch."

"Thank you; you did right. Were there any other inconsistencies besides the connection to DyingFriends?" Lei tried to ignore the flash of the Canon as Ken moved in close to the body.

"Well, Betsy couldn't get out of bed, and she was dressed in a nightgown she'd never worn." Reyes gestured to the body. "Her mother said she'd ordered it online a few weeks ago, and it was still in the box over there." He pointed to an ornate clothing box. "It's wedding lingerie. Sad."

"Her illness was especially sad. ALS—amyotrophic lateral sclerosis. Debilitation, paralysis, then death," Lei said. She'd Googled the neurological nightmare after their first visit to Betsy. She walked over to the garment box, lifting the lid to peek inside with her pen. "Did you dust for prints? Don't see any powder."

"No. Stopped working the scene after I called Dispatch."

"Okay, thanks. Is there a note?"

"Yes. It was in a sealed envelope, and she was holding it. Where she got it was another inconsistency. The mother, name of Annie, said she'd brought the stationery in for Betsy to use a couple weeks ago. Said that was around the time Betsy bought the nightgown. Annie hadn't seen it since. So Betsy must have hidden it."

"Interesting." Lei glanced over at Betsy's body. "She's wearing makeup. Where's the makeup kit?"

Reyes pointed. The kit was on a bureau across the room. Lei caught Ken's eye, and the senior detective turned to Reyes. "Thanks so much. Can you secure the scene outside, move the mother out? We're going to treat this scene as a homicide for the moment. We've already called the medical examiner."

"Okay," Reyes said, giving his golf shirt a tug downward over his potbelly. "Please keep me posted on what you find."

He left and Lei put on gloves, tucked her hands behind her back, and began a slow perambulation of the room in "see mode"—a state where she let her vision roam over the scene without overly focusing, just allowing the information to register and "blip" into consciousness—until something caught her attention.

It was a humble room, with a cheap pressboard bedroom set, a bulbous purple china lamp beside the bed, along with various toiletries where Betsy could reach them, and an empty water glass. Beside the water glass was a pill bottle. Ken photographed it before picking it up, shaking it.

"Ambien. Empty. I bet we find that they were kept elsewhere. I can't imagine Annie Brown leaving this where Betsy could reach it. She had to have some idea of her daughter's state of mind."

"Maybe Betsy could still walk and was concealing that for some reason," Lei said. "Let's check the soles of her feet."

"Good idea. I'm done shooting, so we can move things now." Ken set the camera back in the case, and they lifted the rose-covered comforter up to reveal Betsy's body.

The first thing Lei noticed was a smell of urine and feces wafting up from under the comforter when it was removed, but nothing marred the perfection of the pristine, lace-trimmed cream satin night-gown. Through the fabric, around the woman's hips, Lei glimpsed a bulkiness. She poked the woman's waist. A crinkling sound answered.

"She's wearing adult diapers. Do you think she'd have worn those if she could walk?" Lei looked at Ken.

He shook his head. "Seems unlikely." He bent to inspect Betsy's feet. "They look totally clean."

Lei bent down, shone a high-powered flashlight on them. The toenails had been recently painted. In fact, everything about this woman was perfectly groomed. She'd ritualistically prepared for her suicide, had apparently wanted to look her best. Lei touched the sole of the foot, pressed gently. Rigor was setting in, so the flesh was hard, but the skin was thin and soft.

"She wasn't walking, Ken. This skin on her feet is like a baby's butt. It hasn't touched the ground in months." Lei straightened back up. "She was planning for this."

Dr. Fukushima, in scrubs and with her medical kit, appeared in the door. "Got another suicide, I see."

"Looks like. But we're thinking it's another one of those fishy ones," Lei said.

"I'd imagine, if you two are on the scene."

"We interviewed this woman a few days ago in connection with a website we're investigating. She had ALS."

"Interesting." Fukushima advanced, her sharp brown eyes moving quickly around the body. "I think it's significant that from the waist down mobility was compromised, but she still had full functioning in her breathing and arms. ALS doesn't usually progress that way. Maybe I can tell something more in the post."

The two agents straightened up, looking at each other. "We were trying to establish if she was walking, because her makeup kit is across the room and she is dressed in this fancy nightie from that box over there." Ken pointed.

"Aha. Where's the note?"

"Actually, don't know. Can you find Reyes, Agent Texeira, and locate the note?"

"Sure." Lei had begun to find the smell of Betsy's diaper suffocating, and she was happy to walk through the tiny apartment to the front stoop. Reyes and his partner had strung crime scene tape around the area and helped Betsy's mother pack a bag. The woman sat weeping on the steps while the detectives interviewed some neighbors who had gathered.

Lei sat beside her on the wooden step. "Mrs. Brown. I'm so sorry for your loss."

More weeping. Mrs. Brown had long dark hair threaded with silver, and the streaming face she lifted to Lei was surprisingly young and unlined. "She didn't need to do this. She wasn't a burden. It was my joy to take care of her!"

Lei reached out, rubbed the woman's shoulder. "I need the suicide note. Do you know where it is?"

"The detective tried to take it. I wasn't ready to give it to him." Mrs. Brown reached into the pocket of the flowered muumuu she wore, took out a crumpled card-stock envelope, handed it to Lei. Lei stifled the apprehension she felt about opening it. It had been torn open roughly.

"Where was this found?"

"She was holding it in her hands." Mrs. Brown covered her face with her hands, but the sobbing had stopped, to Lei's relief. Crying still made her edgy.

"May I?" Lei held up the note.

"Yes."

Lei eased the note out of the envelope with gloved hands. The card was a plain drugstore style, printed with *Thank You* in gold leaf.

"She asked me for a box of 'thank you' notes. For when people brought her things, which they did sometimes." Annie Brown stared ahead. "She never wrote any though, until this one."

"Did you have any idea she was suicidal?"

"Yes. I didn't think she was dealing with her diagnosis well. She would get angry and throw her food, then cry when she saw it just meant I had to clean it up. Lately, though, I thought she was improving. She was still on that site a lot, but her mood was much better. She was even cheerful. I thought the worst was behind us. I knew the illness would progress and she'd get more paralyzed, but I thought she was working through it. Accepting it."

Lei was familiar with the burst of happiness and generosity some suicide victims exhibited once they'd made a commitment to kill themselves. She wondered if she'd have made the same choice Betsy had if she'd had ALS. She didn't say anything, not wanting to interrupt Annie's flow. "She bought that nightgown, said she wanted to pretend she was going to have a wedding night. I thought it was sweet, a good sign." Annie shook her head. "I was wrong."

"What did you know about DyingFriends? Did anyone from their organization stop by, ever visit your daughter in person?"

"No. She got a lot of comfort from that site, from socializing on there as everyone else in her life dropped her as a friend. They didn't seem to know what to say or do around her."

"Did you see or hear anything unusual last night?"

"No." Annie turned red-rimmed eyes on Lei. "Do you think someone came in? We keep the back door open, and someone could have. Because I wonder how she got her nightgown on herself. It was on the dresser across the room when I tucked her in last night. Also, I keep the Ambien in the bathroom. She only needs it once in a while, and I'd never leave it where she could reach it."

Lei didn't respond to that, asking another question instead.

"Could she walk? Enough to get those things?"

"No. Her nerves were damaged. At the doctor's, they even poked her with a needle to her feet and she couldn't feel it, let alone walk."

"Thank you, Mrs. Brown. I can't imagine how this must be for you. We've got your contact information. We'll call you if we need anything more." Lei got up and went back into the apartment, meeting Ken coming out with a box full of evidence-bagged items.

"Done for the moment. Dr. Fukushima has the scene. Let's go back to HQ and report in to Waxman."

CHAPTER NINETEEN

Sᴏᴘʜɪᴇ ᴄᴀʀʀɪᴇᴅ Betsy Brown's laptop, which Ken and Lei had brought in from the latest scene, down to her office after the team meeting with Waxman. Her quads were still a little stiff from the running hikes she'd done over the weekend. An unfamiliar tenderness on her nose and shoulders reminded her that even with her dark complexion, sunscreen was a good idea.

Sophie had discovered a new interest over the weekend—outdoor run hiking. She enjoyed the challenge of running hiking trails with their uneven surface, vegetation and rocks, and spectacular views. She'd done Diamond Head on Saturday and another one on Sunday, a famous route called the Makapu`u Trail. Looking down at the old lighthouse off the trail had lifted her spirits in a way she couldn't explain.

Sophie went through her protocol in working with a new computer, hooking it up to the write-block imager being the first part of that. When the copy of the computer's data was complete, she could look at what Betsy had been up to.

She sat down at her rigs, thinking about the latest news in the case. Most interesting was a finding just in from the ME's office on Corby Hale. His blood work had come back confirming AIDS, and the tox screens had come in positive for GHB as well as heroin. Gamma hydroxybutyrate, a date-rape drug, and enough heroin to put down a rhinoceros. The boy's heart hadn't stood a chance.

Someone had drugged him, then injected him. But why would that be necessary, if he'd written the suicide note himself and planned to die? She opened the case file on Corby, viewed the photos. She uploaded the photos from the Betsy Brown scene, dragged one to compare them side by side. The similarities were striking in the way the bodies were posed. She wondered what the tox results would be on the young woman with ALS.

Adding pressure to the investigation, Waxman told them that Senator Hale had reacted badly to the news that his son's death was neither accidental nor suicide. The FBI office had begun fielding calls from politicos as highly placed as the mayor and the police commissioner for them to find out who'd killed Corby and find that unknown subject soon.

Sophie popped open a data entry box in DAVID. No one had to know she'd run the case on DAVID; she'd keep the results to herself. But it continued to feel like a compulsion to check the conclusions she came to in "old-fashioned" police work against statistical probability.

She inputted all the new scene information on Betsy into DAVID, including oddities like no prints on the nightie box that was too far across the room and the poignant photo of the woman's suicide note:

Dear Mama,

Thank you. This thank-you note was always for you, the woman who put her life on hold to take care of me. Well, there's worse ahead for both of us, and I've decided it's just not right for me to do that to you; nor should I have to endure the inevitability of this terrible disease. If I had anything to leave to anyone, I would leave it to fund research for a cure

*for ALS. Since I don't, I hope my gift to you, of the next few
years of your life free of me, will be enough.*

*I love you. Please don't cry. The day we found out I had
ALS was the day we mourned, and it was enough for me. I'm
going to a place where I can run and swim and dance again,
and it's heaven.*

Love you. See you there someday,
Betsy

Sophie felt her eyes fill as she read. Imagine having a mother
who loved her so much she'd give up her life and work to care for
her if she was sick. Imagine a daughter who loved her mother too
much to be a burden. That such a terrible disease still ravaged people
every day was a crime—a crime Sophie couldn't do a thing about. It
twisted her insides with a visceral horror.

Sophie set DAVID to work, searching for suicides with similar
commonalities, and while Ying was working on that, went into her
email on Janjai.

The now-familiar icon from DyingFriends was there, providing a
link to the "next level of support, sharing, and commitment in your
dying journey." She clicked on it, read and recorded a screenshot of
the agreement not to disclose, share, discuss, or otherwise disperse
information about this level of the site.

Once through that portal, she grimaced at what she saw. The page
was laid out with gallery tabs of photos of suicides at their death
scenes. They ran the gamut from what looked like peaceful drug
overdoses to an image of a woman in a bathtub—she'd slit her wrists
and appeared to be bathing in blood.

The photos weren't named, just captioned, and the central blog
was an opinion piece that was strongly right to death and, once
again, written by KevorkianFan.

Sophie frowned, her long brown fingers racing as she scanned through the pictures. She stopped at a photo of Corby Alexander Hale III's beautiful young face.

Angel Gone to Heaven was the caption.

Here was the solid link they'd been looking for, between the suicides and the site. She took scores of screenshots of the various aspects and pages, adding comments and admiring emoticons through her ShastaM identity. There were hundreds of suicide photos, and finally she came upon Alfred Shimaoka, seated in his car with his fingers in lotus position and his suicide note propped on the gear changer.

Who had taken the picture and uploaded it to the site? Had it been Corby Hale?

Betsy Brown must be here somewhere.

Her fingers beginning to ache, her neck seizing up with tension, Sophie kept searching—filling her drop cache with screenshots, moving to the next one, aware even as she looked at them of the hypnotic suggestiveness of the pictures. Even the hideous ones, like the one of a man's broken body on the sidewalk from jumping, or the one with a face empurpled by hanging, began to have a surreal cachet.

This gallery would be a very bad place to spend time if you were feeling depressed.

She finally found Betsy's photo, captioned, *Arrayed for her Wedding in Heaven.*" Betsy really did look like a beautiful bride, taking a nap before her wedding night. Sophie punched the intercom button on her phone and called Waxman.

"Chief, I think you should come down here, I want to show you something. I found the tie between our suicides and the Dying-Friends site."

CHAPTER TWENTY

Lᴇɪ ᴡᴀʟᴋᴇᴅ to her truck in the cool dim of the underground parking garage. She'd been able to keep her mind off Stevens's departure by immersing in the case: reviewing the evidence collection from Betsy's site, sorting and reviewing that of the other victims. She'd gone down to the lab with Ken and Waxman, and they'd all perused the "suicide gallery" on the DyingFriends site.

"Someone is uploading these pictures," Ang had said, sitting on her big exercise ball and flicking through the gruesome, sad roster so they could see the range of it. Ang highlighted the photos of their known victims. "Which means these suicides were, if not assisted, at least witnessed and photographed by a DyingFriends member. I'm waiting to be invited to some further commitment to suicide." She'd explained how ShastaM's persona was being invited deeper and deeper into the site.

Once again Lei was impressed with Ang's creativity in how she found a way to burrow into the site—but Lei could see it cost her something too. The agent's eyes were ringed with darkness like bruises, and she looked like she'd lost weight. Lei's stomach had turned as well, but she kept a stoic exterior as she visually toured the gruesome images with the rest of the team. DyingFriends was definitely behind these cases—but how, exactly?

Lei was now on her way to stake out the Woo house in Kahala, and Ken was taking the "bu-car" to monitor their remaining identified DyingFriends member, Robert Castellejos in Kaneohe. They'd debated whether or not to reinterview the two men, see what "level" they'd reached, but Waxman had decided the danger was too great that they'd share the investigation with others on the site and spook the administrator. For now they were going to surveil them to see if anyone paid an "angel of mercy" visit to either of the houses.

Lei's phone rang in her jacket pocket just as she unlocked the truck and hopped in. She took it out, and her throat tightened as she saw *det kamuela*. She got in, closed the door, debated, and finally answered. "Special Agent Texeira."

"Lei, it's Marcus."

"Hi." She cleared her throat to get her voice to work. Somehow she'd managed to forget the Kwon fiasco over the weekend. Stevens had been a big help with that.

"I'm calling as a courtesy to tell you I'm on the way to interview your grandfather in connection with the number you found. I also need you to go on record with a statement about why you called that number and where you found it." His tone was flat.

He was doing his job, she reminded herself, and she knew right now he didn't like it. Knowing that helped her reply.

"I am happy to do so. Let me know where and when. I will not be repeating what I told you about Kwon though."

"And I won't be asking you to. At the moment."

He was going to try to keep her deeper involvement out of it. It was something, probably all he could do. "Thanks for letting me know, Marcus. You didn't have to."

"Yes, I did." He sighed now, and she heard the strain in his deep voice. "Have you told Marcella any of this?"

"No. It's been killing me, but no. Only Stevens knows. My partner Ken Yamada. And you."

"Okay, then. Let's try to keep it that way. Things could get very messy very fast."

"I'm aware." She gave a tiny bark of laughter. "Thank you for believing me."

"For the moment."

"For the moment." She waited a beat, but he just hung up. She put the phone away, thinking about her grandfather, imagining Kamuela pulling up to his peaceful home. She pictured Soga's face going immobile with affront at Kamuela's questions. Whatever the phone number in his wife's writing meant, she didn't think he'd known about it.

On the other hand, last year when she asked him about Kwon and if they'd known about her abuse, he'd told her not once but twice to "let sleeping dogs lie."

Trouble was, she'd never been able to resist giving a sleeping dog a poke.

Lei started the truck and rolled out of her surveillance spot under an overhanging jacaranda tree. Detective Reyes from HPD pulled up to take her place. They were collaborating with several detectives now that the bodies were piling up, and Reyes and his partner had been particularly interested in helping after their sad experience with the Betsy Brown case.

It had been a long, hot afternoon, and the sunset sparkling on the ocean off Diamond Head as she rounded the turn toward her grandfather's neighborhood did nothing to lift Lei's mood. She'd had way too long to sit with a pair of binoculars fixed on a dying man's house with nothing to do but think about the trouble she was in and how much she missed Stevens.

"Shake it off," she said aloud. "It is what it is." Dr. Wilson-isms, she called them, those distillations of wisdom from her therapy work with the police psychologist in Hilo.

She did just that when she pulled up in front of her grandfather's immaculate lawn in his Punchbowl neighborhood. Getting out of the truck, she stretched high, hung low, shaking out her arms and legs from the hours of confined inactivity. No one but the white Home Care Nursing van had come or gone from Woo's house in the four hours she'd watched it.

She worked the knocker on the front door. Her grandfather eventually answered it, and she took one look at his pale face, lines etched deeply beside his narrow mouth, and said, "I'm here to take you to dinner, Grandfather."

He just nodded, his silvery buzz-cut head wobbling on a neck she'd never realized was so fragile, and slid gnarled feet into a pair of rubber slippers on the top step. She drove them to their favorite noodle house and ordered saimin. When he'd had some sips of green tea, a little color came back into his face.

"Detective Kamuela told me he was coming to question you."

Soga nodded but didn't speak. Took a few more sips of tea, slurping it to cool it on the way down. She waited for him to put the tea dish down.

"What happened?" she asked.

He folded his hands, knotted with work and calluses, on the table in front of him.

"He wanted to know, did I know what this fortune cookie phone number was about? I told him no."

"Tell me more."

Soga's eyes, with their heavy eyelids, pierced her with a sad and accusing stare. "He said you found it in the box I gave you, and you called it. The phone belonged to a man who'd been shot."

"Yes. He told me that too."

"He said that the victim was an assassin. That he'd killed a lot of people, including the man…" Words seemed to fail him. He took the wooden chopsticks out of a paper sleeve, ran them against each other to knock off splinters.

"Yes. Charlie Kwon, the man who abused me. I told him I called the number because I was curious. I had no idea it was anything but a possible friend of my grandmother's."

"Your grandmother. She had no friends." Those deep brown eyes looked up at her again, then down. "She was angry, your grandmother."

"You've said things like that before. That she was the one to keep me and Maylene out of your lives. Do you think—she had anything to do with calling this man? This assassin? Having him kill Kwon?"

"I don't know," Soga said heavily. The saimin arrived, a great steaming bowl of savory broth and noodles enlivened with strips of egg, chives, rice cake. They busied themselves eating for a while and Lei noticed that his color was better and he seemed to be relaxing.

"When did you eat last?" she asked.

"I don't remember."

"Does that happen often?"

"I don't need much, at my age."

"Grandfather. You have to take care of yourself." She reached over, put a hand on his. "It's not good to forget to eat."

"For you to tell me these things…" He shook his head, a hint of a smile around his mouth. "You don't eat well."

"You're right. We can both do better taking care of ourselves." Lei finished her saimin, at least all that she could capture of the noodles amid the broth, and pushed it away. "Now. Tell me from the beginning. What did he say to you, and what do you know? I need to be warned about what's coming."

"He came with his partner Ching. They sit with me in the living room. They ask me what I know about the box. I say it's my late wife's things, and I gave it to you for keepsakes. They ask, do I know what's inside? I say letters and photographs, maybe a small little thing or two." He set the bowl aside, still half full. "I ask what this is about. They tell me about this man who shoots Kwon and other people, that he's dead and your number on his phone. You said you got the number from the box. Now I'm worried." His hands, when he brought the napkin up to dab his mouth, were trembling. "I tell them I don't know anything. And I don't."

"But you do, Grandfather. You know my grandmother, what she was capable of."

"Yes." He did not elaborate.

"So would she? Have called an assassin?"

"I don't know. I like to think not, but she an angry woman, your grandmother. She want to have someone to blame for Maylene dying, for you going to live with Rosario."

Lei was increasingly glad that her loving, generous aunty Rosario was the one to have taken her in and not the Matsumotos. Despite the very real affection she had for her grandfather, her grandmother seemed to have been a hard and bitter woman.

"Well." Lei touched his gnarled hand. "Hopefully, he will close his case quickly."

"I hope you are right." They drank more tea, and Soga insisted on paying the bill. On the way back to his house, he said, "When do I meet your fiancé?"

"Who?" A curl had escaped the FBI Twist and bounced in her eye as she turned her head to look at him. "You mean Stevens? He just came for the weekend." Lei felt a blush rising in her neck and was glad the darkness hid it from her grandfather's sharp eyes. "He's not my fiancé."

"But he was. And he should be again." She'd told Soga she had someone when he'd asked, that they'd had problems but were working them out.

"You been spying on us?" She made her voice playful. "We want to be together; it's true. But I don't know how. One of us has to give up our work to be with the other."

"You should get married," Soga said, opening his door at his house. "I don't have forever to see my great-grandchildren."

The blush intensified as Lei pictured Stevens holding a baby. Their baby. It was a flash of vision—his face, filled with joy, smiling at her. The baby a wrapped bundle with a head of dark curls and tilted sleeping eyes.

It was the first time that idea had done anything but terrify her. Now she felt a tug of longing somewhere deep inside. *Probably my dried-up uterus casting a vote*, she thought. Trust biology to win over good sense. She wouldn't know the first thing about being a mother.

"We'll see, Grandfather. Next time he visits, I'll bring him to meet you. You'll like him, I think." She walked him to the door. "Don't worry about that other thing."

"I will try not to."

"Love you." She leaned over, kissed his leathery cheek. "Good night, Grandfather."

The next day's surveillance was long, punctuated only by a phone call with Stevens. Lei told him about Kamuela's phone call to her, his interview of her grandfather.

"When do you go make your statement?" he asked.

"I have to go by Kamuela's station after work. We're doing stupid surveillance of these two DyingFriends members. Sophie said she's seen them in the second level of the site, but not the third, where all the gory pictures are. My day is seriously dragging."

"Better than being the lieutenant of a station with all these balls in the air, schedules to juggle, reports to fill out—and all I'm doing is missing you."

Lei closed her eyes a second, dropping the binoculars into her lap. "I miss you too. My grandfather says we need to get married, get started on babies. He's not going to be around forever." A long pause. This was the weakness that had sent her running away two other times. Stevens must be scared to answer. "It's not sounding like such a horrible idea to me." Lei's voice was small.

"You know how I've felt these last four years," he said, that rough note in his voice. "It hasn't changed."

"Well, maybe I have," Lei said. "I just don't know what to do about me being over here and you being over there."

"I don't know either. But this is getting bad. I keep thinking about being with you. You know. Being with you. It's really distracting."

"Right," Lei said, raising the glasses as she spotted movement at the door of the Woo residence. The old man was coming out, pushing his walker. He looked more like Yoda than ever. "Gotta go. Call you later."

She punched off, set the phone aside. Stevens probably thought she'd freaked out again—she'd have to call him back.

The white care van had gone; Lei assumed the old man was alone as he made his way to the koi pond, pushing the wheeled walker up onto the little rounded bridge. At the top of it, he gave the walker a shove. It trundled down the other side of the arched bridge and tipped over at the bottom.

Clyde Woo clung shakily to the low rail that came to just above his knees, looking down at the water.

Lei wondered what the heck he was doing. And suddenly she knew, as he leaned forward and fell headfirst into the pond, his bright embroidered silk robe fluttering as it trailed behind him and settled over the splash where his body had been.

CHAPTER TWENTY-ONE

"Shit!" Lei dropped the binoculars and radioed Dispatch with her handheld as she jumped out of the truck. She was at least a hundred yards away from Woo's location. "Send an ambulance to this address! I need medical assistance!"

Lei sprinted down the long oleander-lined driveway that led into the estate. She'd had to park just outside, positioned so she could see the house's main entrance, but it wasn't close enough. Flying down the driveway, once again she was glad she wore athletic shoes to work rather than the girly ones Marcella persisted with.

At the pond, she shed her phone, cred wallet, and radio, jumping in. It was deeper than it had looked when she'd walked over the bridge herself, up to her waist, and she waded forward, startling the huge koi, to Clyde Woo's body. He was floating facedown. She reached under his narrow torso and flipped him, grabbing the front of the robe and hoisting him up in a lifeguard tow, hauling him as rapidly as she could to the edge. She lifted him under the armpits and hauled him over the cement lip of the pond onto the clipped grass at the edge.

Woo had begun to heave and spasm, and she rolled him onto his side, where he vomited water. She thumped his back, picking up the squawking radio.

"Dispatch, surveillance subject attempted suicide by drowning. Conscious and expelling water. Where's the ambulance?"

"Five minutes out," Dispatch replied. "Backup also on the way."

Lei set the radio down and leaned over to look into Clyde Woo's face. "Can you speak?"

He just coughed some more, and she realized that at least some of the water on his face was tears. "Why did you stop me?" he gasped. "I don't want to live anymore. This should be my choice."

"Mr. Woo. I'm so sorry, but it's my job and duty to save lives. You might feel differently tomorrow."

Woo just sobbed, and she drew him into her lap and patted his back, feeling the light fragility of his twisted body, the hollow bird-like quality of his bones, and realizing how far she'd come that she could offer such comfort. She felt a complex regret that she'd saved him only for him to suffer more. That's how they were when the ambulance pulled up, lights flashing, followed by a familiar unmarked SUV.

Lei surrendered the old man to the EMTs and stood up, aware her shirt had gone transparent with water. She unbuckled her damp shoulder harness—she'd need to clean her weapon, make sure it was dry.

Kamuela stood in front of her, Ching just behind. "Agent Texeira. Don't know why they called for backup, but I was in the area."

Lei plucked the shirt away from her bra, glad it was a plain white one. "Yeah, I just called Dispatch for emergency assistance. Seems like they did a general support call."

"Well, how handy that you were on the scene." He let the statement roll out into a question.

"I had Mr. Woo under surveillance. Saw him ditch his walker." She gestured to the tipped-over equipage at the end of the bridge. "He threw himself in."

"What were you surveilling Woo for?"

"Can I get into some dry clothes?" She wanted to buy time to confer on how much to tell about the investigation the FBI had stolen from him.

"We have to do a walk-through in the house, see what we can see," Kamuela said.

Ching added, "Marcus, this is probably related to the fishy suicides the Feds have been looking into. I told you about Shimaoka last week, and you had that Hale kid first."

Marcus turned to look at his partner as Lei picked up her phone and the radio along with her weapon. "Detective Kamuela, why don't you guys do your walk-through and meet me at my house? I can shower and change, give you a statement. About that other thing too." This could save her a potentially embarrassing trip to his station. "I have to call in to my partner and HQ. I'll text you my address." She walked off before he could detain her further, shoes squishing, pants rubbing, holding the shirt away from her body as best she could.

The EMTs loaded Clyde Woo into the ambulance and pulled out, sirens blaring. Woo must be in some distress for them to be in such a hurry, she thought, jumping into the truck. Woo might die anyway from the stress of the experience, and she felt a stab of sorrow for him.

She wondered fleetingly if he'd left a suicide note and knew she needed to interview him further regarding DyingFriends now that her cover was blown—but Kamuela and Ching were entering the elaborate doors of the house as she turned on the truck. They would take any note they found into evidence, and she'd get it from them.

She called in to Dispatch as she drove, patching through to Ken at his surveillance site.

"Woo tried to off himself," she told Ken. "Sent the nurse service home and pitched himself into the pond."

"Damn!" her partner exclaimed. "You had a lot more action than I have—nothing moving over here. Did you get to him in time?"

"Yeah, but Dispatch called for backup and Kamuela and Ching

showed up." She told him what was going on so far. "I'm going home to change. They're meeting me there to take a statement. I'm wondering if we should bring them on to the case. We've already got Reyes and his partner—do we need anyone more?"

"I'd defer to Waxman and their chief on that, but go ahead and brief them on where we are. We need HPD happy with us. Just one big interagency family bringing down the criminals."

"This case—it's tough. The criminals aren't as clear. Woo was crying when I fished him out. Told me he thought it was his right to end his life. It's hard not to feel bad for him, for the others." Lei found herself rubbing the pendant at her throat.

"The law is straightforward, and our job is to uphold and represent." As always, Ken's certainty grounded her.

"I know. Thank God that much is clear. It's all shades of gray, except for this system admin who's promoting suicide and may be killing people. Have you thought of that? So far we have two—Corby and Betsy—that we know had some help going down and no trace we can tie to anyone." Lei turned off the truck's air-conditioning—she'd begun to shiver in her wet clothes.

"I had thought of that. He or she is the real criminal. I hope Sophie's getting somewhere with that today; she seemed to think she was a lot closer."

CHAPTER TWENTY-TWO

HOURS after she'd hooked it up, the write blocker finally beeped, letting Sophie know the duplication of Betsy Brown's hard drive was done. The electronic sound broke the spell of tracking the suicide photos using DAVID. She'd begun to try to match the photos to known victims across the United States.

She stood, stretched backward, then forward to touch her toes. Unhooked the write blocker, replugged it into Amara. She could hopefully spin through the hard drive and online activity and burrow into Betsy's deepest level on DyingFriends. She knew there had to be another level beyond the one ShastaM had made it to.

There was too much work to do to leave DAVID on ice, and she'd heard Texeira express it this way: "It's easier to ask forgiveness than permission."

She smiled, thinking of the way Lei charged her cases. She felt the stiff unlocking of her frozen muscles as she moved and knew that minutes she spent exercising would enable her to work for hours more.

The laptop had a password. She dragged another program over from one of the other screens and set it to cracking the password. While that was working, she carried her water bottle to the cooler, filled it up, and went to a quiet corner of the room. Got out her weighted jump rope and did cardio. She ignored the frequent glances from Bateman, whom she knew wanted to catch her eye and engage her in conversation or, worse yet, give her a compliment. She could see the words bouncing around the little agent's head like a conversation bubble, and she just didn't have the mental or emotional space in her head to deal with his crush.

Back at her cubicle, she stowed the rope and checked Betsy's computer—password was cracked. She sat on the rubber ball and dove in.

She was able to see that Betsy had an account with DyingFriends by her traffic patterns, but Betsy had deleted her cookies. On the site itself, her account came up with a *404 User Not Found.*

The system admin had beaten her to it again and deleted Betsy's account.

"Damn," Sophie muttered, realizing as she did so that her eyes were sore and gritty from overuse. She was going to have to keep going with the ShastaM ruse, and she was getting tired of it.

Perhaps Betsy's email would have something useful. She surfed through the email using keywords "suicide" "death" "ALS" and didn't find anything of note. Also on the hard drive, and just as sad and devastating typed as it had been in the young woman's handwriting, was a typed practice copy of her suicide note. It was dated the same day she'd placed the order for the nightgown, two weeks before the day she'd actually taken her life..

Something had prompted her decision on that day.

Frustrated, Sophie stood up and heard the distinctive growl of her stomach.

"You sound hungry," Bateman said from behind her. "Want to get a bite to eat down at the cafeteria?"

"No, thanks," Sophie said. "I brought something from home." She didn't turn her head, didn't smile. He took himself off, and she felt guilty relief.

She logged back into her DyingFriends email on the site, and this time there was a new email invitation for ShastaM: "DyingFriend-s.com is pleased to invite you to the deepest level of commitment and sharing available on the site. Read and accept Agreements to enter."

She read on. This security layer was even stricter about not talking about the site, disclosing things you'd seen or "participated in," and it required a background check. The consent form for the background check was handily provided.

Sophie paused. Fortunately, she had a clean and complete identity and background in place ready for ShastaM's fake social security number. She'd anticipated that at some point, DyingFriends was going to do its own vetting of prospective members. She uploaded the consent, made sure all her blocker programs that hid her computer's true identity and location were in place, and hit Accept.

Sophie knew the drill by now. Nothing more would happen until the system admin had reviewed her.

She got out her lunch from home, microwaved it, and while it was in the oven, looked at the clock—it was already five p.m. She took the vegetable curry out, sat back down at her station with the bowl, and opened the gallery of suicide photos again.

It didn't matter what time it was. The only people she wanted for company were the unnamed dead. Their faces, crying for names, crowded her mind.

CHAPTER TWENTY-THREE

Lᴇɪ ᴛᴏᴏᴋ ᴀ sʜᴏᴡᴇʀ, towel-dried and scrunched her curls, and got into a fresh FBI "uniform." She was sitting at the dining room table with her Glock taken apart for cleaning when the dogs let her know Kamuela and Ching were there.

Kamuela had come in alone. She looked past him to the car, where his partner was working a computer on the console. "Told him I'd only be a minute," Kamuela said.

"Thanks for the privacy. Which statement do you want first?" She led him into the cottage. She cued well-mannered Keiki to sit and give him a sniff while Angel bounced around, yapping. She shushed the little dog by picking her up. "Something to drink?"

"No, thanks. I do have to keep an eye on the time. I'll take the statements on tape, if you don't mind." He set a handheld tape recorder on the table between them. Lei sat down and kept her face neutral, stifling anxiety—this was protocol.

"Sure. Which one do you want first?"

"Let's start with the one about the Bozeman murder." It was the first time Lei had heard the name of the assassin. She was silent, stroking Angel's head, as Kamuela stated the date, the time, their location, and their names. He looked up at Lei, gave a nod. "Tell me how you came to dial Bozeman's disposable cell number."

Lei told him, including the impulse decision to try to make contact with someone who had known her deceased grandmother and how she'd come to have the number.

"So you did not know whose number you were calling?"

"No. I was affected by nostalgia and the message the number was written on. It was an impulse decision." It felt odd to be so personal and truthful about something so dangerous.

"And was there any other reason you might have called the number?"

"No." Was he fishing for the Kwon matter?

"How do you think your grandmother had in her possession the number of a man who has killed at least four people that we know of?"

Lei felt her heart beating with heavy thuds. She looked at Kamuela; his eyes were opaquely brown.

"I have no idea." She was able to say it with conviction. She really did have no idea.

"Thank you for your cooperation, Special Agent Texeira." He punched off. Lei exhaled, and Keiki came to lean against her leg, her eyes worried.

"That's a beautiful dog," Kamuela said. "Have you had her long?"

"I've had Keiki five years. Since I was a patrol officer on the Big Island. This little girl, I'm just dog sitting for an extended period."

"So you started off in uniform?"

"Yeah. Worked my way to detective, did my degree in criminal justice on the job at UH Hilo. Caught some heavy cases, got some attention for it, and Marcella was the one to recruit me for the FBI." She'd told Kamuela her darkest secrets but not even her basic background. "I'd like to get the other statement out of the way, the one about Woo. Did you guys find anything in the house? Because I need it, if you did. It's an active investigation."

"Into what, exactly?"

"A website and assisted suicide." Lei told him about Dying-Friends and where they were in the investigation. "Did you find a note in the house?"

"No. So either Woo's decision was a spontaneous one, or maybe he accidentally fell in?"

"Didn't look like it. He really let that walker go with a push at the top of the bridge, looked down at the water for a minute, then just keeled in headfirst. After I fished him out, he said it should have been his choice to end his life, so it wasn't an accident."

"We didn't find anything about DyingFriends either."

"You wouldn't. They're cagey at the deeper levels on the site. I wonder if Woo just didn't have anyone to leave a suicide note for. He said he was estranged from his family when we first interviewed him."

On that sobering thought, Kamuela set up the tape recorder and she made her statement about seeing Woo apparently fall and how she'd come to rescue him. "There is an active investigation ongoing regarding a series of suspicious suicides, and the FBI was keeping an eye on Woo for his safety."

Kamuela turned off the tape recorder, stood up. "I look forward to putting this whole Bozeman thing behind us. I just want to find his killer. I don't plan to hunt down all the 'clients' he hit targets for unless my chief directs me to, and I don't know if it's even possible. Your number was one of the only ones on his phone. How he got his jobs, I haven't been able to determine. So unless some new evidence turns up, it's one of those cases where it's better to let sleeping dogs lie."

Lei started at the detective's use of the familiar phrase. "Very true," she said. "When Stevens and I work out our long-distance issues, we'd love to do something with you and Marcella."

"Sounds like a plan. I'll call you if I need anything more." The entire Kwon situation lay between them unspoken, and Lei hoped it stayed that way—at least until she found out how her grandmother had had Bozeman's number in her keepsake box.

She followed Kamuela out, waved to Ching just as her phone rang again. It was Ken.

"How'd that go?"

She filled him in. "I'm going to the hospital to interview Woo. There was no suicide note at the scene. Are you anywhere near Woo's house? Maybe you can pick up his computer."

"We need a warrant for that, and at this point I don't think we have probable cause," Ken said. "There's no evidence that he even was truly attempting suicide, and if he was, that DyingFriends had anything to do with it."

"He was committing suicide."

"Well, get confirmation at the hospital."

"Okay." Lei sighed, grabbing an apple as she locked the house on the mournful dogs and headed for the truck. "I gave my statement to Kamuela about why I called Bozeman the hit man's phone. Are you near a computer? Can you look him up? I want to know what his background is like."

"I'm not, but I will and I'll get back to you. How did that go?"

"Kamuela was gracious. Stayed with the reason I called Bozeman's phone—curiosity—and left the Kwon thing out of it. I'm hoping that will be the end of it."

"Do you know why your grandmother had his number? Really?"

Lei got into the truck, switched to her Bluetooth, clicked it on. "No. But I'm beginning to think she might have been the kind of woman who would hire a hit man. I haven't heard one good thing about her, even from my grandfather, who won't say straight up, but I can tell he suspects she did hire Bozeman to kill Kwon. Said she 'had a lot of anger' about all that happened to the family but was too proud to reach out to me when I was living with my aunty Rosario. I'm beginning to think I'll never know. But at least we know who killed Kwon."

"A lot of unanswered questions," Ken said. Lei's phone beeped with a second call, and she looked down—it was Stevens.

"I'll call you after my interview with Woo," she said, and rang off, taking Stevens's call.

"Hi, Sweets."

"Hi. I need a nickname for you. Lover Boy? Hot Stuff?"

"No, please no. Why'd you hang up on me? The subject of kids?"

Lei remembered where their conversation had ended. Woo's dive into the koi pond had completely distracted her.

"Don't blame you for thinking that. I actually had to run off and save a man's life." Lei filled him in on Woo's suicide attempt and her statements to Kamuela regarding Bozeman the shooter. "I may still need to have you retrieve the disguise I wore to visit Kwon and make a statement as to where you found it."

"Happy to do it if we need to. Seems like Kamuela decided to believe you."

"Seems like it, thank God." Lei navigated the light traffic leading to the Queen's Medical Center in downtown Honolulu. "But what are we going to do about getting together? Now that I've had you, I'm missing you worse than ever. We can't live like this."

"I like the sound of that. How about you come over to Maui next weekend? See my place. We sold the house in Wailuku Heights, and I've got a nice little apartment in Kuau—close to my station and right on the ocean."

Lei's mind filled with images of Kuau—that aqua-blue stretch of breezy Maui coastline with its tiny hidden beaches. "God, that sounds amazing." She navigated around a slow-moving camper and made a left into the parking garage at the Queen's Medical Center. "The investigation's heating up. I just don't know when I can get away."

A long pause. Lei bit her lip.

"There's always an investigation heating up. This is how it's going to be for both of us," Stevens said. "We both have jobs that take more than your average pound of flesh. I just know I can't be without you much longer without having some sort of breakdown." He uttered a mournful-sounding howl.

Lei laughed, relieved he'd decided to be playful. She pulled into a parking slot. "Yeah, here it is six p.m. and I'm going into a hospital for another interview. This isn't working, but which of us is going to suck it up, give up their job, and move?"

"I'll look at the transfer postings if you will."

"You know there aren't any Bureau offices on Maui."

"Maybe it's time there was a liaison branch over here. C'mon. You know what a hassle it was last year, coordinating everything with that interagency case."

Lei leaned her head on the steering wheel. "It would never fly. Waxman still thinks I'm a loose cannon. That would be giving me too much rope."

"I don't know. Another way to look at it is that you're an agent who's a self-starter and knows how to take initiative."

"That's not a big value in the Bureau that I can tell."

"Well, then. There's always local. Omura still asks about you, and she's the big cheese now at Kahului Station."

Lei sighed. "Michael. Let's just agree to do some homework on it. We don't have to figure this out right now."

Saying goodbye felt so awful she almost wished she hadn't taken his call.

"Mr. Woo is in a coma," the nurse said, consulting a chart. "He came in with cardiac arrhythmia and some mini strokes complicated by his current diagnosis. His systems are shutting down."

Lei felt a clench of regret. "So he's dying. Can I see him?"

"Sure. Just through the window, though. We've got him in intensive care." Lei followed the nurse to the viewing window and looked in at the diminutive figure in the bed. He was propped up, tubes and lines appearing to be what animated the slight rise and fall of his chest. He still looked like Yoda, with his bald, freckled skull with a few antennae-like hairs surrounding it, those wide transparent ears.

"Who's his doctor?"

The nurse looked at the chart again. "Shimoda. He's due to see him tomorrow morning."

"I need to interview him for an investigation. Does he have an emergency contact listed?"

The nurse scanned through her folder, frowned. "No one listed. He was unconscious when he came in, but he had been here before, so we knew who he was and had his insurance on record."

"So the hospital hasn't contacted anyone?"

"No one to contact."

"Okay." God it was sad—Woo dying alone and no one even to call. Lei knew what she was going to be working on this evening. "He had a home care service. Maybe they know something. Someone must be here for him."

The nurse shrugged. "Some old people don't seem to be missed."

Lei felt a flush of heat blow through her body. "Everyone should be missed."

She spun on a rubber heel and stomped off, already on the phone with Dispatch, running a deeper background on Clyde Woo. She went to the deserted waiting room. Apparently, he'd been married, but his wife was deceased. Parents deceased. Had been an only child. She was eventually able to get the number of his lawyer.

She dialed it after getting the man's personal cell, glancing at the clock on the wall that gave the time as seven p.m. "This is Special Agent Lei Texeira with the FBI," she said briskly when the phone was answered. "Your client, Clyde Woo, is here in the Queen's Medical Center in intensive care and is not expected to live."

"Cyde who?" She could picture the man's confused face. He sounded as old as Woo.

"Clyde. Woo. Little Asian multimillionaire. Looks like Yoda."

"Oh, Clyde." She heard the head smack the guy gave. "I'm retired, you know. I turned my clients over to my son." He gave a name and number. "Sorry to hear that Clyde's gone downhill."

"It was, apparently, a rapid slide in that direction," Lei said, jotting the number on her trusty spiral pad. "I'll give your son a call. I'm looking for who his next of kin is, his heir. Someone to inform of what's going on with him."

"Oh, I can tell you that. No one. He's a bitter old man. Had some cousins, but they're all estranged and live on the Mainland. My son never met him, but his office has the will. Clyde was leaving everything to the Honolulu Zoo."

"Oh." Lei digested that. "Well, thanks."

She hung up and decided not to call the lawyer son until the next morning. She was passing by the nurse's station when the young woman waved her over. "Mr. Woo's vitals are failing. Did you reach anyone?"

"No."

"Well, you seem to care what happens to him. Perhaps you'd like to sit with him in his final hour?" For the first time, Lei really looked at her, noting a round, plain face animated by intelligent brown eyes. She must see so much death, and now she was calling Lei on her bluster a few minutes before.

"All right," Lei found herself saying. "No one should die alone."

The nurse gestured. "I'd tell you to get sterile, wear scrubs, and all that—but I don't think it's going to matter to Mr. Woo at this point. You know where his room is."

Lei nodded and walked to the door of the room. She paused outside, did some relaxation breathing. Was she really going in to sit with a relative stranger, one she'd just tried to save, while he died?

She turned the knob, pushed the door open. Went over to the small open area beside the bed, dragged a plastic chair over. She found herself breathing through her mouth because there was a smell in the room—that unique combination of decay and ammonia cleaner that seemed to inhabit every hospital to varying degrees. The nurse came to the doorway, pointed to the monitors.

"See that one? It's his heart." The blipping line on the monitor seemed to be skipping at random intervals. "He has arrhythmia, and notice the time between beats is getting further and further apart.

This is his oxygenation monitor. The blood isn't getting oxygenated." It was marked with a red line, and Mr. Woo's oxygen was well below it. "Over here is his respiration monitor." Lei could see another blipping light. It was also slowing down. "It won't be long now. They say people go easier when someone's with them. You could hold his hand." Those sharp, dark eyes were challenging. "Someone should care."

"I don't know why it has to be me," Lei said miserably. "Why don't you sit with him, hold his hand, and watch him die?"

"Because you're here for this one. I have others to see to who are going to make it." She withdrew.

Lei winced at the woman's directness and sighed again. She steeled herself and picked up Mr. Woo's liver-spotted hand. His palm felt soft, silky. She had a sudden flash of memory: holding a pet mouse as a very young child. The texture of its coat, its trembling delicacy as it rested in her hand, were just like this.

"You're not alone," Lei said, feeling self-conscious, awkward. "I can't tell if you can hear me, but I'm hoping you can." She looked at the monitors, and the heart one seemed to be stabilizing, beating a little more regularly.

"I tried to find your family and let them know you were here. You were right when you told me they weren't around, and I'm sorry about that. I understand why you tried to take your life today." She looked down at the gnarled hand, smoothed the back of it gently. "But no one should die alone."

That hand tightened suddenly, and she looked up into Mr. Woo's open eyes. He was focusing on her, and he opened and closed his mouth. "Water," he whispered.

Lei thought of calling the nurse but decided to get him the water first. She poured from a nearby carafe into a waxed cup holding a sponge on a stick. Held the sponge to his lips. He sucked weakly.

"How are you feeling?" she asked.

He turned his head, and she took the sponge away.

"Like I'm dying," he said, and one side of a smile pulled up his mouth. She remembered the nurse saying he had had strokes.

"Well, you aren't dying alone. I'm here." She rubbed that silky palm. "Just rest."

"You came to ask me questions," he whispered.

"I did. But they really don't matter now."

"Yes, they do. I left DyingFriends."

"Why? The site was such a comfort to you."

"They wanted me to do something I didn't want to do."

"What was that?" Lei fumbled for her phone. "I need to record this. Can you say it again? What did they want you to do?"

"Help someone else die." He pushed each word out past stiff lips. "Take a picture and post it to the site. Then someone would help me die. I decided to just do it myself. I didn't need anyone's help." He coughed, and Lei glanced worriedly at the monitors, all showing irregularities.

"We need your computer for the investigation. Can we have it?"

"Yes," he said. His eyes closed then, and his chest lifted in a spasmodic breath, settled.

Lei leaned over to speak into his bat-like ear. "It's okay, Mr. Woo. You're not alone, and you helped me and others by telling me. You're going to a better place. Just relax; take it easy."

She didn't know that he was going to a better place. She didn't know what Mr. Woo believed, what he'd done in his life, where he would go in the next life. She just knew she hoped he'd be walking somewhere wonderful in his beautiful patterned robe. "God, please give him peace."

In the dim light of the room, accompanied by the random beeping of machines, she felt peace come, moving over Clyde Woo's struggling body like a warm blanket.

Lei continued to rub Woo's hand to let him know she was there. The beeps of the machines got further and further apart, and finally whole minutes went by without anything at all to break the silence.

The nurse came to the door. "Well done."

"He knew I was there. He woke up right before the end," Lei said, blinking, reluctant to let go of Woo's hand.

"They often do."

"Wish you'd told me that."

"Well, they also often don't." The nurse moved briskly around the bed, turning off the monitors, removing the blood pressure cuff, unclipping the IV cord. "I've notified the doctor on call to pronounce the death."

"Well." Lei stood, put her chair back in the corner, cleared her throat. "I'm glad you made me sit with him."

The nurse stopped, smiled, extended her hand. "I didn't 'make' you do anything. My name's Theresa. Theresa Rodrigues. You have a heart, and that's a good thing in a cop."

"If you say so. Met this guy two days ago, and I'm the one at his deathbed. It pretty much sucks. Lei Texeira." Lei took out her card, handed it to the nurse. "You care too. Must be hard keeping that up, doing what you do."

The nurse shook her head a little, pocketing the card. "Compassion makes us human, but it does take a toll."

"Mr. Woo was leaving his millions to the Honolulu Zoo. You ever been?" Lei felt the awkwardness of her overture, but Theresa's directness and passion for her work intrigued her.

"Of course. I heard one of the giraffes gave birth, and I'd like to see that."

"Well, I've never been. Let's do it." They walked out of the room just as the doctor arrived, and Theresa was caught up in the procedure of dealing with Woo's body. Lei walked away down the hall, feeling bittersweet gladness at finding a genuine human connection in the midst of death..

CHAPTER TWENTY-FOUR

MORNING'S SPARKLE made the previous night's events seem like another world as Lei walked back to her office after the team briefing with Ang, Waxman, and Ken. She'd reported in on the events with Clyde Woo, played the recording for them, and now was on her way to his house to search it again and pick up his computer.

Ang followed her out of the conference room. "You doing okay?" The other agent's brows had pulled together. "I wouldn't like sitting with a dying man. This case is really depressing me. Looking at all those suicide photos, looking for ID's on them—it's tough."

"You know, it wasn't that bad," Lei smiled at Ang, stopping outside her office. Ken had gone back to the workroom to look through their evidence again. "It was good to do the right thing by him, and it was peaceful. When he went. I don't think he was suffering. He'd already done a lot of that."

"That's good to hear, at least. Don't tell Waxman, but I'm using DAVID to match the suicide victims in the gallery to known cases."

"Good. It's easier to ask forgiveness than permission."

Ang laughed. "I knew you'd say that."

"Yeah, I've never been much for the finer points of procedure. I get how a defense attorney could tear DAVID apart, but I have a feeling it's not going to matter much in this case."

"Well, I hope to get an email today and get in to that final level on DyingFriends. That's probably where Woo ended—assisting another member's suicide before one of them offs you. It's good to have a solid testimony on tape and confirmation on that."

"Woo did good before he died. Now I'm off to get you another computer." They got on the elevator, Lei to go to the garage and Ang to go to the tech lab. "Hey, I'm sorry I couldn't shoot pool with you and Marcella the other night."

"Just as well. We drank too much." The tech agent got off the elevator with a little wave. "We'll catch you next time."

Lei was walking toward Mr. Woo's house, already looking strangely deserted with leaves blowing through the entry, when her phone rang. *Lt omura* had appeared on the screen.

"Special Agent Lei Texeira."

"That does have a ring to it." Omura's crisp voice had a note of humor. "But I have an idea for a different title for you."

"Hey, Lieutenant," Lei said. "How's it going?"

"It's Captain Omura, as I told you last year, but how does 'Lieutenant' sound to you?"

"What do you mean?" The front door of Woo's house was open. She would definitely lock it. Thieves would be there in minutes if they knew, and they probably watched the obituaries.

"I mean I'd like to offer you a job. See if I can get you back from the Feds."

Lei stopped just inside the door to give the call her full attention. "Did Stevens put you up to this?"

A feminine snort. "Hardly. Don't know and don't care what's going on with your romantic life. Just looking for a good cop to work next to me in a male-dominated workplace. Someone I know I can count on to take initiative. That's a quality I've come to value over time, and you always had good instincts. Here's the deal: The legislature approved another lieutenant position. It's a new one, so I'm not under pressure to give it to someone who's been angling for it. And I want to bring you back, Texeira. You could have a future in the Maui Police Department, and I'm hoping the bright lights and big city aren't as appealing as Maui."

Lei rocked back, taking this in. Omura must have thought she was hesitating because the captain went on. "You can keep your years of service in the Hawaii Police Department, continue to build on them, and the years you spent as a Federal cop will still count. Also we have a generous salary package." She named a figure that was more than what Lei was making or would make for some years as a junior agent. "Unfortunately, I don't have too long to keep the offer open. Two weeks, and then I have to hire someone or lose the position. So think it over and let me know as soon as you can. You're my top choice."

"Wow," Lei said, looking around the great big sunken living room for Woo's computer. "Thanks so much. I will give it some serious thought and get back to you by the end of the week."

"You do that." Omura rang off with the decisiveness that had made her both intimidating and effective as a leader. You always knew where you stood with Omura, Lei thought, unlike Waxman. She spotted a laptop on a side table next to a La-Z-Boy where Woo must have watched TV and relaxed.

Lei unplugged the machine and power cord and did another quick survey, still distracted by the turmoil the phone call had elicited. There was nothing to see but the remains of a life in an empty setting. She definitely had something to think about.

She decided not to call Stevens about it just yet. He'd just pressure her to take the job, and many of the reasons she'd joined the FBI still stood: the movement around the country, higher-level cases, the latest in equipment and technology.

Looking around the beautiful and expensively-appointed room, she remembered that Clyde Woo was also someone who had put his work first. But in the end, it had been cold company.

CHAPTER TWENTY-FIVE

SOPHIE HAD DECIDED to clear her head, and now she ran the rugged Koko Head stair trail, Pandora playing some German thrash metal through headphones to spur her on. Hike running was good because it took all her concentration to move at speed on trails that were never intended for that. Finally, an exercise that took all she had and gave something back. She had Fight Club later on but had already checked Alika's schedule and knew he wouldn't be in, which had bled the anticipation out of going.

Sophie wondered, with the one brain cell that wasn't totally engaged with the perpendicular trail with its rail-girder stair dividers, if he was avoiding her. Ever since she'd said no to the women's fight circuit, he'd been mysteriously absent. She could call him, she thought, jumping a large rock, landing light on her toes and bursting away from the ground. She had his number.

But no.

Maybe just to find out where he was, set up a real coaching appointment.

No. It would be too awful if he figured out she liked him that way and wasn't interested. She'd rather die. She probably would die. Alone, as so many of the suicide victims in the gallery had been...

Sophie reached the top, a stupendous display of clouds, ocean, rugged green slope, and   sweeping vista. She stood, panting. Breathing it in, taking it in, feeling endorphins from the exertion flood her system along with appreciation for the natural splendor all around her.

The dark thoughts fled.

There were important things for her to do, and maybe tonight would be the night she tracked the system admin. She closed her eyes and inhaled, the wind cooling her flushed skin, feeling literally on top of the world.

Sophie turned and headed back, running even faster downhill.

Kamala was slow warming up, so Sophie did some stretches over her home exercise ball. Fight Club had been good. Marcella had shown up and brought Kamuela with her, so they'd had fun orienting him on the sport. Sophie grinned, remembering. Marcella had improved so much, she was able to take the big detective down at least once.

Spending time as a threesome didn't seem so bad when they were doing Fight Club.

Sophie had heated up a frozen fish and noodle dish and ate it as she read through the emails that had come in the intervening hours. Sure enough, the link she was looking for had arrived. She clicked on it and followed it to the next portal.

On this screen, two choices awaited her click: "DyingFriends in Your Area Live Chat" and "The Ultimate Solution."

She clicked on "The Ultimate Solution" and was confronted by a bold printed contract. It read as Lei had led her to expect from Woo's disclosure. The contract designated a commitment to the "ultimate solution" to end his or her suffering, with areas to fill in the subject's top three suicide choices. Once that was submitted, the subject made a commitment to assist or support in the suicide of another member in their local area by one of their three chosen methods, photographing the body and uploading it to the DyingFriends site when complete.

The contracted member could choose the method and the time, effectively surprising the suicide victim. All notes must be written ahead of time and photographic evidence of their completion submitted to the system admin via email for the contract to be enabled.

This was it, Sophie thought, her heart speeding with excitement. Hopefully, the system admin would vet her contract and suicide note personally, and when he did, she could finally track him.

The suicide notes were to be handwritten, photographed, and uploaded to the site. A link she could click on led to "examples of the most effective notes." Effective for whom? In what way? She wished she understood the psychology of the site administrator. She hesitated to click on the "examples." She'd looked at more than enough already in the suicide gallery.

What she should do was write ShastaM's suicide note.

Sophie seldom had any use for paper and a pen, so none were immediately handy. She looked around her workspace—as usual, nothing there but the keyboard, the monitors, the mouse pad, and a mug of cold tea from the morning. She got up, went to her bill-paying area at the other end of the desk. She did most of that online too, but some vendors continued to send paper bills, and in a file drawer she found a yellow legal pad and a ballpoint pen.

She paused. Would ShastaM use a yellow legal pad?

No. The identity she'd been developing was more feminine and girly, traditional even. She needed a card of some kind. She remembered her father's desk, a formal affair in one corner of the living room. She went across the room, pulled out drawers until she found a stack of embossed all-occasion cards. One of them would work.

She sat on the gilt chair at the shiny black lacquer desk, the card open, one of her father's black rolling-ball gel pens in her hand, poised above the creamy paper.

It felt real, this note. Maybe it was all those dead faces she'd pored over in the last few days; maybe it was the depression and loneliness that had dogged her in spite of all her efforts to outrun it, outfight it. But when she put the pen to the paper, the words flowed easily.

Dear family,

First of all, you need to know this was never about anything you did or didn't do. I always knew you loved me the best you could. It was my fault I never felt it, never took it in, and somehow landed on this planet feeling alone and different.

I take responsibility for that and even for how this choice to escape my pain and loneliness is, at the heart, a selfish one.

This once, I choose me and what's best for me and trust that you will understand someday. And even if you don't, that you come to accept that I did what I had to do.

I love you.

Shasta (Mom)

She signed it with the series of three smileys she'd been using as an online signature. If there was a part of the note that felt faked, it was that.

She spread the note open and used her phone to photograph it. Sent it from the phone to Kamala's hard drive. She'd have to upload it to the site from there, behind the masking program, or Kevorkian-Fan, as she'd come to think of the system administrator, could track it to her phone. She sat up, feeling disembodied, as she often did lately, looking around the spacious, elegant space.

It would probably bother her father to know what she'd just done at his desk. It had been overlong since she called him, and a pang of guilt made her thumb to his number on the phone and call it. She tore the card into thin strips and dropped them in the wastebasket.

"Hello." Her father had a resonant voice that had reminded her of Morgan Freeman.

"Hello, Papa. How are you?"

"My girl." His voice felt like a long-distance hug. "Having wild parties in my apartment?"

She gave a little bark of laughter. "Hardly. Your Internet bandwidth is always tapped out, though. How's Washington?"

"Crazy people, crazy traffic, crazy politics, but I'm doing my tour of duty." An ambassador, he had rotations between Southeast Asia and Washington. "Looking forward to retirement. In fact, either we're going to be roommates or I'll be kicking you out next May."

"Really, Papa? You always say that, then don't do it."

"Really. I put my papers in. It's not like I need the money, and lately, I really don't need the stress."

"Well, good. I hope you do it this time." Sophie looked out at the view—perhaps she would miss it more than she thought. Or, they'd try being roommates. The thought made her smile.

"So what's up that you called?"

"Nothing. Just hadn't talked with you in a while and…I wanted to tell you I love you."

A pause. She racked her brain. Had she ever said that to him before on the phone? She didn't think so.

"Are you all right?" he asked, voice sharp with alarm. No, apparently, she hadn't.

"Fine. Really." She reached up, played with a bit of hair, rolling it between her fingers. "Just wanted to tell you that. Also I found a new sport, and it's fun." She told him about run hiking. "I want to take you when you come."

"That can be my first project. Getting in shape," he said. "Well, I'm glad there's nothing wrong. And in case you didn't know it and I don't say it enough—I love you too. There's something in the mail for you."

He was a gift giver. Always had been. "Great, Papa. I'll look forward to it, and the apartment is clean and beautiful whenever you decide to drop on in."

"I kind of wish you'd mess things up," he said. "It feels like no one lives there but your computers whenever I come. Mess the place up for me, will you? Really live in it."

She smiled. "Okay. I'm having a rave here this weekend. I'll tell everyone you said so."

"You better." She heard the smile in his voice. "Have fun. And I love you." He rang off.

And she really felt his love, for the first time in a long time. She was beginning to suspect that was her fault, not his. Sophie walked over to the formal couch with its cream leather cushions and velvety throw pillows and tossed them around. One landed on the floor, and she left it there.

"There. Someone lives here," she said aloud and walked into the bedroom to fill out the rest of her suicide contract.

Sophie got up in the pitch-dark of her room at the beeping tone of her phone alarm, which she'd set to wake her at five a.m. Dressed in the silky tee she wore to bed, she padded over to her computer bay and turned Kamala on, apprehension and anticipation clenching her belly. Today was the day; she just knew it.

Sophie walked into the living room and immediately spotted the cushion on the floor. "No, I'm not going to pick you up," she said aloud, and went into the kitchen, turned her electric kettle on, and walked to the bank of windows.

Sunrise was just beginning to gild the silhouette of Diamond Head with a rime of gold against cobalt-purple sky. Night was pulling back, yielding its hold, but the full moon still hung over the ocean—a silver sequin on the dress of a new day.

Sophie began a sun salutation: Inhale, arms up in a point above her head. Exhale slowly as she spread them, fingers wide, bending over to touch the floor with her palms. Inhale as she put one foot all the way back in a runner's lunge, exhale as she extended the other and hoisted her butt high, arms straight so she formed the pyramid shape of Downward Dog. Inhale as she brought the right leg in, keeping the left out in lunge position. Exhale as she brought that leg in, staying doubled up over straight legs, face between her knees.

Inhale, unrolling the spine one vertebra at a time, lifting the arms arrow straight above her head, palms together. Exhale as she spread them wide in a fan, bringing them open, down, and back to center.

Palms touching.

Breathing.

Feasting her eyes on the morning.

Filling her eyes with beauty and her mind with peace.

Calm settled over her. She would know what to do when the system admin revealed himself, and she could finish her double life as ShastaM with its haunting overtones. She couldn't wait to be done with this case.

Her teakettle whistled.

Sophie broke the pose and poured her tea, returning to Kamala, who hummed with readiness to work. She opened her email.

The system admin had responded, and she immediately set her trace program working on his message even as she read it. It appeared to be a personalized note.

"Dear Shasta,

Your decision to join those who have participated in the ultimate solution is not an easy one, I'm sure. I found your note moving and a true declaration of liberty. Since you have chosen peaceful means of departure from this world, take that note out and leave it somewhere prominent. Live with it in the days to come. Make sure it says exactly what you want it to say, and revise it if you need to. The personal details, location, and means of departure of someone in your area will be emailed to you as soon as they are available. When you've assisted them on their journey, you will be met by another member of DyingFriends.com who will assist you on yours.

Peace to you in your final days. Thanks for reaching out through the forums, and I hope DyingFriends will help many more people in your situation.

Sincerely, Lightbody the Gatekeeper."

So, who was KevorkianFan? Was Lightbody even the real site admin, or was this a final deflection? KevorkianFan was the one whose beliefs were driving the agenda of the site. His position had been clear through his "right to death" editorials.

Once the IP tracker had something to trace, it was remarkably fast. She pinpointed a location and using satellite mapping, was able to view the large house where Lightbody lived. Sophie reached for her phone and speed-dialed Waxman's cell.

"Chief, I have the DyingFriends administrator's address. It's off island, but at least it's in Hawaii."

CHAPTER TWENTY-SIX

LEI AND KEN climbed out of the Bureau's helicopter in well-marked black body armor. A mercifully smooth flight from Oahu to the Big Island had brought them into the parking lot of Lei's first station as a police officer. Well-worn South Hilo Station, where she'd started her career in law enforcement, looked just about the same. Captain Ohale, burly with a few more threads of gray in his buzz cut, had come out to greet them. Several officers and the SWAT team were already gathered around the vehicles they'd use for the raid.

"Captain!" Lei gave her former commanding officer a hug, the Kevlar vest making it awkward. "Great to see you again, even if the circumstances could be better."

"Hated to lose you to the Feds," Ohale said, brown cheeks lifting ever-present Oakleys up with their wide grin. "But fun to see you flying in on a helicopter, girl. Hear you been tearing it up over there."

"'Wherever I go, there I am.' As Dr. Wilson would say."

"Speaking of, I know she'd love to see you if there's time." He whacked her shoulder in a friendly fashion. "So, we pulled together a team for a takedown, like you guys called for. Who's the perp you're after?"

Ken had come to stand beside her, and she introduced them. Ken gestured for the other officers and SWAT to come in, and they formed a circle around Lei and Ken. Everyone looked unfamiliar and intimidating in their black body armor and weaponry, just as they should.

"Hopefully we can catch this guy off guard. He's the administrator of a website that promotes assisted suicide, and we suspect, may have been an 'angel of mercy' in murdering several people himself. We have no idea what weapons he may have, but we can expect an unknown subject or subjects who are prepared to die," Ken said.

The drivers of four vehicles plugged the address Ken distributed into their vehicles' on-board GPS, and radio silence was enforced in case the unsub was monitoring the police band. The team's order was established: SWAT would break down the door, the FBI agents would follow, and additional local police officers would guard the perimeter to make sure the unsub didn't escape out the back.

Lei and Ken jumped into an unmarked Land Cruiser with two SWAT in front. Lei glanced back to see Captain Ohale watching them pull out, hands on his hips.

She hadn't realized how good it would feel to see him again, and even with preraid adrenaline up, she was a little nostalgic as they roared through downtown Hilo, thinking of the things she'd enjoyed about working with local law enforcement. The new job offer, compartmentalized into a niche, felt like it was pressing on the back of her brain.

All the downtown Hilo buildings seemed to have a tinge of mildew from the damp. Towering tree ferns and orchids decorated almost every house. For once it wasn't raining, though everything was lush as she remembered.

Lei frowned as she realized they were traveling through her old neighborhood at the back of town, a quiet area of tin-roofed cottages built in the 1960s connected by a necklace of exterior electrical poles. And for some reason she couldn't put into words, she wasn't even surprised when the house they pulled up to and surrounded was the sprawling compound of the Chang family, crime lords of the Big Island.

They had history, she and the Changs—and it seemed today they'd be making more.

She felt her heart rate spike as she turned to Ken. "I know this house. This is the Chang crime family compound. There will be a lot of people in the house, and they'll be well armed. We've got to move fast and surprise them, or this could turn into a siege."

Ken's dark eyes widened as he absorbed the ramifications. He lifted the radio to his lips and passed that on to the squad leader. Somewhere deep in the house, a large dog had begun an aggressive barking that raised the hair on the back of Lei's neck.

"Let's move fast," she repeated, squashing her helmet with its built-in comm unit down over her rebellious hair. She checked her Glock, patted the flash bangs in her pants pockets and her backup weapon on her hip as she followed Ken. The SWAT unit, six officers strong, was already at the front door with their door cannon while the backup police took up positions behind the parked vehicles. She and Ken split up to crouch behind the SWAT officers, weapons out in low ready position.

"Police!" the team leader yelled, and swung the door cannon. The door, splintery and old, held. Lei heard running feet and the report of a pistol from the window beside the door. Someone was already up and shooting.

The officer swung the cannon again, and the wood blew apart, revealing the reason for the door's resistance: a steel core. Another officer took hold with the team leader, and they aimed the cannon right at the handle area. This time it blew inward, but now rifle fire, peppering their vehicles, had joined the chaos.

Lei, jittery with adrenaline, made herself as small as possible crouched behind the SWAT officer in front of her, and ran in behind him. The SWAT members peeled off, taking down the shooter behind the window and spreading out through the house. Lei and Ken headed toward the center of the house—the source of the menacing barking.

Lei felt her world telescope down to what she could see and hear through the helmet: the burr of static, voices reporting in, the thunder of her heart in her ears, eyes scanning for targets, breathing constricted by the body armor. There was no room in this world for doubt, hesitancy, or compassion—there was only shoot or be shot.

The interior of the house was dimly lit, a maze of rooms punctuated by dark unidentifiable humps of furniture. The barking of the dog led them toward one final door. She crouched on one side, Ken on the other, and they heard the menacing snarl of what was on the other side.

Lei knew the day had finally come that she might have to shoot a dog. She was very clear that she'd rather shoot a human any day, but there wouldn't be a choice if she were being attacked.

Ken made eye contact, gave a head nod. She reciprocated, and he stood and kicked in the door with one well-aimed blow just below the handle. It flew inward and he stepped through, aiming his weapon inside. She sprang in behind him, ready for the leap of the dog and braced for gunfire.

CHAPTER TWENTY-SEVEN

A SLIM YOUNG man dressed in fatigue pants and an undershirt held one hand up in the air. The other restrained a great brindled pit bull by its collar. He stood in front of a desk with a bank of computer monitors on it and appeared unarmed. In the other corner was a hospital bed, dimly lit by the green and blue light of monitors. A shrouded form lay there unmoving.

"On your knees!" Ken bellowed, and the man dropped to his knees, now using both hands to hold back the dog. It was frantic to attack them, jaws gnashing and spraying spittle, eyes slit. He appeared to be barely hanging on.

Lei hit the light on the wall. The fierce white of the overhead fluorescents broke the aggressive spell, and the dog sat back on its haunches, still barking.

"I have to put him in the back," the man said, and Lei and Ken moved in to cover him as he wrestled the dog to the back door. As soon as the animal was secured on its cable tie out in the backyard, he knelt, and Lei moved in to cuff him as the SWAT leader called the all clear.

There was something familiar about this young man. She thought he might be Healani Chang's grandson, a boy with an attitude and a red do-rag she'd busted for tagging back in the day.

"Glad you held your dog," she said in his ear. "I didn't want to have to shoot him. Are you Lightbody?" He turned his head so quickly toward her she knew the answer was yes. She hefted him up. "Let's go."

"We can't leave my grandma here without care," he protested as they went back into the house, the dog barking hysterically behind them.

"We'll call it in." Ken got on the comm to Dispatch to send someone from Animal Control. "Who is someone we can call for your grandma?"

"My sister. She lives in Hilo."

Lei handed the young man off to Ken as they moved toward the front of the house. She approached the bed.

Healani Chang, Big Island crime boss, looked back at her. Chocolate-brown eyes, always her best feature, were sunken in grayish fleshy pouches. Someone had done her thick silver hair in braids. She wore a scarlet muumuu, stark as blood against the white sheets. An IV and urine catchment bags hung from beside the bed, and the sheets were tucked up under stumps where her knees and feet should have been.

Lei took her helmet off, tucked it under her arm. "Mrs. Chang. It's been a long time."

"Not long enough." Healani's husky smoker's voice was the same. "I knew it would be you, in the end. Somehow I always knew. Wish I'd killed you years ago."

Lei stood for a long moment, staring at her enemy. The hate in the woman's hard brown eyes hadn't changed in the years since they'd last stared each other down, but she was surprised to feel nothing but a wary sorrow, looking at the wreck the woman had become. "What happened to you?"

"Lung cancer. Diabetes took my legs. I've got only a few weeks to live, they say, and I'm not spending it in jail."

Lei looked toward the door, but Ken and the young man had gone to the front of the house with the rest of the gangsters the team had rounded up. They were alone.

"That your grandson? The kid I picked up for tagging?" Lei distinctly remembered running the boy down as a teen, tackling him four years ago.

"Yes. He's a good boy. Went to college. Not in the game."

"He's not in the drug game; he's in a different game. Do you know what he does on those computers?"

"He has an online business. Brings in plenty of money that way. Legit." Healani's ragged voice had gotten stronger. "You leave him out of this."

"Mrs. Chang. We aren't here for you. We're here for him." Lei measured each word and bit it off. The fight drained out of Healani Chang's eyes, and the life with it.

"Can't believe none of them got you," Healani said. "I should have killed you myself." Her voice was so low Lei had to lean in to hear it. Lei could tell the news about her grandson was a crushing blow by the leeching of color from her puffy face. Lei frowned, but before she could say another word, she found herself looking into the black bore of a weapon the woman had brought up out of the bedding.

Lei dove, banging her head on the steel bed and her chin on the stand of the IV rack. She was stunned, flat on the floor and seeing stars. She heard the boom of a pistol report in the enclosed space, then a second one.

She was too dazed to get up and was unsure where Healani was aiming next. She stayed down, waiting for the spinning stars in her vision to subside. She cursed herself for not searching Healani's bed. The woman was deadly no matter her age or disability.

She heard the rushing thunder of boots, heard them stop in the doorway, heard her partner yell, "Lei! You okay?"

"Gun!" Lei yelled back. "She's armed!"

"Not anymore." Ken came forward to stand in front of her.

"What happened?" Lei could see him looking around, his brows drawn down in concern.

One of the squad appeared in the door. "Oh shit."

Ken reached down and helped Lei up. Her head spun, and she clung to him, turning to look at the bed—and wished she hadn't. Most of Healani's head was gone, and gore covered the wall behind her body.

"Oh God," Lei said. "Oh. God."

She felt visceral horror rise up and squeeze the breath out of her lungs. There was a hole in the side of the mattress where Healani had taken a shot at Lei.

"Where's your weapon?" Ken's voice was sharp.

"Holstered. I never saw it coming."

"Give your weapons to me." She was barely aware of handing him her Glock and her backup weapon, she was so dizzy. She needed Ken's help to walk back out of the house. Her legs had gone rubbery, vision doubling in and out. He supported her outside, and she dropped to the ground. "Are you injured?" he asked.

"I hit my head. I don't feel well." She rolled to the side and vomited, narrowly missing his boot. He cursed.

"Medic! First aid over here!"

Lei closed her eyes, feeling the roughness of the uneven grass of the Chang front yard against her cheek and utterly lacking the where-withal to do anything more than lie there. She must have a concussion. She felt something damp wiping her hands.

"Just rest. You're going to be okay." Ken's reassuring voice. An ambulance pulled up, and Lei opened her eyes. Lying facedown on the grass, cuffed a few feet away with the other suspects, the Chang grandson stared at her, and she recognized the implacable hatred in his narrowed eyes.

She closed hers to shut it out.

Hours later, they descended off the helicopter, and Lei and Ken accompanied Terence Chang III, aka Lightbody, off the helicopter and into the Prince Kuhio Federal Building. He'd been formally charged with multiple counts of third-degree murder and conspiracy to commit murder. Through all the proceedings, he had never asked for a lawyer.

Lei's head hurt, thumping with pain along with every breath. The EMTs had diagnosed her with a minor concussion, but once she told them about her head injury on Maui, they wanted to put her in the hospital for observation.

She'd declined and followed Ken and the prisoner toward Conference Room B, where they conducted hostile interrogations. Waxman walked up to her, accompanied by Sophie. The tech agent looked tense.

Ang frowned as Ken guided Chang into the interview room. "I thought he'd be older," she said.

"Texeira." Waxman stopped Lei with a hand. "I heard you were supposed to be in the hospital. You have a head injury on an old head injury."

"I'm okay, Chief. I want to be in on the interview."

"I want you to go home. Call for someone to keep you company and put compresses on it."

"No, sir." Lei pulled herself fully upright, looked him in the eye. "I need to see this through."

He stared back for a moment, then sighed. "Okay. You can join me in the observation room. But I want Sophie in the interview with Ken. She'll know what kinds of questions to ask Chang related to the website."

"Okay." Lei exchanged a glance with Ang. She trusted the tech agent—Sophie'd know what to ask Chang even more than Lei did, and that old history wouldn't distract from the interview. "It might be good to sit down for a while."

Lei followed Waxman into the dim cave of the observation room as Sophie followed Ken into Conference Room B.

CHAPTER TWENTY-EIGHT

SOPHIE FELT ALL her senses sharpen as she stepped into the bare room behind Ken, who had attached the prisoner's handcuffs to a ring on the steel table. The room smelled musty and closed up, and she realized how seldom she'd been in it—her job was usually behind the reflective mirror on the other side.

Overly bright fluorescent lighting bleached out Lightbody's black undershirt and bent head. He was mid-twenties, medium-height, slender-built, with the olive-tan skin of mixed Asian and Hawaiian heritage.

Sophie brought her handheld tablet to make notes, and she had an Internet connection open to her computers so she could ask him site-related questions. She sat down beside Ken, who'd turned on the recording equipment at the door. They were both piped in to monitors and clearly visible to Lei and Waxman on the other side of the mirror.

Ken stated the date, time, and names of all present and started in. "Tell us about the philosophy behind DyingFriends and how it got started."

The young man, Terence Chang III, rubbed the skin of one wrist. Sophie could see it was red and abraded from the cuffs.

"Agent Yamada, I wonder if Mr. Chang needs to be cuffed. He doesn't seem like an ordinary criminal," Sophie said.

Ken glanced at her, one brow raised, but went with it. He reached over with his key and undid the cuffs. They dropped free with a metallic clang.

"All right, Mr. Chang." Sophie placed the tablet on the table, touching it with her long fingers as she gazed at the young man. "I am an admirer of your work. The DyingFriends site is an extraordinary accomplishment."

Terence Chang looked up, eyes widening slightly. She flattered him some more.

"I'm a technology specialist for the FBI, and I routinely crack into databases and track their source within hours. It took me an extraordinarily long time to penetrate your site and track you down, and in the course of the investigation, I came to admire both your skills and your passion for your cause. This is your moment to share your vision with us. Help us understand what you were trying to accomplish."

"I did accomplish it." Terence sat back with a return of what looked like a natural arrogance in his demeanor. "I wanted to help people who were mentally or physically dying adjust to their circumstances, make it easier. Help them by having some control and say over the process."

"What got you interested in something so different from your family's usual business?" Sophie chose her words carefully.

"My grandmother. Her situation." He folded his lips tight.

"Your grandmother," Ken said. "According to Agent Texeira, who was with her when she died, she didn't know about the operation that was going on literally under her nose."

"Fucking Texeiras. Tutu always said they'd be the death of her, and they were." Chang almost spit the words. Sophie started and glanced at Ken, seeing in his narrowed eyes this wasn't an avenue they wanted to pursue. Terence went on. "Tutu inspired the site. I'm glad she's free of her body now." Chang looked down, rubbed the red mark on his wrist. "She was sick with diabetes first. Then the lung cancer. She was a powerful woman. She wanted me to go legit. So I did."

"And yet here you are, under arrest," Ken said. "I wouldn't call that legit."

"It's a matter of perception. Society just hasn't caught up with us. Someday everything DyingFriends stands for will be legal."

Sophie felt a shiver of anxiety at the utter conviction Terence Chang conveyed through his words. "I don't know about that, Mr. Chang. Sometimes mistakes are made. For instance, I got a call from the ME's office, and Betsy Brown? Remember her?" She held up the tablet, displayed Betsy's photo arrayed in the bridal nightgown. She saw by the slight pinch of his nostrils that he did recognize her. "She thought she was dying of ALS. She was misdiagnosed. She had Guillain-Barré syndrome, a viral paralysis that is nonfatal. She would have recovered."

This time, Terence Chang's face blanched. Sophie went on. "Someone assisted her suicide, and that person is a murderer."

Ken leaned forward. "Who was it? Help yourself. Give us something."

"Was it KevorkianFan?" Sophie asked.

Chang shook his head. "It doesn't matter. People should have a right to die when they want to. It's a basic human right and covered under 'freedom to pursue life, liberty and the pursuit of happiness.' Sometimes pursuing life, liberty, and happiness means pursuing death."

"But not everyone should die when DyingFriends promotes them to. Corby Alexander Hale III. He was nineteen. Yes, he had AIDS—but he could have lived almost a normal life span with proper medications and treatment, possibly even long enough to see a cure. Your organization took that choice from him."

Chang shook his head again. "It's about freedom. He chose his path. I merely helped him achieve his own goal."

"So you're admitting to that you assisted Corby Hale at his suicide?" Ken zeroed in on Chang.

A long pause before Chang answered. "I believe I'll call for my lawyer now."

Damn, Sophie thought. They'd pushed him too hard, too soon. Her earbud crackled with Waxman's voice. "Offer him a phone, and see who he calls. We'll get back to this later after the lawyer meets with him."

Ken took out his phone. "Who can we call for you?"

"Bennie Fernandez," Chang said. "He represents our family."

Sophie heard Lei's voice groan aloud in her ear. Fernandez was the premier defense lawyer in the state and had been a thorn in their side on many cases. Ken looked up Fernandez's number for Chang and dialed it. Sophie looked back at the young man from the doorway as he sat on hold with the firm.

"I get what you were trying to do. You are a true pioneer." Sophie wanted to leave him with the feeling of having an ally. She closed the door gently and followed Ken into the observation room, where Waxman and Lei waited.

"Good job, right until the part where you tried to get him to take the rap for murdering a senator's son," Waxman said dryly.

Ken shrugged. "He was going to lawyer up eventually. We'll keep building the case against him—verify when he's traveled and alibis for the deaths, et cetera. We've got this guy. We don't need a confession."

"I don't think so." Waxman shook his head. "I think you're going to have to prove this case, and that's going to be tough. And what the hell was that about the Texeiras?" Even in the dim light, Sophie could see the paleness of the other agent's skin, freckles across her nose standing out like blots of paint and the bruises on her face darkening. "Lei, are you feeling okay?" Waxman asked.

"No. And, sir, I have a history with that family. Long, sad story."

"Do I need to know it right now?"

"No, but you should know it eventually. Actually has nothing to do with this case."

Waxman gave an abrupt nod. "Texeira, go home immediately. In fact, Ken, why don't you run her home? It'll take at least that long for Fernandez to get here and confer with his client."

Lei rubbed her eyes. "Yeah, I think I need an ice pack or two. I can always review the tapes." They left, and Sophie looked at Waxman. They both looked over at Chang, head bent over the phone.

"I'm glad you didn't let Texeira go into the interview," Sophie said. "We'll get more out of him without her there."

"Do you know any of this 'long story' she alluded to?" Sophie asked. Waxman's pale brows had come together, and she felt her throat constrict with worry. She knew Lei had been under scrutiny since she joined the Honolulu office, but her chief needed all the facts to best handle the case.

"What history?" Waxman snapped.

"I know this from Marcella. You know she and Lei are close." Sophie sketched in what Marcella had told her about Lei's background in Hilo and the multistranded web connecting her and the Changs. "I wonder if that's why Healani Chang took her own life—being defeated by Lei might have pushed her over the edge."

"Texeira's off the case," Waxman said flatly. "And I'm going to want her interviewed separately about the showdown. If Terence Chang tells this to Bennie Fernandez—and he will—it could compromise our whole prosecution. I'll see if Dr. LaSota can make a house call. She's in town." He got out and worked his phone, and Sophie stared through the glass at Terence Chang, who was still rubbing his wrists.

"Sophie, you can shut the site down, right?" Waxman had finished his calls.

"I can, yes, but we need an order to do it."

"I'll work on that, get a judge to issue an injunction so no more suicides go on while we're investigating."

"It's too bad for the legit part of the site. A lot of people are helped by it. It doesn't get weird until the deeper layers."

"Can you disable just the deeper layers?"

"Not without Lightbody's cooperation, if he's even the site administrator. We're still missing KevorkianFan, the author of all the op-ed pieces. I need to get into the operating system and make modifications. I'm not backdoored into all that."

"Well. I want you to go back in alone and try to get that cooperation from him. If you can't, I want you to shut the whole site down," Waxman said.

"That I would be happy to do." They both watched the next-generation crime boss of the Chang family, sitting arrogantly relaxed in the interview room. Sophie had a bad feeling she couldn't put into words.

CHAPTER TWENTY-NINE

Lᴇɪ ᴡᴏᴋᴇ up from a Vicodin-assisted nap to the barking of the dogs warning her there was a visitor. She pushed a handful of curly hair off her forehead and encountered the knot where she'd hit the rail of the bed there. Her jaw, where she'd landed, still hurt too. Both had left nasty bruises. Considering the bullets flying around that morning, she thought they'd all gotten off light. Shot-up vehicles, two of the Changs in the hospital but expected to fully recover, and one suicide—all in all, not bad.

Lei walked to the door and was surprised to see Dr. LaSota, FBI psychologist, accompanied by an unknown agent, standing outside the gate. She hurried across the yard, shushing the dogs. "Come in, Dr. LaSota. This is a surprise. I expected a debrief but not so soon or at my home."

"Yes, I'll explain inside." The diminutive brunette psychologist, pressed and perfect in her FBI gray, gestured to her companion. "This is Special Agent Pillman."

Lei shook the agent's firm, square hand. Hard brown eyes assessed her. "Call me Hank."

"Nice to meet you, Hank. Come in, please." She led the way into the little cottage, got through the dogs' antics, and ushered them inside.

Something was up. She'd anticipated a debrief, but not until the next time she went in to work. She'd planned to take another day or two off, let her head get back to normal now that Terence Chang was safely in custody. But if she'd identified "call me Hank" Pillman correctly, he was with Internal Affairs Division.

She offered them refreshments, and when everyone had a glass of ice water, she sat down at the little table with them.

"So, Hank. I expected an interview with Dr. LaSota or Dr. Wilson, but what brings you here?"

He flipped open his cred wallet, showed her the unique badge that designated Internal Affairs. "You can call your union rep to be present for this interview."

Lei's heartbeat picked up. Black spots encroached, and she felt the throb of the headache resurging. She held herself very still, one hand creeping down to pinch her thigh. "Am I in trouble? What is this about?"

Dr. LaSota, sharp, dark eyes observant and taking in every move Lei made, took out a tape recorder and set it on the table, pressed Record.

"You have been apprised of your right to a union rep," she said. "Are you waiving that right?"

"For the moment. Until I know what this is about."

"All right. We'll get started, see where this goes. Tell us about the events of this morning's raid, step by step."

Lei took a sip of water and tried to focus. Her thoughts felt elusive, little fish slipping through her fingers. She tracked back and described getting the address and the call to do the raid, communicating with South Hilo Station and SWAT, flying into Hilo, converging on the residence.

She paused for another sip of water.

"Was that when you realized you were raiding the Chang crime family's house, or was it earlier?" Hank asked.

So that was what this was about.

She realized in that moment that the head injury really had dulled her thought processes. How had Internal Affairs found out about her relationship with the Changs? Waxman had to have called them.

"I recognized the Chang residence when we arrived at the coordinates of the location we were sent to. We didn't have Lightbody's name, just the location of his computer. I didn't know until we pulled up to the house."

"So did you say anything to anyone about your involvement with the Changs in the past?"

"It hasn't been relevant. When we got to the residence, I told Ken I knew this family and that they would be heavily armed. We were about to do a raid, and a dog was barking inside the house. There wasn't time for a lot of second-guessing."

"So at what point did you realize you shouldn't be participating in the raid?"

"At no point did I think that." Anger had begun to build. "It's pure coincidence that he's a Chang. We followed the evidence. Nothing more."

"And how interesting that Healani Chang shot herself while you were alone in the room with her," Pillman said. "Isn't there a feud between your families?"

Lei sat back, found her hand had come up to cover her mouth. "What are you saying? That I killed her?"

"Are you saying that?"

"I think I will call for my union rep now. Do I need a lawyer as well?"

"Lei. May I call you Lei?" Dr. LaSota leaned forward.

"No, you may call me Agent Texeira." Lei's head really was throbbing. "One thing I will say before this interview is over is this: I have a head injury and I need to get it looked at. If I hadn't had it, I would have appreciated the situation I'm in more clearly." She got her phone out. "I need to go to the hospital. I was supposed to stay there in Hilo, but I wanted to continue with the investigation."

"Uh-huh. Right," Pillman said.

"You can check with SAC Waxman, with anyone on the team. When Healani pulled her gun, I hit the ground and whacked my head on the metal bedframe. My chin on the IV stand." She pointed to her face. "Waxman sent me home to rest from the interview. I was supposed to go to the hospital on the Big Island."

Dr. LaSota had a crease between her arched brows and seemed a little worried. She gave Pillman a quelling glance as he started to say something more. "We'll take you there ourselves. You shouldn't be driving if that's the case. We can verify everything she's saying, Agent Pillman."

In the back of their black SUV, Lei texted Stevens, Marcella, and Ken: *Going to hospital. Head injury in raid. IA investigating me b/c of Chang involvement.*

This was no time to suffer stoically alone. She needed all the support she could get. Dr. LaSota, sitting in the passenger seat, had called Lei's union rep. That worthy individual said he appreciated the heads-up but didn't want to come until they resumed the interview, which he assumed would be after Lei had recovered from her injuries and a doctor had signed off on that. Pillman looked irritable at that news.

"So I don't need a lawyer?" Lei asked.

"We aren't charging you with anything at this time," Pillman said over his shoulder. "We are just trying to get to the bottom of what happened."

"I don't understand where you're going with all this. I did nothing wrong."

Neither of the other agents answered.

Lei went through the paperwork at the emergency room, feeling like a suspect with the stoic agents standing behind her. Her phone rang with Stevens's call, and she answered it, standing in front of the admissions clerk.

"I'm getting the next flight out." His voice was tight with anxiety.

"You don't have to." Lei glanced at LaSota and Pillman, reveling in the sound of his voice and the comfort it brought. "I have company."

"Yes, I do. I'll see you soon." He rang off. She was bolstered by his immediate support. Marcella and Ken arrived together a few minutes later, and she grinned at the sight of them in spite of her sore face.

"Good," Pillman said, as they approached. "We need to interview both of you."

"Have a little decency," Ken said. "This is my partner, and she's here with a head injury. Let's see if she's okay first. And I want to be the first to meet with you. I have some evidence to discuss."

Marcella came to hug Lei, careful not to jostle, and stood close enough that Lei could feel her body heat.

"I'm sure this is all just a misunderstanding," she said to the agents, with her best dimpled smile. Unfortunately, LaSota appeared impervious, and so did Pillman.

The nurse arrived at that moment and helped Lei into a wheel-chair. "Off to get a CT scan," she said. "Only one person can accompany the patient."

Marcella stepped in. "Lead on."

After the CT scan, they admitted Lei for observation, and she was propped up in bed, sipping water from a straw when Ken came to the door.

"Your turn, Marcella. They're using an empty exam room for the interviews," he said.

Marcella tweaked one of Lei's curls as she got up to leave. "Don't worry, Sweets. This is just Waxman getting a bug up his ass. You've done nothing wrong."

"Good thing I took some steps at the scene to protect you," Ken said. "Agent Pillman was almost disappointed I'd taken your weapons and checked them—not discharged. I also swabbed your hands for GSR. I showed them the evidence that you never, at any time, discharged or handled a weapon at the scene." Lei dimly remembered handing him her Glocks, the damp swab on her hands. She'd barely registered what he was doing at the time.

"I owe you, partner. Big-time. I had no idea they'd go in this direction with this." Lei felt sick at the thought of being prosecuted for Healani Chang's death. "Thanks for the quick thinking."

"I know how a defense attorney thinks, and I hadn't just gotten a concussion." Ken took Marcella's seat beside the bed. "Just wanted to get some insurance for you after what you'd told me about the Changs a while ago."

"Those assholes," Marcella said. "I've got a few things to say on the subject." She stomped out.

"Just relax," Ken said. "This'll blow over. Stay cool. You've been through worse with Waxman, right?"

"Yeah." Lei's head hurt too much to think. She closed her eyes. "Can I have a pill yet? The pain is really bad."

"Yes, young lady, you can." An unfamiliar voice. She opened her eyes to see a doctor reviewing her chart. "You have a concussion, which means there's some swelling around your brain. I want to keep you here overnight for observation since this is a two-time injury. Now that we know what's going on, it's okay for you to have something for pain."

He signaled, and the nurse who'd been standing by injected medication into Lei's IV, and in mere moments, she felt herself slipping into blessed darkness.

CHAPTER THIRTY

"YOU'VE GOT that boxer brain syndrome now." Stevens drove her home the next morning in a lime-green Ford Fiesta he'd rented at the airport the night before. "We can't have you banging your head anymore. Period."

"Apparently not, though getting shot point-blank by Healani Chang didn't really appeal either."

The contusion on her head had migrated, giving her a black eye, while the bruise on her chin swelled that side of her face. She felt better physically, but miserable with apprehension about what would happen next. Did they really think she'd shot Healani or provoked the woman's suicide somehow? And if that wasn't enough, there was always the Kwon murder and Marcus Kamuela to worry about.

At the house, the dogs, lonely and missing dinner, were beside themselves, and that drama took a while to settle. Lei let Stevens handle it and went straight into the shower. She was glad when he joined her there.

"Make me forget all this," she whispered, plastered against his wet length, leaning in to him. "Make me feel better."

"My pleasure," he whispered in her ear. And very gently, he did.

Their cocoon lasted only a few hours before Lei's phone buzzed with a text from Ken: *Heads-up. Waxman and goons on the warpath. They'll be calling you to come in any minute.*

Lei got out of bed, hurried to the closet. "IA and my boss are going to call me in. Should I look professional, or look injured?"

"How about both?" Stevens propped himself up on an elbow. "They shouldn't be doing this so soon."

"I'm sure it's because Dr. LaSota's in town. She's always on a schedule."

Lei's phone rang with the summons once she was dressed. She looked at her hair and face, appalled, in the bathroom mirror. Stevens came up behind her and touched the ripe black shiner that had developed as blood moved down from the knot on her forehead and collected under her eye. "The clothes are professional and the bruises look heroic. The hair?" He pulled a curl. "Uniquely you. Don't change a thing."

"I love you." She turned and hugged him. "What happens in this meeting is what makes my mind up about Omura's call." She'd finally told him about the unexpected offer and its deadline. "With the case heating up, I've hardly had time to think about it. I wondered if you had something to do with Omura's call."

He snorted. "Me tell Omura anything? Good luck with that. No, I didn't even know about it—though I confess to crying in my beer to Pono about the whole situation. I'm sure he's working the 'coconut wireless' to get something for you."

Pono Kaihale, her first partner and one of her oldest friends, was still looking out for her on Maui. Lei was warmed by that thought as she said goodbye to the dogs and left Angel and Keiki looking mournfully after them through the gate.

Lei was relieved to find they'd put her in Conference Room A, hoping that meant a more friendly interview. Her union rep, Herb Takayama, a Buddha-like little man with round spectacles that echoed the dome of his head, wedged in beside her on the too-small love seat. Waxman, LaSota, and Pillman sat on the bolted-down armchairs.

Takayama opened the questioning after they were apprised of the date, time, people present, and that the proceedings were being recorded. "First of all, I'd like see my client fully recovered from her injuries before she's interviewed regarding—what is it, exactly?"

"We are trying to establish what her relationship was with the Changs, a known crime family," Pillman said. "There is a conflict of interest with the situation that could endanger our prosecution of the case against Terence Chang."

"What conflict of interest?" Lei felt the heat of anger flush her cheeks. Takayama shook his head, but she ignored him. "Yes, there was a prior relationship with the Changs. They hated me and my father and tried to take both of our lives in the past, but I thought that was all over with after I talked with Healani Chang when I was an officer at South Hilo Station. There has been no contact, threats, or evidence of interference from the Changs for either of us since. Our tech agent Sophie Ang followed the evidence, and I went where I was sent to do a raid with no prior knowledge of whose house we were raiding. All we had was an address and a username."

"We're concerned that Terence Chang will paint it that you had a vendetta, that he's been set up in some way—even that you had a hand in killing his grandmother."

"He can say what he wants. The evidence is what led us to him, and the evidence will back me up."

"Tell us about your confrontation with Healani Chang." Dr. LaSota's dark eyes were expressionless, her pencil poised above a yellow legal pad.

Lei took a deep breath, closed her eyes a moment to remember the feelings she'd had looking at the woman on the bed. She pictured the proud set of Healani Chang's head, the fog of grief that had come over the woman's eyes just before she pulled the gun on Lei.

She described their exchange. "When I told her we were there for her grandson, it was a blow to her. I think she was hanging on for him, and finding out he was the reason for the raid—well, she got out her gun and said, "I should have killed you a long time ago." I dove for the ground. She fired a round at me that went through the side of the mattress but missed me. Then she shot herself."

A pause while they digested this.

"Why didn't you search her? She should have been patted down immediately."

"There was the dog situation to deal with. It distracted us." Lei described what had happened with the animal. "It took both of us to cover Chang as he dealt with the dog, which saved its life, quite frankly, and Chang knew it. Then Ken took the suspect out the front, and I approached Healani's bed. Yes, I should have immediately searched her, but you had to see how pathetic she was."

"She's been as active as ever, managing the 'family business,' according to reports from local PD," Pillman said. "You should have assumed she was armed."

Lei shut her mouth. She wasn't going to agree with her mistake on tape.

"So, you at no time touched her weapon?"

"No," Lei said definitely.

"So you didn't stage the suicide."

"What? I thought Ken told you he'd pulled my weapons. Neither were discharged!"

"You used her weapon."

"There was no GSR on my hands!"

"Your partner isn't exactly an unbiased witness."

"Really? This is where you're going with this?" Lei could feel the concussion pressing against her eyeballs along with tears. "How did I get these injuries, then?"

"You staged the suicide, then dove down and hit your head to lend credence to your story."

Lei couldn't speak. Her throat had closed completely, and spots danced at the corners of her vision.

"That's one theory," Waxman said, addressing Pillman. His pale brows had drawn together, his mouth tight. "It's good for us to be prepared for what the defense will raise, so I agree we have to thoroughly investigate this situation. However, I want everyone to know that I've never seen Agent Texeira act with anything but sincerity. Impulsiveness, yes, sometimes not the best judgment—but murder? I think not."

"We're leaving," Takayama said. "Any further interviews will be accompanied by legal counsel." He tugged Lei's arm and pulled her out the door.

She couldn't believe that things had taken such a turn for the worse, that even what her partner had done to protect her was being questioned. Even so, it warmed her to hear Waxman come to her defense.

Stevens stood up from the chair in the hall, took one look at her face and folded her into his arms. "That bad?" he said into her hair.

"Worse," Lei whispered hoarsely. "Pillman thinks I murdered Healani Chang."

She felt the outrage shoot through his body in the sudden clenching of his muscles, in the sharp intake of breath, in the way he straightened up, reaching for the door. This time, she clung to him, holding him back. Takayama harrumphed, reminding them of his presence.

"Better to let the investigation take its course," he said. "These things are unpleasant, but my sense is that the evidence will support Agent Texeira or be inconclusive. Just sit tight, and you can retain legal counsel as a preventive measure. Here are some of the lawyers we've used successfully in the past." He handed Lei a slip of paper with names and numbers on it. "Absolutely no further meetings with your administration without me present."

On that note, Waxman came to the door, stepped out, and closed it behind him. "Texeira."

Lei wanted to hide her face in Stevens's rigid chest, but she made herself turn to face her boss.

"I'm required to take your ID and sidearm for the duration of the investigation. You are off the case and are not to discuss it with your coworkers."

"Yes, sir. Ken already has my weapons." She handed her cred wallet to him. Behind her, she felt Stevens radiating leashed heat against her back. It was the only good thing in the world.

"I want you to know, I don't believe this trumped-up bullshit for a minute." Waxman had hectic red spots on his cheeks "Hang tight. This will blow over."

"Yes, sir," Lei whispered.

Stevens clamped his arm over her. "I'm taking her home. Don't contact us without Mr. Takayama present."

CHAPTER THIRTY-ONE

THE NEXT DAY, Sophie and Ken ushered Robert Castellejos into Conference Room A. The bald-headed cancer patient, looking tanned and relaxed, smiled as he sat on the love seat facing them. He'd carried in a leather folio slung over his shoulder; the metal detectors had let it through but Sophie tensed as he reached inside. He only produced a couple of jars of clear golden honey, which he set on the coffee table before them.

"Brought you something to sweeten your day."

"Thank you. We are not allowed to accept gifts, however," Ken said. "This is a formal interview that is being recorded, to question your involvement with the DyingFriends site." Ken recited the date, time, and attendees for the record. Sophie was conscious of Waxman's watchful presence in the booth next door, but her earbud stayed silent.

"Yes. I'd like to make a full confession." Castellejos wore tidy chinos and a brown T-shirt with a honeybee on the front. "Bennie Fernandez, my dear protégée Terence Chang's lawyer, contacted me yesterday that Terence had been arrested in connection to deaths related to the site, and I'd like to set the record straight."

Whatever Sophie had been expecting from the beekeeper, it

wasn't this. They'd been stonewalled in attempts to interview Chang further until Bennie Fernandez had called them with the unexpected news that Chang wanted to cop a plea in return for information on KevorkianFan, the "mastermind of the site." He'd implicated Castellejos.

"DyingFriends is my project. I recruited Terence to provide the technical skills to run the site—the boy's good with computers and believes in the cause. At no time did he ever participate or assist at any suicides. If you check his alibis for the dates of suicides in the photo galleries, you will see that they hold up. I, however, have been quite the traveling man."

Castellejos reached into his folio and produced a handwritten log along with a stack of Visa bills. "I've traveled all over the United States fulfilling the last wishes of DyingFriends members. This log contains their names and times and dates of death. These Visa bills document the tickets they gifted me with and my travel to meet them. I've personally witnessed the last moments of more than three hundred people who have chosen to exercise their freedom to die with dignity."

Sophie felt her face freezing into a mask of immobile horror. She'd spent hours poring over those photos, seeing everything from jumping to hanging to overdoses, and the thin, tanned, smiling face before her, sitting in his honeybee T-shirt, just wouldn't compute as their executioner.

Ken cleared his throat. He reached over and pulled the log and Visa bill close. "Robert Castellejos, you have voluntarily submitted records documenting your involvement with these deaths. You are under arrest for the assisted suicide deaths of these voluntarily submitted names." He recited the Miranda warning.

Castellejos waved a hand. "I waive my right to counsel. I have no need for such things. I've made my peace with spending my last days in prison for a cause I'm dying for anyway. I won't allow Terence Chang to be charged with 'crimes' I've committed." He made air quotes as he said "crimes."

"All right. I'd like that in writing, if you don't mind." Ken pushed a legal pad over to him, and the man picked up the pad and wrote, reading aloud as he did so. "I waive my right to counsel and make a full confession of my assistance in the suicide deaths related to the site DyingFriends."

Sophie forced her paralyzed throat to form some words. "So you are KevorkianFan."

"And you are the lovely and deceitful ShastaM." Castellejos's warm brown eyes shone with the light of fanaticism as they rested on hers, casting a hypnotic spell. "I detected your phishing, but not until poor Terence had already bought your bogus suicide note. Very authentic, my dear. May I suppose you've had your own thoughts of suicide? It really is a viable option and part of your right to life, liberty, and happiness as guaranteed by the Constitution."

Sophie's mouth opened and shut. Waxman's voice crackled in their ears. "Don't listen to this man's poison; we are not providing him a stage for his rhetoric. Focus on the logs and victims; get a confession of each name while he's willing to talk."

Ken opened the log. "Let's begin with our most recent murder victim, Betsy Brown, and work our way back, shall we?"

"Ah, Betsy. Lovely young woman. Didn't she look beautiful in her special gown?" Castellejos went on to describe helping Betsy prepare with her gown and makeup, bringing her the water and the medication, sitting with her until her heart stopped. "It's my honor to help people who have chosen to leave this world do so on their own terms."

"Betsy wasn't dying. She had Guillain-Barré syndrome, a rare viral infection that she would have recovered from." Sophie found her voice again, and it vibrated with outrage.

"Yes, Terence's lawyer informed me of that. What you need to understand is that the right to death is a basic human right, just as is the right to life. Perhaps Betsy wouldn't have chosen this path if she had known that; perhaps she would have. It doesn't change the fact that she had a right to choose when her life ended. I don't concern myself with verifying details of diagnoses. Human rights are what's important."

Sophie felt her hands ball into fists, her arms tightening. She'd never wanted to punch someone in the mouth more than she did at that moment. Ken put a hand on her arm. "Let's move on to Corby Alexander Hale. What was your involvement with his death?"

"I doctored the boy's drink. He was a little ambivalent about his commitment to suicide; he told me that. I gave him a little relaxation drink when I met him at a gay bar the night I picked to help him fulfill his commitment. He'd chosen a pain-free way to go—I imagine it was actually quite pleasant." Castellejos smiled. "I imagine, after the grief passes, the senator and his wife will actually get a lot of political mileage out of this with the sympathy vote."

Sophie stood and paced behind the chairs, needing to discharge her rage and not sure she could keep from attacking the man. She thought of Lei in that moment, the other agent's physicality and emotional volatility. She'd never really understood it—until now.

Castellejos worked imperturbably back through the log with them recording every word—nailing his own coffin shut tighter with each disclosure and unfazed by that fact. In the end, they were hearing the confession of a dying man with nothing much to lose.

Sophie took pleasure in erasing every virtual trace of Dying-Friends from the Internet late that night—but she didn't know how she'd ever erase the memory of Castellejos's smiling death's head face from her dreams.

Lei carried Angel into the community room at the Youth Correctional Facility. This wasn't her usual scheduled visit, but after Stevens had left and she'd spent another day in bed, she realized that seeing her young friend was the only thing she could think of that might cheer her up.

They'd let Consuelo meet her in the rec room alone, and as usual, the Chihuahua went into rapture upon seeing the girl. Lei smiled, watching them play, and finally Consuelo sat on the couch holding the dog and gestured. "Lei, come sit. What happened to your face?"

"Injured on the job. I have some free time. Thought I'd come see my favorite juvenile delinquent."

"Well, I have some news too. I'm getting out early. They need my bed, apparently, so I'm being furloughed to a work-study program." Consuelo's pretty face was animated and she jumped a bit on the couch so that her glossy black hair bounced. "I'm getting a job. They're already looking at some maintenance programs where I could work. I even get to go to classes at East Oahu Community College, and I come back to the group home in the evenings."

"So good, that news!" Having Bennie Fernandez on a case was great when the defendant was someone you cared about. "When does this start?"

"Next week. They said I could have Angel there at the group home. She could be a therapy dog for all six kids who live at the house."

"Nice." Lei felt a pang as she looked at the Chihuahua. Angel had really worked her way into Lei's life even though she'd always known the arrangement was temporary. As if sensing this, Angel hopped over and licked her hand. She petted the dog's sleek head. "I'm so happy for you. Well, it comes at a great time for both of us. I have an opportunity I'm considering." She told Consuelo about the offer from Captain Omura on Maui. "Without the FBI, I never would have met you. Thinking about leaving feels like giving up, like I couldn't cut it." Lei found herself touching the metal disc at her throat.

"Don't you think there will be other people you will help through the police department? I mean, some of the stories you told me were awesome." Consuelo smiled.

"I know. It's just a tough choice."

"You're so good at what you do; it doesn't matter who you work for and you know it. By the way, I'm starting my first college class soon."

"What is it?"

"Journalism. Then political science. Maybe I'll do politics someday."

Lei felt a wide grin stretch the bruises on her face. "Perfect."

"I guess I had to get stuck in here to see that I had other choices than to do what I did. You're the reason I didn't give up back then when I wanted to kill myself, and you're the reason I know I can do it even though I'm not the best student."

Lei hugged the girl, the dog sandwiched between them. She thought of DyingFriends and of the vulnerability of suicidal teenagers, who could, if supported, go on to lead productive lives. Thank God the site was shut down—Sophie had texted her that, and that she'd be by to tell her about the case soon.

On the way home, Lei's cell rang.

"Hi, Lei. It's Marcus." Lei wondered when her breath would stop freezing at the sound of the big detective's voice.

"Hey, Marcus. Any news on the Bozeman thing?" *Be proactive not reactive.* Another Dr. Wilson-ism.

"That's what I'm calling about. We got Bozeman's shooter. Grieving wife of a client he'd offed. The lady extorted Bozeman's name out of the business partner who'd ordered the hit, then shot him. Tracked Bozeman, shot him too. Lady's a badass. I wish we could give her a medal instead of locking her up, but oh well. Everything's all tied up on the case."

"Wow, she sounds like a force to be reckoned with. So . . . everything's tied up?" She gave a delicate emphasis to the word "everything." Kwon lay between them, an unspoken ghost.

"Yup. Everything. Case closed." Kamuela's voice was brisk.

"Well. Thanks for the call. That's really good news."

"Yeah. Marcella and I want to go out with you and that mystery man of yours."

"I know. Soon, I hope. Thanks again." Lei hung up, and breathed a huge sigh of relief.

Kwon was finally behind her for good.

CHAPTER THIRTY-TWO

Sᴏᴘʜɪᴇ ᴘᴜʟʟᴇᴅ the Lexus up to the curb on the quiet side street where Lei Texeira lived. She took a minute to close her eyes and lean her close-cropped head on the steering wheel, gathering courage to go talk about the case and its aftermath. She was still haunted by all she'd seen and by Castellejos's utter lack of remorse.

She'd had no idea IA would get involved regarding Healani Chang's death and that they'd investigate Lei for murder! Her stomach clenched at the thought of Lei's stress, but she hoped her visit would help a little with that.

Sophie took one more breath, blew it out, and stepped out into the pearly light of approaching dusk in Honolulu. The plumeria tree by Lei's gate was in bloom, and the yellow throats of creamy white pinwheel blossoms emitted a sumptuous scent as she rang the bell set in the metal gate frame.

The reaction was immediate—a chorus of barking. A deep, bellowing bark was punctuated by a shrill timpani bark, and two dogs burst into view, matched perfectly and yet never more different. One was a big Rottweiler and the other, a teacup Chihuahua barking so hard she flew off the ground on stiff legs.

Lei followed the dogs out to the gate. Her bruises were fading but still evident. "Sophie, hi! Come on in."

Lei opened the gate, and Sophie entered, hesitant because of the dogs' cacophony. "Meet my dogs. Keiki, sit. Angel, sit." Lei did a hand signal and the dogs shut up and sat. "Put your fist out, Sophie, fingers down. Let them get a sniff of you."

Sophie did so, realizing in that moment that a dog might be something she was missing out on. She'd never had a pet, and the empty echo of the apartment came to mind. Imagine having the company of a dog on her runs, happy toenails clattering across the teak floors to greet her. Her father couldn't complain the place was unlived in with a dog at home. She smiled and knelt, stroking the dogs' smooth heads.

"They're beautiful. I think I might like a dog."

"Lots of great animals needing homes at the Humane Society." Lei led the way back into the cottage. "You're never really alone when you have a dog. So what brings you to my house? I should tell you, I've been forbidden by Waxman to discuss the IA aspects of the case at all while I'm being investigated." She went to a cabinet, took down a couple of glasses. "Can I get you something to drink? A beer?"

"Okay." Sophie sat down on one of the small aluminum chairs. Maybe some alcohol would make this easier. She looked around the tidy, bright little space. "Cute place."

"It's perfect for me and the girls." Lei poured a couple of Heinekens into the glasses, brought them to the table. "To the successful shutdown of DyingFriends. You made this case, Sophie, and you're going to make it for the prosecution."

They clinked the glasses in toast and Sophie sipped. "Did Ken call you about KevorkianFan's confession?"

"No. What's the latest?"

"Bad news on Terence Chang but good news on the real monster behind the site." Sophie drank more, chugging down half her glass while Lei watched, tilted brown eyes wide.

"Thirsty? There's more where that came from."

Sophie burped behind her hand. "I'm sorry. I'm just having a hard time since the interview with KevorkianFan. Turns out he's Robert Castellejos, the cancer victim."

"What?" Lei's shock looked genuine. "Seemed like such a nice guy. Gave me some honey." She gestured to the jar on the counter.

"I hope you didn't try any. Throw it away. God knows what he put in there!" Sophie pushed the glass away, looked at Lei. "Terence Chang rolled on Castellejos as the power behind the site. Castellejos came in and made a full confession on the assisted suicide of more than three hundred victims. Guy's a psychopath but sees himself as a patriot."

"Holy God." Lei stared at her for a long moment, then picked up her glass and drank. Set it down. "What happened with Chang?"

"We cut him loose. Going to get a year or so for his administration of the site in return for testimony about Castellejos."

Lei frowned. "That kid hates me. I better watch my back."

"Yes. I'd agree with that. I think we'll see more from Terence Chang in the future. He's got the attitude to step into Healani Chang's shoes as head of the family, but we've got him under surveillance and on an ankle bracelet at the moment. Marcella told me they're investigating you as if you might have shot Healani Chang. It's just crazy."

"That IA guy? Pillman? What a piece of work. I get that it's his job to investigate irregularities in the department, but he doesn't have to like it so much." The beer appeared to burn Lei's throat going down, and she coughed.

"Well, I just came to bring you up to speed. I know we aren't supposed to discuss the IA investigation, so all I'll say is this: None of us believe that shit, and Ken's got evidence backing you up. It will blow over."

"Thanks for that."

"We've also been able to prevent at least three more deaths so far by intercepting communications that were in motion from the site. A lot of people will have an opportunity to live a little longer, and maybe that will make a positive difference. I don't know."

"I know, right? Tough case. So sad—a bunch of dying people helping each other die faster. I felt so bad for the DyingFriends members. Even Chang—he seemed to really love his grandma and hate to see her suffering. This is one case I'm happy to be done with."

"Speaking of happy. Marcella told me your boyfriend is back in your life." Sophie wished she wasn't the only one of their trio without anyone to come home to.

"Yeah. We're good." Lei's face moved from interesting to truly beautiful with her big smile. "We've sure been through some hard times. I'm hoping they're going to come to an end soon. One way or another. Thanks for coming by."

"I'm glad I did. Hang in there." Sophie stood up, headed for the door. Lei followed.

"You know, everyone keeps saying that. I just don't know what I'm hanging in there for anymore."

"That sounds ominous." Sophie petted the dogs' heads and they trotted with her to the gate.

"I have more than just work on my mind these days. I'm thinking of making some changes."

"I bet, with a guy like Stevens. I'd be happy to just have a dog at this point."

"You should get one. Go by the pound; they'll all be begging for you to take them home. I can't go there at all myself. I'd be overrun. Thanks so much for coming over."

"I'd like to be friends," Sophie said impulsively, feeling a flush in her cheeks at her awkward words. She was so bad at this.

"Of course. I've wanted that for a while." Lei smiled. "So next time you and Marcella shoot pool, count me in. Better yet, we can just go."

"For sure." Sophie went through the gate, clicked it shut, and stopped for one last touch of Keiki's broad nose, pressed through the bars.

Yes, a dog would be a good place to start.

That night, Sophie's new companion, a two-year-old yellow Lab named Ginger, refused to stay in the laundry room. The dog employed a variety of behaviors from scratching to howling to convey the message that she wouldn't be separated from her new mistress.

Sophie ended up with company in her bed in the cool dark cave of her room. While not exactly what she'd had in mind, Ginger was most definitely warm and hairy, and Castellejos's hypnotic eyes were banished from her dreams.

CHAPTER THIRTY-THREE

THE NEXT DAY Stevens drove Lei in his old Bronco from Kahului Airport toward his place in Kuau on Maui. Lei gazed out at the wind lashing the sugarcane fields in a familiar dance off of Hana Highway. Her phone vibrated in her pocket and she pulled it out, frowning at *dr. lasota* in the little ID window. "Special Agent Texeira."

"Dr. LaSota here." The psychologist's voice was crisp. "Just wanted to inform you that the investigation into Healani Chang's death has been ruled a suicide."

"Okay. I guess." Lei glanced at Stevens and met his concerned eyes.

"Yes. And furthermore, our Internal Affairs investigation has come back with no evidence of wrongdoing on your part. You are in the clear."

"Thank you." Lei gave Stevens a thumbs-up sign.

"We are, however, entering a note in your personnel file that you are not to be involved with any further investigation of the Chang family."

"Great. I don't want anything to do with them, either."

"Good. Also, I'm personally sorry if this investigation added stress to your injuries." The doctor's voice had softened. "I didn't like the direction things took."

"I didn't either. Thank you." Lei clicked off the phone after the psychologist hung up. "Looks like I'm in the clear over Healani Chang's suicide."

"Thank God," Stevens said. "We can really relax and enjoy our weekend together now that the Kwon thing and that investigation are over." He reached over to squeeze her leg. "I hope you like my apartment."

He turned into the small parking lot of a condo complex outside the beachfront town of Paia and parked the truck in front of a three-story tan cinder-block building facing the turquoise sea. Coconut palms gyrated in the wind around the sides of the building, and the parking lot was trimmed in plumeria trees and brilliant magenta bougainvillea.

Stevens lifted Lei's stuffed carry-on backpack out of the backseat of the Bronco while Lei opened the tailgate and unlatched the door of the big dog crate where Keiki lay, expressive brown eyes anxious. Angel had gone to live with Consuelo at her group home, and Lei missed the little dog already.

"C'mon out, girl."

The big Rottweiler jumped down from the Bronco, and Lei clipped the dog's leash on, letting her sniff and investigate the lot. Maui really did have something uniquely wonderful about it, and it was in the wide-open spaces and warm breeze that tossed her hair.

Lei thought she could smell the salty tang of the ocean just on the other side of the complex. Her chest was tight with excitement—she was finally here.

"I scored a unit on the bottom floor," Stevens said. "Come see." He carried the backpack along the cement walkway to a teal-green apartment door marked 101. He set the backpack against the wall. Stuck the key in, turned it, gave the door a little push. It swung inward.

Lei could hear the sound of surf echoing through the sliding door at the front of the apartment. The rhythmic swish was amplified by the walls like the song in a shell. A lance of sunlight reflected off the ocean, bounced off the ceiling, and lit the way in.

He stood still for a long moment, then slowly turned to face her.

"What? Is something wrong?" Lei felt her chest tighten. Was he regretting this? She'd finally learned what she needed more than any job, and she wasn't going to let any more time go by without telling him so. There were big steps ahead to take, but she'd made up her mind to get through them one by one.

Keiki gave a happy bark, trotting ahead of them into the apartment, leash trailing. The sunlight from the sea reflected off the floor, lighting Stevens's eyes. There were flecks of white in that crystal blue like ice floating in an Arctic sea. She could stand there, in the doorway, looking into those eyes all day. He seemed to feel the same, looking into hers.

"You're here," he said. "You're really here."

"Yes." Lei felt tears well up. She was so happy and so scared. "I have something I want to ask you."

"What?" His dark brows drew together in confusion as she dropped to one knee, hands twisted together.

"Will you marry me?"

She'd broken his heart so many times. She'd deserve it if he broke hers. She shut her eyes, bracing herself.

Stevens threw his head back and laughed, a sound of hilarity and joy that made the tears she'd been holding back overflow.

"Yes. Yes, God help me, I will." He reached down to haul her up by the elbows. He hugged her, crushing her with such power she gave a little wheeze. He swung her up into his arms as if she weighed nothing, and she squeaked and laughed through the tears. Stevens stepped over the threshold with her in his arms and kicked the door shut with his heel.

The backpack sat out on the sidewalk for a long time, forgotten.

Monday morning, Lei walked into the meeting she'd asked for with Waxman. He'd beaten them to the conference room, as usual.

Lei carried a piece of paper in a sweaty hand, and Marcella and Ken followed her in as she laid it in front of the special agent in charge.

"My resignation. Effective immediately."

She'd texted Marcella and Ken of her intentions, and their set faces reflected stoicism and support as they seated themselves on either side of her.

Waxman picked it up. Read it. Steepled his fingers as he did so. Removed his glasses, rubbed his eyes, sighed. "Where's your union rep?"

"He advised me against this. I just want to get it over with. I have another job offer on Maui."

"And a relationship there too." Waxman put his glasses back on, looked at her. "I'm not blind. And I know this IA thing has knocked you on your ass. I was prepared for this, and I have a proposal for you. How would you like to remain on in a titular capacity as our special liaison to Maui? Whenever we have cases there, you'll be our go-to support and communications agent."

Lei felt hope fluttering. "I would love that," she managed to say. "I hate to leave the FBI. But I don't know how that role would work with my new job. It's a full-time lieutenant position with the Maui Police Department."

"Congratulations on that. I'm sure Captain Omura and I can work something out that will be beneficial to all concerned." Waxman leaned forward. "I also want to let you know the investigation into Healani Chang's death has come back with no evidence of wrong-doing on your part. Personally, I never doubted it." He reached into his briefcase, brought out her two weapons and cred wallet. "For the remainder of your time with us."

"Thank you, sir. I hope I will be able to be an asset to the Bureau on Maui." She took the items, shook her boss's hand.

Waxman smiled. "It's been a pleasure working with you, Agent Texeira. You'll be missed around here."

Out in the hall, Marcella embraced her. "Damn girl. Thank God

Waxman came up with something to keep you connected to the Bureau!"

"It was such a hard decision, but Stevens and I—we're getting married." Lei held out her hand for Marcella and Ken to see the simple engagement band with a channel-set diamond, which they'd picked out that weekend. "You both better come and be in my wedding."

"Oh my God!" Marcella exclaimed, grabbing her hand. "You're doing it!"

"Congratulations!" Ken swept her up in a bone-cracking hug, a first from her physically reserved partner. "Count me in. Do I get to be a bridesmaid or groomsman?"

"Your choice." Lei felt those easy tears that had plagued her since the head injury rise up, and she blinked them back as she smiled at the two agents who'd become her closest friends. "I wouldn't trade this experience for the world. It was great working with you, and I learned so much from both of you."

"It was mutual," Ken and Marcella said in unison, and they laughed as they walked down the hall.

Turn the page for a sneak peek of book six of the Paradise Crime Mysteries, *Shattered Palms!*

SNEAK PEEK

SHATTERED PALMS, PARADISE CRIME MYSTERIES
BOOK 6

Detective Leilani Texeira wished she'd come to this enchanted place for some reason other than death. She picked her way down the steps of the raised jungle boardwalk, turning her head to look upward at the canopy of interlaced branches of native koa and ohia trees. Droplets of moisture and golden light fell around her on an understory of massed ferns. She'd heard of the native forest sanctuary accessible from atop Haleakala volcano but had never taken the time to visit. Now she wished she could linger and take in the multitextured beauty of the place instead of hurrying on with their grim errand.

"So many shades of green," Lei murmured, ducking under a lichen-covered branch crossing the walkway. Her curly brown hair caught on it anyway, and she gave it an impatient tug. The ranger who'd found the body, a wiry older Japanese man with the weathered skin of someone who'd lived his life outdoors, glanced back over his shoulder.

"This is what we call a cloud forest, not a rainforest, because it's mostly watered by mist. All the plants you've seen since the helicopter landing area are native Hawaiian species. We've worked hard to keep the invasives out of this area."

"Invasives?" A solitude pierced only by unfamiliar, sweet bird-song brought Lei's heart rate down after the lurching helicopter ride to the remote area.

"Introduced plant species. There are thousands, and they are smothering the native plants and taking away feeding from the indigenous birds. The biggest enemies of this forest are pigs, axis deer, and goats, and the reason this area is so pristine is that we've fenced the entire top of Haleakala to keep them out."

"Interesting." Lei glanced back at her partner, Pono, following her, another ranger bringing up the rear.

"I do my part as a hunter." Pono's smile turned up his mouth behind a trademark bristly mustache. "Plenny game up here, and they're all good eating."

"Well, I don't know what all this has to do with the body you found." Lei wove her way around a giant curling fern frond bisecting the path, her athletic body moving easily even with the elevation.

"I didn't touch the body, of course, but I think he looks like some kind of hunter," Ranger Takama said. "He's in camo gear. I'm no expert, but even I could see what killed him was an arrow, so it was probably a hunter up here that shot him by mistake. If it weren't for the smell, we wouldn't have found him at all."

That smell had been steadily increasing, a sweetish reek that clung to the inside of Lei's throat like mucus.

"We leave the boardwalk here." Takama gestured and stepped down off the boardwalk. Lei jumped down beside him into thick underbrush made up of ferns and bushes. "Normally, no one but authorized personnel are allowed off the path."

The smell of decomp almost made Lei's eyes water. She dug a vial of Vicks out of her pocket and rubbed some under her nose, turning to hand it to Pono, who'd joined her beside the boardwalk. Takama also helped himself, and they followed him, feet sinking into the deep, soft leaf mulch on the forest floor.

Crime scene tape already marked the area around the body. A

first responding officer jumped to his feet, holding the scene log on a clipboard.

"Good morning, sir." The young man spoke in the nasal voice of someone whose nose is blocked. Lei spotted white cotton sprouting from his nostrils.

"Hey. Nice up here if it weren't for the smell." She took the clipboard, and each of them signed in.

Passing the tape, Lei spotted the hand first, extended toward them from beneath the ferns, palm up. The tissue was swollen and discolored, masked in a filmy gray gauze of mold that seemed to be drawing the body down into the forest floor. Lei could imagine that in just a few weeks, the body would have been all but gone in the biology of the cloud forest.

The victim lay on his stomach, his head turned away and facing into a fern clump, black hair already looking like just another lichen growing on the forest floor. The body was at the expansion phase, distending camouflage-patterned clothing as if inflated. A black fiberglass arrow fletched in plastic protruded from the man's back.

Lei and Pono stayed well back from the body. Lei unpacked the police department's camera from her backpack, and Pono took out his crime kit. The modest quarter-karat engagement ring on her finger caught a stray sunbeam and reminded her of her upcoming wedding, with all of its accompanying stress. She pushed the thought out of her mind with an effort—she had a job to do.

"How close did you get to the victim?" Pono asked Takama.

Ranger Takama pointed to a in the leaves. "Here. I didn't need to touch the body to see he was already beyond help."

"Good," Lei said. "Hopefully, we can backtrack a bit to where he's been and identify the arrow's trajectory."

"I can help with that." The second ranger accompanying them finally spoke up. A tall, ponytailed young man with large brown eyes, he'd been introduced by Takama as Mark Jacobsen. "I've been doing tracking for the Park Service for years."

"All right," Lei said. "Pono does his share of hunting, as you heard, but I'm sure we can use your skills."

Pono and Lei got to work, photographing the area surrounding the body, then the body itself, finally moving in closer to check for marks and trace.

Lei thought the man appeared to have dropped where he stood. There was very little disturbance in the leaf mold around the body, and the ferns were unbroken except for a few near his feet. A deeper boot impression marked the ground behind the body. The man had a canvas bag attached to his belt, and the pockets on his pants bulged.

"About ready to remove some of these pocket items," Lei said. "Ranger Takama, do you know when the medical examiner will be arriving?" The Park Service's helicopter had brought them up the volcano, then been dispatched to fetch the ME and equipment for transporting the body.

"They're on their way."

"I'll go with Ranger Jacobsen to see if we can identify the area where the kill shot came from," Pono said. He and Jacobsen bent over to assess the damage to the plants and moved away into the ferns.

Lei was already intent on the items dangling from the victim's belt. She detached a cloth bag with a metal clip first, shooing a slow-moving blowfly away. Rather than opening the pouch here, she slid the whole thing into an evidence bag. It was light, but she could feel shapes inside. She sealed and labeled it, setting it in her capacious backpack.

Squatting on her heels, Lei reached gloved hands carefully into the man's combat-style pouch pockets, gently tugging out the contents and slipping them into separate bags: a serious-looking bowie knife in matte black and a plastic bottle with a squirt tip of something chemical-smelling, labeled in Chinese characters. Another pocket yielded a metal handle wound with almost-invisible net, fine as human hair. In another pocket was a tiny tape recorder. She pressed the Chinese character on what looked like "play," and a recording of a bird sounded, a single piercing *Tweee! Tweee!* It stirred something in her blood just to hear it. Lei wished she knew what kind of bird it was.

This man appeared to be some sort of bird catcher. She continued on, eventually unearthing a cell phone—a cheap burner. She removed a pistol—a matte black Glock .40—from a holster at the man's hip. That he was armed in a setting like this was alarming. She heard vegetation rustling, heralding the approach of more personnel.

"Try not to crush the plants." Takama, who'd been so quiet that she'd forgotten about him, chided Dr. Gregory as the medical examiner crunched into view, two assistants carrying a gurney behind him.

"Hey, Phil." Lei greeted the ME. She'd worked with him on several cases prior to her departure from the FBI. It was good to be back working with both her first partner on the force, Pono, and the portly doctor with his love of bright aloha shirts. Today's shirt was covered with large graphics of the Road to Hana, the bright red of the Guy Buffet stop signs echoed by red patches on Dr. Gregory's pale cheeks.

"Could have done without the helicopter ride up here," Dr. Gregory said.

Lei remembered he hated heights.

"And you gotta love a four-day-old body."

"So that's how long he's been dead, you think?" Lei asked, sliding a sticky loop of wire, the last item from the man's pockets, into an evidence bag.

Gregory leaned over the swollen body and sniffed. "That's my guess, pending further analysis."

Lei gestured to the mold-covered hand. "Do you think maybe the maximum decomp environment up here sped things up? I don't remember seeing mold like that on a body before."

"It's true that this is a totally natural biological environment," Gregory said, taking out small round magnifying glasses and hooking them over his ears, then leaning in for a closer look. He gave no sign that the stench bothered him. "That may have contributed to some exceptional mold and mildew growth. But it's not actually that warm up here. Heat is a greater breakdown accelerator than any other factor."

"From the equipment he was carrying, it seems like he might be some kind of bird catcher."

Gregory's thick blond brows snapped together. "Only scientists with special certification are allowed to capture and handle these birds, and they usually work in teams. If he's a poacher, that sucks. Let me see any bird-related evidence. I'm an avian admirer, and I'd hate to hear that anyone was capturing native birds. They're highly endangered."

"Okay, will do." Lei was already thinking of the lumpy contents of the bag she'd taken off the body and dreading what she might find inside.

Gregory's assistants set the gurney up as best they could with Takama fussing around the ferns and other undergrowth that they couldn't avoid crushing. Lei withdrew from the body, walking back toward the boardwalk to get some fresher air.

She was labeling the last of the evidence bags when Pono appeared. The big Hawaiian startled her by looming up beside her. Light on his feet, he moved through the forest without breaking a twig or disturbing the leaves.

"Pretty sure we found where the arrow was fired from. Want to take a look?"

"Of course." She got up.

"It's a hunting blind," he said over his shoulder.

"Thought that wasn't allowed up here."

"'Course it isn't."

Lei picked her way carefully after Pono through the dense vegetation, bending to keep from breaking the brittle ferns and foliage as much as possible. He led her to the base of a massive old-growth koa tree.

The native tree, with its sickle-shaped leaves, spread in opulent umbrella-like splendor to shade the forest floor. A few strategically placed knobs of wood were nailed on its silvery trunk, and peering down from the center of the tree, his face almost lost in shadows cast by the sun on the leaves, was Jacobsen. "Up here."

Lei turned to Pono. "Did you find any trace up there?"

Pono shook his head. "No. Went over it with a light and magnifier. No hairs, nothing."

"Damn. Is there room for two?" The area where Jacobsen was sitting looked hemmed in by a circle of branches.

"Sure. Once you get up here, there's plenty of room," Jacobsen said.

Lei reached up and grasped the trunk, setting her foot on the first knob. She hauled herself upward using arms she worked hard to keep strong, hair catching in the branches again. It was only a few minutes until she sat beside Jacobsen on a smooth branch that had been bent over and nailed down as a seat.

"So what do you think this spot is used for?" Lei's voice instinctively lowered to match the soughing of a tiny wind in the branches, punctuated by birdsong. The forest was not a place that invited loud voices, and once again Lei wished she'd taken the time to visit earlier.

"This is an observation station. Probably birds. This area is the habitat of some of the rarest birds in the world. One of them, the Maui Parrotbill or *Kiwikiu*, lives in koa trees and feeds on the bark and insects."

Lei squinted at the knobbed, silvery bark of the koa tree as Pono's buzz-cut head rose to join them. Once again her partner surprised her with the smooth, silent way he moved, settling his muscular bulk easily beside her on the branch seat. He pointed, and she sighted down the brown expanse of his arm.

"See? I think this is where the shot came from. Note the downward angle into the body."

From where they sat, Lei could clearly see the body, the arrow still protruding, as Gregory covered the man's hands and the assistants arranged a black bag beside the corpse so they could roll the body into it.

"Seems like a significant distance to get the arrow so deep into the body." Lei squinted, imitating an imaginary bowshot.

"Compound hunting bow, I imagine. More power and accuracy."

"Glad I have you on this case," Lei said. "This is foreign territory for me."

"Oh yeah? I'll have to take you out hunting some weekend." Pono grinned, a flash of teeth. "You and Stevens can get your first blood."

"Thanks. I'll pass. What I can tell is that there's a lot more going on up here than anyone knew about."

"That's true." Jacobsen's warm brown eyes were concerned, his brows drawn together. "The Park Service certainly wasn't aware of these activities, and I don't think the Hawaiian Bird Conservatory, who manages the preserve area, was aware of this hunting blind either. Takama and I work closely with them, and we'd have heard about it."

Lei frowned as she studied the forest floor, dressed in lush under-story vegetation. "Do you think the shooter was hunting the bird catcher? Or was he just sitting up here and the vic passed by? Was it accidental, or intentional?"

Pono glanced at her. "When we answer those questions, we'll solve the case."

Download *Shattered Palms* and continue reading now!

ACKNOWLEDGMENTS

Aloha dear Readers!

Twisted Vine is the book my subconscious has been planning since *Blood Orchids,* first in the series, came out. Preparing for *Twisted,* I wrote all the "loose ends" and subplots I needed to tie up on the whiteboard next to my desk while I was still completing the challenging manuscript that was *Broken Ferns.*

I started looking for a crime for this book well ahead of time. I look everywhere for ideas: the news, rumors in the community, blogs, articles, newspapers, TV shows. Some of my favorite crime exposes have been in People Magazine and Vanity Fair—truth is often stranger than fiction!

I needed something *no one had done before*, something the FBI would get involved with, something new and unique.

I've included a lot of crimes in the series, from the "basics" of the genre like rape, robbery and drugs to the finer points of money laundering, identity theft, sex trafficking, burglary and of course, murder. It's challenging to find something really different in the crime mystery genre, and I was coming up dry.

In my therapy practice I saw a series of depressed people—and as part of "motivational interviewing" a technique in which there is open dialogue about why a person engages in a given behavior, and the reasons behind it, I had serious discussions with people struggling with suicidal thoughts. These talks delved into the reasons behind this complex problem—and I realized I wanted to explore the issue of suicide and right-to-death, just as I have many social issues of Hawaii and current times through my fiction.

I came home one day with the idea of an assisted suicide "club," a variation on the ever-popular "strangers on a train" scenario, updated for modern times with chatrooms and passcodes—and best yet, I'd never heard of such a plot.

It's challenging to write modern crime fiction with only a basic knowledge of computers, and I'd dodged that bullet by having Lei be a bit of a technophobe, clinging to her spiral notebook and flip phone. Enter Sophie Ang, a character who had begun to capture my imagination when she first appeared in *Broken Ferns*—a woman of mystery, of foreign birth, and of contrasts: an MMA-fighting female agent who's a genius with computers. So much of this investigation was taking place online that I gave her a second point of view in the book—and if you've read my other fiction, that's unprecedented. Only the "bad guy" and Lei get a point of view—but through the device of Sophie's perspective, I wanted the reader to better understand the process of tracking criminal activity online.

From the moment she appeared on the page, Sophie Ang was in danger of taking over this important book of Lei's. The tension between writing from Sophie's POV and working through so many delicious subplot threads (Marcus Kamuela and the Kwon murder! The relationship with Consuelo! The twist at the end and the IA investigation! Stevens and Lei's reunion!) kept my fingers flying, and I blazed through this story in a mere three months.

I've really come to love Lei and Stevens, and I want to see them move forward into life together and struggle with the same things we grapple with: marriage, children, temptations, aging, health, and careers even as I continue to explore the way the twisted vine of the past reaches its tendrils into the present.

Many thanks go to retired Capt. David Spicer who provided valuable feedback on the procedural aspects and particulars of dead bodies and suicide victims. Thanks to Jay Allen, internet detective extraordinaire, who took time out of his busy schedule to read several of the Sophie scenes and advise me on write-blockers and other computer arcana used in computer investigation work. Thanks also to Dan, Holly Robinson's computer engineer husband, who also gave small but important language tweaks to a world I don't pretend to understand.

Matt Rogers, another writer friend, does MMA and he helped with the scene between Alika and Sophie—thanks for the "spiral ride," Matt!

My editor, Kristen Weber, earned her money as I fired the rough manuscript off to her "on deadline" before taking a month with my husband to travel the National Parks, out of internet range most of the time. Thanks Kristen! And thanks always to my awesome beta readers Holly Robinson (whose literary influence has single handedly deepened my characters and sharpened my writing more than any other) Noelle Pierce, Bonny Ponting and now, my mom Sue Wilson. Each of you had a hand in shaping and developing *Twisted Vine,* and I'm forever grateful.

Most of all, thanks to my amazing husband Mike Neal, whose creative flame fans mine. We truly rediscovered love, adventure and companionship on our epic road trip while *Twisted Vine* was at the editor—and because of my years with you, I know the best is yet to come for Lei and Stevens too.

If you liked the story, *please leave a review*. It's the best thanks you can give any author!

Much aloha,

FREE BOOKS

Join my mystery and romance lists and receive free, full-length, award-winning novels *Torch Ginger & Somewhere on St. Thomas.*

tobyneal.net/TNNews

TOBY'S BOOKSHELF

PARADISE CRIME SERIES

Paradise Crime Mysteries
Blood Orchids

Torch Ginger

Black Jasmine

Broken Ferns

Twisted Vine

Shattered Palms

Dark Lava

Fire Beach

Rip Tides

Bone Hook

Red Rain

Bitter Feast

Paradise Crime Mystery
Special Agent Marcella Scott
Stolen in Paradise

Paradies Crime Suspense Mysteries
Unsound

Paradise Crime Thrillers
Wired In
Wired Rogue
Wired Hard
Wired Dark
Wired Dawn
Wired Justice
Wired Secret
Wired Fear
Wired Courage
Wired Truth

ROMANCES

The Somewhere Series
Somewhere on St. Thomas
Somewhere in the City
Somewhere in California

Standalone
Somewhere on Maui

Co-Authored Romance Thrillers
The Scorch Series
Scorch Road
Cinder Road
Smoke Road
Burnt Road
Flame Road
Smolder Road

YOUNG ADULT

Standalone
Island Fire

NONFICTION

Memoir
Freckled

MIAMI GUNDOWN